PENGUIN BOOKS

LADY MACBETH

Born in London of English parents, Nicolas Freeling has spent his life in Europe. Since 1964 he has lived in Strasbourg, handily between France and West Germany. In his own words, 'This has made for the intricate problems of the expatriate writer. There are privileges and also handicaps.'

Nicolas Freeling has a world-wide readership and has received every honour known to crime writers. His books have all been published by Penguin, including the 'van der Valk' series set in Holland and the more recent 'Castang' books, which have a French background.

LADY
MACBETH

NICOLAS FREELING

PENGUIN BOOKS

PENGUIN BOOKS

Published by the Penguin Group
27 Wrights Lane, London W8 5TZ, England
Viking Penguin Inc., 40 West 23rd Street, New York, New York 10010, USA
Penguin Books Australia Ltd, Ringwood, Victoria, Australia
Penguin Books Canada Ltd, 2801 John Street, Markham, Ontario, Canada L3R 1B4
Penguin Books (NZ) Ltd, 182–190 Wairau Road, Auckland 10, New Zealand

Penguin Books Ltd, Registered Offices: Harmondsworth, Middlesex, England

First published by André Deutsch 1988
Published in Penguin Books 1989
1 3 5 7 9 10 8 6 4 2

Printed and bound in Great Britain by
Cox & Wyman Ltd, Reading
Filmset in Times Roman

This book is for
Wolf: gardener; Paracelsus-lover.
And to the memory of
Stanley Ellin: crime writer; my friend.

ACKNOWLEDGEMENTS

I must thank, here, my friend Camille Claus; who drew the Rhinemaidens, and made my wife – who is Dutch – a present of 'Eternity in Rotterdam'.

Grandfontaine: 1986.

I must thank, too, Monsieur le Ministre de l'Intérieur of the French Government, 1986– : Monsieur Charles Pasqua, who is responsible for the Police, and in a rhetorical moment said, 'Whatever my boys do, I'll back them up.'

'Nobody ever looked less
like Lady Macbeth'

Raymond Chandler, *The Little Sister*

PROLOGUE

You'll have to put it at the very start, I said. Narrative. Headings to each section. Or your reader will get hopelessly confused. Like this: Narration by Henri Castang.

Because we, the professionals, are used to handling material of this sort. But if you're not careful, it won't make much sense to the man in the street. I can see all sorts of difficulties.

Look – a criminal case-history, call it a dossier if you like, starts mostly with statements made by the police. Made *to* the police, in the first place, *by* the people concerned. We type them out in résumé form. Chap signs at the bottom, agreeing that this is a true and faithful account of what he had to say. Can't put it down word by word, question and answer. Much too long; not to say incoherent, irrelevant. People ramble, full of ums and ers. Probably all lies anyhow. They change their stories, you know, to suit the facts as these appear.

Yes, *you* know all this. You are a sociologist, criminologist and so forth. You have an orderly, academic mind. But the reader needs explanation. Editing, that's right.

We send these papers to a legal officer. The Procureur, correct. The District Attorney, he'd be called in the States. If he decides there's a case to answer, he names a magistrate. The judge of instruction, that's right. He – she – builds up the dossier, summons witnesses, interrogates them. The clerk types it out.

At the end, this is the colossal mass that you see carried into court and dumped down in front of the presiding judge. He refers to it, often. The law states that the proceedings in court must be oral. So he has to go through it all again word by word.

9

Man, you can't make a book out of this. It'd be as long as three phone directories.

Yes, you could edit it. You'd have to. You're turning it into fiction, then, aren't you? Look, let's say you are describing a scene where you were not present. To make it interesting, readable, you've got to put words and thoughts into direct speech, no? Dialogue and monologue, am I right? It's fiction. All right, it's midway between fact and fict, that's your affair. You can build a sort of text, I suppose, as lecture-room material. For study by students.

Yes, you could even publish it, if you're that way inclined. The people concerned aren't going to sue you for libel, are they? So start at the beginning. Make it clear what goes on. From this moment, okay? Like this:

I am a Commissaire, a senior officer of Police Judiciaire, that's the CID. My home, my work, my district for which I am responsible are in the north.

Yes, this will all be clear as we go along. We are at the end here of an enquiry into a suspected crime. I am in the city of Strasbourg, at the home of two friends. Arlette and Arthur Davidson. They were concerned in this affair. In fact it is through them that I was brought into it.

And you take it from there, Arthur, okay?

Editorial note: A.D.
I have little to add to that, for I have done almost exactly as he said; I have edited. There is a 'fictional' element, in the sense of ghost-writing, as publishers call it. The 'As Told To' of pop singers or tennis stars who employ a journalist to put their ramblings into readable shape. I am that journalist. I am something better; because I am a trained academic, accustomed to handling source-material with truth and precision. The reader has my word for it that no dialogue or monologue in the pages that follow is not firmly based upon what I have read and heard direct

from the witnesses. This is a factual case history. I have 'edited' as little as possible. For any confusion in chronology, or repetitions in narrative, I must accept sole responsibility. Since it is seen through my eyes, inevitably a certain distortion has taken place. I am not a novelist. I cannot prevent the voices of the different narrators from sounding, too often, like my own.

Of myself little need be said. I hold a visiting professorship here at the University of Strasbourg. My vocation is in criminology, a discipline in which I am an advisory consultant to the Council of Europe, here in this city. This material has been collected with a view to eventual publication, in a form yet to be determined. In unpublished form, at considerable length as Henri has pointed out, it can be used as source material for graduate students. For the present purpose I have omitted much and condensed more.

I must add a note of explanation concerning my wife.

Arlette was the fount and origin of this story. The pivot, itself small and unimportant, upon which it turned.

She had a longstanding interest in criminology, in what I might call the pathology of society. Her first marriage was to a Dutch police officer. He was killed in the course of duty: it left a lasting mark upon her. As is natural, from her marriage to myself she has maintained this interest.

For some years she ran a little advice bureau. This was of value: she helped many bewildered and frightened people towards a better understanding. It was never an 'enquiry bureau': she was in no sense a private detective. But her experience, as well as curiosity, led her to enquire into the causes of many obscure human relations, and this was here the case.

She has been in much distress of mind. She feels, to some degree, responsible for this affair, which developed into a tragedy. It was, she has said, her errors of judgment, leading to what in an emotional moment she has called 'irresponsible meddling', which set this affair in motion.

As Henri has said – he has become a friend – professionals are not emotional.

So she is at the beginning of this tale. But Henri began it. And it starts in fact with him. Because he had already met another 'Lady Macbeth'. So that I send him back, to narrate his story, from its true beginnings.

HENRI CASTANG . . .

An old cop used to say to me "You think too much." In any police official, a major weakness.

"I don't mind your being bright." The tone quite kind. "You think in this abstract way." It is a French failing. "A cop, you know, shouldn't allow himself to think much." Talking as usual from behind the newspaper he was pretending to read. "He's there for focus. From low to high definition when a microbe swims into the field. Collect your material, okay. Analyse. Synthesize, okay. Don't philosophise so goddamn much."

All true. I never have succeeded in cutting out the bad habit.

Seeing that the punch had taken effect – this old pro was expert at the right hook to the liver which jolts the chin up – he held off on the left uppercut which would have downed me.

"Too late to change you fundamentally," again in the 'kind' voice. The bright eye peeped out over the newspaper. "Part of your defensive system." Light jab, to keep me from counter-attack. "Learn to feel, boy." This man of sixty could call me boy without humiliating.

I go often to the Russian Tea Room. At lunchtime on a busy day, instead of going home. At breakfast even, when Vera has forgotten to buy coffee, which she quite often does. In office hours upon occasion; moments when my stomach heaves at the thought of Madame Metz with her paper cup of Nescafé and her dewy moustache. I like the antique feel of the place. You can even get Russian tea there, if you ask, in a tall glass which fits in a filigree silver holder. There are few places left like this. Real marble tables, dusty green plush banquettes, dirt-encrusted mahogany. Ice cream in cylindrical silver vacuum-jars. Polish bortsch. Stroganoff. Ornate porcelain beer-pump.

13

'Petrovich' the older generation still calls it though there hasn't been a Petrovich since 1956. The students say 'RTR' with the modern love of acronyms, or 'Thé-Russe' the way Americans say Maitre-dee.

There are two waitresses. Elena and Olga, sounding Russian enough and they're both Spanish. Creates a comic effect. Olga is I think South American. Indian blood there; very beautiful, with reddish lights in her skin and hair. Small, with a perfect upright carriage, floats along, delicious bottom in her high-waisted trousers. Never in a hurry. Sings to herself as she works. Gentle eyes and mouth. You know, I'd use the word 'tender', devalued as it is; almost as bad as gay. Risking both the slightly acid twist the word will give Vera's lip and being thought a praliné by whomsoever – the reader proud of being a hard nut inside the chocolate.

Elena is a handsome, hardy woman, a little too old for prettiness, for her face is marked by the experience of suffering known and the anxiety of that to come. She has an entertaining way of beautifying her top half, quite unlike Olga who beautifies nothing at all and contents herself with soap and water. Splendid hair which snaps and pops with cleanness, enhanced by clips and combs and her large collection of dangly diamanté earrings. Her wide low-necked blouses are changed twice a day. Her eyebrows are thin high arches, like Marlene Dietrich but she has not an actress's eyes, melting in self-admiration: they are professionally alert.

Comically, below the waist she is tight trousers, black washed out to stormcloud grey and her walk is not pretty: she forces it from the waist, and standing upright sticks her thin bony behind out a bit. She has large, nervous arm gestures.

Over-observing am I, d'you think? I sit in this place often enough with nothing to do. They are both excellent, professional waitresses. Breakfast is a busy time; it's that kind of café, on a crossroad much frequented by municipal employees, and not just typists who whip in for coffee but heavy men in overalls with powerful Polish stomachs who were out hosing streets and storm

14

drains before dawn: massive appetites for the fried-egg-and-bacon sandwich of the north, the farmers' pancake; here cheap and known to be good. Comic, again, in this faded art-déco interior. It is in the afternoons that the 'tea-room' atmosphere is uppermost, when housewives with bulging shoppingbags rest their feet and are tempted by cake.

"Hallo darling." Elena is fond of me since I am polite and untroublesome. Not that fond: she calls everybody darling, of any sex, until hassled, when she mutters irritably in Spanish about thick northern peasants. Her voice is high, harsh. She pours my coffee so vehemently that it almost splashes. Her hands are shapely but formidable with a suggestion of sudden terrifying slaps.

"Olga sick?" Winter has come this last couple of days, and not in bedroom slippers but with a vicious polar wind which brings the tears to the eyes at street corners.

"No – the baby," darting off.

I didn't know Olga had a baby. Why should I? Olga's fluid dancer's body is as unselfconscious as a cat. Elena has the eyes and shoulders of a mother, the strong needlewoman's hands, the soft breasts that move liquidly inside her blouse. Olga is durable too and tough but her lithe body does not look maternal. I should not sentimentalise. She is competent, and will cope. But I worry about this baby; that's bronchitis weather, out there. How young is this baby? Does it look like her? Is it fragile?

Elena comes pouncing back, scribbles my check, tears it off and slaps it on the table. I have noticed before the strange and touching code she uses. These printed forms have in the top corner a space for a waiter's number, in the case of error or complaint at the desk. However hurried the rest, this part is always carefully done; a tiny drawing of two hearts side by side like a valentine, and in neat caps LOVE. The cashier, who is the 'management', a youngish dour man in shirtsleeves, is I suppose her husband. Olga's checks have just an O on them. I fumble for change; she is already mopping with her strong forearms.

"You've a hard day ahead, I'm afraid."

"I think so, darling. I think so."

Everything goes in cycles and the Tea Room too: I might not be there in three months and then find myself there three times in one week. Two – no, three days later I pottered in for a beer at that slack time of the morning just before lunch. The menu is the usual conventional list of such places but they have plats-du-jour, the lunchtime specials, and the nice old habit of writing them out on a slate stuck up on the back wall. I dislike standing at counters, went to a table. The waitresses were sitting in 'their corner'; Olga got up to serve me.

"Baby better?" She glimmered and said yes. Elena did not notice me as I left. She was staring in front of her with an elbow on the table and a forgotten cigarette between her fingers sending up a thin ribbon of smoke: the campfire at dawn. A long day, for those women, though they make good tips, of which they doubtless declare about one tenth to the tax inspector: no business of mine, God-be-thanked. But I noticed the manager was missing today. The counterman took my money and the owner, an elderly man not often seen, was there fussing.

I was in the street before he came running after me, taking my arm in a confidential way.

"Commissaire, Commissaire – a word in your ear if I may." He smelt of expensive hairtonic and had no hair, an unsurprising fact when one reads the advertisements which fill our newspapers and magazines for baldness cures. Vanity and credulity go together to nourish as profitable a legalised fraud as I know of. "A matter of delicacy," glancing about him for spies.

I allowed him to pilot me upstairs. Very snug. Having a shop is all right but owning the whole building is cosier still. I got sat in a panelled room with leatherbound editions behind glass, where he insisted upon pouring me a porto and giving me a not-very-good cigar before unfolding his troubles in felt-lined phrases. They never will say anything straight. These are the people who say 'a certain number of' instead of 'some' before a crowd of parroting journalists decided it was more elegant that way. I didn't catch his name, which sounded Greek. Something like Periphrasis. After unfolding the giftwrappings and a certain quantity of tissuepaper within I managed to understand that the manager or cashier or administrator was nowhere to be found. I used my cigar to stop my mouth. A phrase like 'We're a happy little family here' might mean anything from undeclared personal income to catching his wife in bed with the cook, and not wanting the press to get to hear of either. It takes a few police-periphrases to get some basic realities into their head. If a crime is known or suspected there is a legal officer to notify called the Procureur. If I am to enquire into anything I will have a few bluntish questions to ask.

The man was in such a stew, gabbling about good name and reputation and whatnot; ten minutes of syrup-pouring before I could get a salient fact. The fellow had disappeared. His wife knew nothing. Nobody knew anything. All quite unaccountable. The Peripatetic gentleman seemed chiefly preoccupied at having to sit at his own cash desk. We agree; tough titty.

"Hand in the till?" No no, the system's foolproof. Mm? Is it ever, in the lemonade trade? One makes little arrangements with suppliers. Double billing say; three or four per cent between official and unofficial invoices.

No no: Joseph had been with him a number of years.

All the more reason?

No no. Embarrassment here made it pretty clear that he was in the duplicate accountancy racket himself. I said mildly that I was not an incometax inspector. The criminal brigade would like something rather more concrete, to justify taking an interest. So Joseph is a trustworthy, confidential employee (rather under-paid, seemed to me). You watch him carefully. To protect your interests, quite. So you know him pretty well. Anything there to suggest his stretching his income outside your sphere? Gambler? Womaniser? Little supply of cocaine?

Good heavens no, Commissaire.

Look, something's worrying you and you better make up your mind to spit it out because either I leave it alone altogether or I get to the bottom of it.

The whole staff is upset. Everyone's acting queerly.

So? Less bad. Would the gentleman care to make this request formal. We are not the Gestapo. Before nosing in people's private lives we must have some official notification, complaint or . . .

But it's no business of mine, Commissaire! I simply felt it my duty to bring to your attention . . . damned bourgeoisie, always intent upon dodging responsibilities.

Very well. We'll ask Madame Joseph to step round to the commissariat and see what she has to tell about this disappearance.

But after working hours, Commissaire.

You'd prefer it if I sent a couple of officers around to enquire upon the premises? Oh oh: perish the thought.

Having thus reminded him that we too have working hours, once back at the office I had the dogsbody step around the corner with the little printed form that says Affair Concerning You, with no-time-to-be-lost.

Elena was as sulky and suspicious as could be, put-upon and as balky as a frightened horse. Joseph was a good husband and a good father, a good provider and a decent honest quiet man. She was a good housewife and a good mother. Even if it is never anything but work work work she makes no complaint. They are honourable people, ask anybody, she's never put a finger to anything dishonest in her days. What have the police to do with her? No, she won't make a complaint. Perhaps he has family troubles. Something back in Poland. Something which worried him which he had decided not to tell her. No he was not active in any political or syndical party or movement or anything like that, just ask the priest, my girls are good girls, they're Children of Mary. We're ten years in this job and spotless and Mr Peristalsis can't dare suggest the slightest hint to the contrary and put that in ya pipe 'n' smoke it.

One has to accept, with poor people, that they can be totally inconsistent, contradict themselves flatly five times in as many minutes and it makes no difference: they aren't to be budged. Logic of the bourgeois sort means nothing to them.

She left hating me. Don't come to her for any cups of coffee, Castang. Just because I'm a waitress you think you can treat me as dirt?

"Vayvay!" Miss Véronique Varennes, known as VV on account of this rather music-hall name, is the junior of my four subordinate officers and the only woman. A tall girl in her late twenties with a lot of fair hair and bone, sharp features and a crude manner: beneath this a good heart, good lungs and a sound stomach. If I omit mention of admirable legs and a fine pair of breasts it is because she is a competent police officer as well as a straight clean girl. She will do this job without upsetting anybody. I outlined the job.

"You tell this Periprick flat that you're on my authority and under instruction. It'll be quiet at this time. You probe the teeth of the staff, nice and gentle and you take pains not to hurt. Go easy with this girl Olga. Pretty girl such as you incline to be harsh with. She has worked a good few years with this woman, close tandem, and will know most of what there is to know. In private; there must be an office or at least a changingroom for the staff."

I rang up the Proc's office. A commissaire of police is also a legal officer, with considerable legal powers, but the Code of Procedure is explicit in defining and limiting these. We are pretty circumspect – and have to be – about busting into people's houses and routing about in their cupboards. In situations of flagrante delicto, the jargon expression meaning that either a crime has just been committed or, we have strong reason to predict, is actively planned, only then may we indulge in the more masculine sorts of intervention. We dislike having courts throw a case out for a procedural fault, ticking us off for excess of zeal while they're at it.

The secretary, our good Madame Metz, had – some time ago – made the routine trace enquiries of hospitals, municipal authorities, the gendarmerie and the like.

A Pole. Well, there do exist unofficial groups of Solidarity-in-Exile and the like. There are also religious affiliations, confraternities of this and that, which do not seek publicity. So one has a little word with one's opposite number in the political police, the one which is forever changing its acronym.

We aren't yet, you see, quite at the stage of modernisation where one is supposed in the popular imagination to get all this just by pushing a few buttons and typing a name on to the computer terminal. And even if we were, it would be naive to suppose that human beings are quite as easy to bandy around the telex as airline reservations.

Nor, just because a person is Missing, can one make assumptions of any criminal act or intention. Good, if you have a photo of Our Accountant, jauntily stepping off at Las Vegas with his little black bag full of used currency in small denominations, you might ask politely whether this is part of the therapy recommended by his analyst.

Least of all does one start mumbling about Foul Play. People, often those of the most bland and blameless aspect, have characterial eccentricities outdoing the most lurid inventions of fiction. There are nine hundred and ninetynine other explanations of a disappearance, and some of them pretty fancy.

It was close to closing-time when VV got back. She has not yet a great deal of criminal-brigade experience, and I went, metaphorically, around her own teeth (she has lovely white teeth) with a poking object before heaving sighs and reaching for the phone.

You see, where I am is only an 'antenna', meaning a small mobile group, of the PJ. In the jargon, I am a satellite of the big Regional Service of the Police Judiciaire; whose headquarters, for the North, are in Lille.

We do not – for example – have specialised sections for narcotics or minors, violent banditry or equivocal finance, and if I come across anything a little more sophisticated than we can readily cope with I must make application to my superior, the Divisional Commissaire. The same applies to scientific work.

20

Lille and the other big centres have technical and laboratory facilities: we do not. I had to ask for – and ask permission for – a couple of specialists, people trained in collecting samples and removing them for analysis. This has to be done. All one's conclusions will be questioned in court by a regiment of 'experts', many of them with axes of their own to grind.

Olga is only an ignorant simple woman, goodhearted, brave and furiously loyal. Her lies are gallant, enormous, and stitched with white thread. Varennes is hardly a forensic heavyweight, but she is a pro. Put a trained pro and even a promising amateur in the ring together, and the result is a foregone conclusion. VV has been taught the art of the treacherous question which seems innocent, and treachery will always have the better of generosity.

So I had to 'provide myself with a substitute'. The Procureur is an important legal official, and likewise a considerable local notability. It doesn't do to interrupt his dinner. He has thus a stable of young lawyers who 'substitute'. It is they who may be seen in court, occupying the prosecution throne. And since the law exacts the Proc's physical presence at a scene-of-crime it is they who, like me, go without their dinner. Mr States Attorney turns out only upon important and glamorous occasions.

Go home. Say rather pettishly to Vera that I don't want any dinner because I will have to go out again at short notice. The truth is that I have no appetite whatever for food. Vera, understanding this perfectly, still replies, equally pettishly, that it is a fine thing to prepare dinner for a man who then says he doesn't want any, that it is a meal which will not warm up well, that it is unhealthy to drink instead of eating, and similar standard pleasantries of a subacid nature. We have to wait for these clowns out of Lille, who have probably stopped on the road for a beer.

It is thus a frightening crowd which comes to beset a lonely frightened woman. We are all very polite and quietly spoken.

There was never much doubt, and there is less still when it is noticed – and it is – how very scrubbed the kitchen is. This is a houseproud woman and everything about her is clean, but this is too clean.

There are simple questions about times and places. The children are sent to look at the television. Very soon the matter is raised of the clothes worn. Elena's lying is just as pathetic as was Olga's.

A strong active woman, singleminded about a task, can manage remarkable feats. Alone, for she was determined to involve no other person, she had wrapped the body in old sheets. She had stripped then and taken a shower – that needed no explaining. Dressed in old working clothes she had got her horrid parcel out of the house. An extraordinary feat singlehanded. Getting it into the back of the car had been bad. Done by stages, resting at intervals. She knew that bodies stiffen, that any delay would make the task harder yet, but this she was going to do and did.

The Substitute intervened here. He had left the conduct of enquiry to me, up till now.

"Madame, could you tell me why you took such immense pains to get it out of the house? You must have known that such an attempt to evade justice would be futile?"

She looked at him as though he were off his nut.

"What d'you think I care about justice? I should run the risk of my children coming down and finding this?" He had the grace to mutter "I beg your pardon."

"I thought of going to the cemetery," she said. "But then I would have been found at once. I went to the garbage dump. That was bad. I could not ask forgiveness of God. I asked him to forgive me, for that."

Véronique got up without a word and went to telephone. I did not envy the task of the municipal police at the garbage dump. Elena sat quietly at the kitchen table, her hands folded. She looked without curiosity at the antics of the technicians. I had explained to her that scrub as one may there is no getting rid of blood: in the lab the smallest fragment shows the size of a dinnerplate.

"Shall I make you some coffee?" she asked.

"Only two small questions now, Elena. The gentleman here will see you in the morning, and he won't make it difficult. Just for me now. Why?" Her eyes were bloodshot and the orbits bistred: she had had no sleep. But she looked at me without fear or hatred.

"I knew that he had been with another woman. I could smell her on him."

"Yes. And finally – will you show me how?" She seemed puzzled for an instant, as though unable to remember and unable to understand that. Then she put her hand to the drawer of the table where she was sitting. The usual muddle of corkscrews and beer openers, potato peelers and nutcracker. My own kitchen drawer is just the same. So I dare say is Mr State Attorney's. Vera keeps little twists of string which she cannot bear to throw away.

Elena scrabbled about and came up with a cook's knife. A professional's, thirtytwo centimetres, twenty of them triangular steel blade. She reversed it courteously to give it handle first to the startled technician.

"This is Véronique," I said. "She's a sensible girl and she understands things. She'll help you pack some clothes and things you'll need. You tell her everything the children want and she'll stay with them. In the morning we'll get the lady who will look after them, and – well, you have my promise, you'll see them soon." VV's expression was drawn in the obstinate lines of I-get-all-the-shitty-jobs, but she is both kind and trustworthy.

Elena got up calmly and then, as is often the way, she broke down utterly, covering her face with both hands.

"Blood," she said, holding her arms out, her eyes tracing the line from fingertip to shoulder. "Blood." She brushed her fingers down from her forehead to her neck and chest and down to her thighs. "Under the shower, the water was full of blood. I drew bucket after bucket of water. I made a terrible noise. I can't understand why they did not wake. I told them he'd had to go to Poland in the night." Well brought up, the Substitute got her a

23

glass of water. He is a nice young man. He will not pursue her, in court, vengefully or with venom. With severity, at first, and then he'll ask the jury to temper that. Three years, would be my guess. But I could not stop thinking of Lady Macbeth. 'What, will these hands ne'er be clean.' Scrubbing at the spots. Elena's lifetime will not be enough to scrub it all clean.

I got home at last. Since Véronique stayed with the children, in a nightdress lent her by Elena but stopping short, I should imagine, of using a dead man's toothbrush, I had the job of bringing her to the Women's House of Arrest.

Vera was still up, knitting and with the radio on. Late night jazz programme from France Musique. I sat sort of slumped with a badly-needed cigarette. The fluted voice, of monstrous affectation, was explaining about blues. Teach yer granny to suck eggs! Enigmatic but graphic English phrase taught me by my friend Geoffrey Dawson.

But it started again, a slow hard beat from the drummer on his cymbal, and the harsh hoarse flourish of Jack Teagarden's trombone. And then the famous whisky-voice.

> Won't you come along with me! –

"Food?" said Vera.
"Beuh!"

> We'll take the boat – to the land of dreams –
> Steam down the river –

"Cup of chocolate?"
"Are you trying to make me sick?"

> The band's there to meet us –
> Old friends to greet us –

"At least a cup of tisane. Come on – a linden tea."
The voice had gone confidential.

> Basin Street
> Is the street –

"Honey and lemon."

– always meet.

"You've been smoking too much too."
"Oh for the sake of peace all right then, but do stop fussing."
"I do not fuss. I care."
"Yes but shut up, do, I'm trying to listen."
The voice had changed again. A minor key? – I am no musician; I am never quite sure what a minor key is, though as the Proc says about Porn I recognise it when I see it. Slurred, drunk nostalgia.

> Glad to be,
> Yes sirree,
> Where welcome's free,
> Where I can lose –

Lose my Basin Street Blues. The trumpet broke in, great big happy gold tone. Henry Allen, is it? I turned around to try and concentrate upon what she was saying. Least one can do. She is my wife. She loves me. And what is more, if I were to come home smelling of another woman, I'd keep a sharp eye on the kitchen drawer where the knives are kept. My gun, which I do not use but am obliged by regulation to keep, I have locked in a bottom bureau drawer. I don't like it, although our present Minister of the Interior, and his sidekick, known as Charley and Bob, are to us still better known as Smith and Wesson (purely private police joke). Vera says she does not understand the mechanics of guns, and would not know how to use one. If circumstances arose, I rather think she'd be a quick learner.

The English keep saying we, that is 'The French', have no sense of humour. I'd agree on the whole. Probably few French people would, which supports the imputation. What is 'French' anyhow? I am married to a foreigner, and have never at any time felt much convinced by the nationalism concept, but I am a servant of the state. That implies constraints.

Thus, when Professor Davidson started mumbling round his pipe about collecting the 'documents in the case' I felt pretty wary. Throughout my connection with this matter I was way outside professional umbrellas. Unprotected, and it is important to myself, my wife, and my children, to stay protected. Professionally speaking.

The English make too much of their sense of humour. Take a look at their journalism. Every subheading, relentlessly determined to be funny; so rarely better than facetious.

I wasn't very proud either of the rôle I had played. Arthur said he saw. He's nice; like his wife; I like them both. They're both a pest. She, particularly.

"I do see," said Arthur.

"So leave me out, okay? A whisper of this in official circles and I'd be busted. Believe me, the government has no sense of humour. And no interest in fairness."

"No no. Like any case history, disinfected. Even if it gets to publication, anonymity guaranteed, as the cure-for-baldness people put it. But I don't want to cook it more than need be. Avoiding euphemisms."

"You mean like the illiterate are really just educationally subnormal?"

"Huysmans described a stiff prick as an apanage in emotion."

"He was emotionally deprived, no doubt."

"I have a colleague," said Arthur, "who studies the contents of dustbins. Sociology is largely listening at the bathroom door."

"How like the police it does sound. Only we never have the time."

"Trailing clouds of glory do we come," said Dr Davidson, whom I was to learn enjoyed a phrase, "but leave in a haze of exhaust fumes."

I have learned he can be relied upon. He will be making literature, no doubt, from police prose. But I said yes to him, in the end.

Editorial note: A.D.

Castang has a natural distrust of professors. I don't blame him: the very word sociologist is a big initial handicap to common sense and clear thinking. The definitions are as loose as the screws of its priesthood. It is notorious for the most unreadable jargon. Our notions of crime still rest largely upon the Mosaic Law: beyond that it's just antisocial behaviour. Since nearly all behaviour is aberrational and most of it criminal, a code of conduct is needed and nobody has so far done better than Moses. The injunction not to covet your neighbour's wife is extremely sensible. Bourgeois society has muddled all this. Crime becomes anything from the goings-on of Gilles de Rais to adolescent delinquency, which is mostly the wish to attract notice.

I have limited my own studies to what are termed crimes against the person. It is typical of the bourgeois that they give more weight to crimes against property. In this we can detect the flaw of economics. When discussing production and consumption we use the word 'goods' when we should be speaking of bads. Talk about Wealth and the Gross National Product (Denis de Rougemont enquired whether this included the earnings of prostitutes) is as meaningless as it is destructive. Economists are very silly people, though few are actively vicious.

I ramble, but so does sociology.

The reader should be warned, finally, that the great difficulty throughout these pages was the bringing of Lady Macbeth back to life. Alas, she was not available for interview.

ARLETTE DAVIDSON . . .

I can rival anyone when it comes to gabbling at a tape. I write things down, too. I got told by my husband that my word-of-mouth was 'disjointed'. In using these academic expressions Arthur is being defensive. He is fond of saying things are otiose, nugatory. He called my early efforts 'woolly-minded adumbrations', and I told him that these pedantic turns of speech betray the usher. He would not dream of putting on this pompous hectoring manner with students; get pelted with tomatoes if he did. He then withdraws into ironic self-deprecation.

All right, I adumbrate. A shadowy outline is all I have. There are no proofs, no solid evidence. As everyone was at pains to point out, one can't build a legal case on the nasty feelings I got in my gut. Like the insurance adjuster in *Double Indemnity*. One can only go and look. Well, that is what I did.

It is a fact that Sibille has disappeared. There are more facts. I cannot conclude by saying 'The fact is that Guy killed her'. I can and do say that I know. The point is that Guy knows. I intend him to know that I know. That will also be a fact, for him to realise and to face. Some men do; others do not. Men are forever boasting of their logic, their clearheadedness. The percentage able to face a fact, place it in the equation, is I have noticed small.

Guy Lefebvre. He is or was a neighbour, out there in the country. I am not really countrified: I function better in an urban environment. But I inherited a cottage out there in the wooded hills of the Vosges, from my first husband. Arthur likes being out there, wearing peculiar clothes, with a thoroughly English exhibitionism.

Facts: the Vosges form a range of ancient, much-eroded mountains averaging about a thousand metres in height. Ian Fleming once called them hillocks: by English standards they'd be enormous. They are still beautiful, and fairly unspoilt though much menaced by pollution, and they make a formidable barrier between the Rhine valley, to the east, and the Meuse and Moselle valleys to the west, splitting Alsace and Germany from Lorraine and France. A hematologist tells me that Alsace blood has no element in common with Lorraine blood: that fact is interesting. I know something about marrying across frontiers. I have done it twice. I asked Arthur why Smith or Schmidt seemed to have no equivalent in Latin languages. He answered that 'Faber' means maker. Lefebvre is something like Schmidt. That awful b and v again as in Spanish but the other way round, the b is silent.

But Guy is not French at all! At the risk of boring pedantries, religious persecution in France caused the emigration of huge numbers of French Protestants. The Huguenots, that's right. They fled to Germany, to Flanders, to England. Louis XIV's version of the final solution: as silly, as impoverishing to France, which has never really recovered, as later efforts. There was a lot of genocide too. They were the Sioux and Cheyenne of the south. France's loss was England's gain. Guy's forefathers prospered. I wonder why he came back to France. Something went wrong there. My belief is that this sort of split in a personality is where one starts looking, when later something funny happens. And Guy married a Scotch woman. Nothing odd about that, but might it be a further disjointing factor? Wouldn't a psychiatrist start looking there too?

Guy is a nice man, and I make no bones about that. He is also an interesting man, and was an interesting – and valuable – neighbour. He had a house then in the hills, and had made a wonderful garden. He is a landscape designer: architect I suppose one says. He had this large uneven piece of ground, bought 'because it was so cheap' he said with unFrench candour. He used the contours with great skill. It's acid ground. He had great masses of rhododendrons and azaleas. And there's plenty of water (it rains all the time here): in the boggy bits he made a lovely iris garden. The sandstone is a dark red, most attractive. Guy had a lot of rich clients in Germany. One saw a good deal of him, and we often talked. We weren't 'friends' – I don't think he has many friends. A withdrawn person and not very sociable.

Sibille, though, I became friends with: you can call it that. Quite; here is the first weakness in my argument. There wasn't affection between us (I am being scrupulous). We are both sociable women (hm, this present tense is giving trouble). She is hardheaded, a good business woman. Without her Guy would never have become what he is: successful and sought-after.

Artist or craftsman? – that boring old question. And often I believe the answer depends on business sense. I doubt whether Guy would have done more than make ends meet, on his own. Sibille kept accounts but it takes more than that. Guy could respect a deadline but the bourgeoisie are notorious nonpayers of their bills. It takes two to keep a contract. She was the motor, and she was the canaliser of a specialised reputation.

I have to skip about in chronology, which is tiresome. I had better explain that this neighbourhood time was five years ago. They moved; sold the house here (at a good profit) and went south. We lost sight of them.

Guy, when planning a garden, made an elaborate and beautiful picture of his design, his vision. His original training, I believe, was as a draughtsman. He did perspectives, to scale, in indian ink (and watercolour, gouache, crayon; I get lost amid the technical media but when I say that he greatly admired William Blake . . .). It was a good selling argument: clients were delighted and hung them in the hall.

But a garden takes a generation to come to maturity. Trees are – I mean they have life and ideas of their own. There are always accidents, and neglect. One could say, I suppose, that these designs are halfway between imagination and reality. Guy did fantasy pictures too. Sibille started hunting out openings in the art-dealing world, and this was happening when I ran across them both in New York. But any reader will be getting impatient with me by now, so that I will come to the present, and fill more of the background in later.

The English couple – they are very nice – who bought the house from Guy and often drop in of an evening, were full of an unexpected visit. Gossip. One gets much taken up, in the country, with any little thing out of the ordinary. I do not despise gossip. Arthur grumbles about his privacy (a perfect disgrace, flybuttons undone and pipe-ash all over) but secretly enjoys it. The English are good at making gossip amusing.

"There of a sudden appears this rather grand car. All agog. You remember that estate wagon, grotty Volkswagen all earthy and turfy at the back, smelling delicious. Out gets Guy, very friendly but seeming oddly embarrassed with a long involved tale about customers in Germany." Fair enough, I'd have thought: he had maintenance clauses in some of his contracts, but was always conscientious about how things were getting along. He doesn't just take the money and run. A type of integrity beyond ordinary commercial honesty (and that is rare enough). It singles him out. You feel he cares. I have said it, he's a most attractive personality.

"Rather over-voluble, lot of explaining one didn't want to listen to. But one's fond of old Guy, you know, so of course we said stay to dinner, won't you stay the night . . .

"Oh, much the same. Bit older, bit fatter and greyer. Rather smarter, kind of gaberdiney whipcordy, but looking oddly dishevelled. Been grubbing about in the woods by the look." There are often rather good bonzais to be found by the side of the woodcutters' tracks, which got trampled on when seedlings and have acquired decorative distortions.

"Yes. Alone." Sibille always was along on business trips; was indeed indispensable to them. "So we filled him up with single malt and sooner or later, where's Sibille? He pulls a sickly face, and it appears she's left him."

She'd not made much of this, with most people a commonplace if a sad one, but it pulled me up straight away. Remember, I knew Sibille pretty well. There were things we had in common.

Argue it as much as you like. A lot of marriages break after twentyfive years. The word menopause gets uttered. Sure. I'm in my fifties too, and God knows Arthur is trying. That biological upheaval is violent and takes startling forms. Women can go pretty dotty. But it doesn't alter basic traits of character.

Sibille was a fiercely proud woman. Also ambitious, tenacious, hard if you like and selfwilled. Only words, but I look at them more closely because I've had them all used about me.

I have never got over this basic stumblingblock. I just don't believe in Sibille walking out. Arthur goes pooh, and says I'm swamped in my own subjectivity. All right, I'm an obstinate woman.

For a start, when you take a woman out of her native habitat the effect is profound. She loses family and neighbourhood links. The belonging is important to her: the roots are there for a purpose and are not so called for nothing. At student age, one is delighted to be rid of all that junk. Later one realises how much one has cut off.

A man transplanted finds compensation in work. His living to make, the purpose and achievement; he has so much to fight for. The whole success thing. Just the same for a woman, you'll argue, and if she marries then she identifies with her man's effort.

Certainly, but the man has a wider field. Promotion, hierarchy, material reward, social acceptance in a peer group. The woman has only her home and her children, to express her identity.

Times have changed, since I was twentyfive? Yes. Not all that much. When I went through the hard time, losing my man when my children were barely grown, it was a great reinforcement to me that I'd already been through a hard mill, transplanted lock and stock from the Mediterranean littoral where I grew up to a northern country. They thought of me in cliché terms, there. Hard, acquisitive, avaricious French woman. A 'good cook' – oh yeah!

I had to come to terms with what I was. And am. I did. The point is that Sibille had to, too. She got dragged out of Scotland into France when quite a young girl, and her social background changed totally too.

And Sibille is childless. I don't know why, the why might be of interest; in former times a man was sterile now and then, or she was – but now that it's a matter of choice . . . that can come pretty heavy, with bad guilt feelings. One has a precarious vagabond existence, a child is a drag, one keeps putting it off.

I'm pretty sure this house here was the first they'd owned. Guy put every scrap of his being into his gardens. This was genuinely creative; he made it from nothing. While building up the clientèle. Once he'd opened the door in Germany it snowballed, by recommendations, word of mouth, and a garden is its own advertisement, but those early years were rough, with Sibille belting about arguing, persuading, scrounging credit. While I had a civil-service husband whose world I could not enter: I stayed home and raised brats. Guy has not much push. It had to come from her. She was driven in upon herself. It nags me that this is all such truism, so many boring everyday commonplaces. Anyone reading shrugs. It has happened to them, it happens to everyone.

Ambitious, you bet. She wanted a lot, and whole areas of her unused. Isolated, here. She was proud, and secretive, but she sometimes let me see things. You see, I liked her. She felt passion, and frustration. She wouldn't admit to fear or anxiety and she'd never clutch or cling.

And finally she got it made. He was getting jobs all over Europe, and real money coming in. Paintings – but I'll come to that. Sibille did something comic. She bought herself a castle. Oh, quite a small castle, but real enough. She told me, upon a time, that in Scotland she'd been brought up in a castle, but a nineteenth-century fake. The family was something baronial but penurious. I thought it touching.

It was in New York that I heard about this. Don't get the idea that I lead a grand existence. Arthur flits about – there are conferences or whatever. All the international bureaucracies are well-heeled. Quite a lot of expense-account travel. The lollipops, he calls them. He cronies with academic pals in those terrible clubs that are full of portraits of Past Presidents, in huge paralysing gilt frames, frowning upon the female sex. And I trudge about being cultural. But on this occasion I was in Lord and Taylor, thinking about a new frock, and doubtless I should have been in Bloomingdales. Who should heave in sight but Sibille. Lucky her, she's slenderform down to the ankles, while I worry about my behind. Over some female chat we made a date for drinks that evening. Arthur (the effect no doubt of that club architecture) is addicted to the kind of place with buttoned leather sofas and we all found ourselves in the Algonquin. I realised Sibille wanted to preen a bit. Poverty days are now over.

Arthur was in vein, full of witticisms and aphorisms or whatever he calls them, being Robert Benchley, and I'm sitting there in the new frock being Myrna Loy. Guy was exuberant, in the throes of a fantastic love affair with cast-iron architecture: God, were he and Arthur showing off to each other!

And Sibille was the lady of the manor. What had happened? His imaginary gardens, that clean draughtsman style unbending into baroque fantasy, had gone to town. New York is full of Piranesi. Arthur was delighted with the Bowery Savings Bank, which is mind-boggling anyhow, getting a garden in the middle where they keep the petty cash. It began, said Guy, with Madison Square Garden, which is neither square nor a garden so he made it both. Tree ferns in the Grand Central train shed, sequoias in the Apthorpe Apartments and giant lianas invading Tudor City. A dealer – they're always on the lookout for novelty . . . no, that sounds denigrating: Guy had genuine talent as an architectural painter, and a sense of style, and what sounds like Belgian comic-strip drawing in the sci-fi mode was actually far better.

Sibille had chatted up the dealer into giving gallery space and they sold like hot-cross buns. Which are something English, I've never found out just what. I am rambling badly, I realise, re-living a happy hour getting pissed in the Algonquin, resurrecting the splendid Stanford White buildings long since knocked down. The little round church! Penn Station!! All with the trees Guy chose as specially suitable; in, out, or coming through the roof.

Sibille beamed, looking young and beautiful. She has the looks which by electric light in these surroundings become magnificent. At last happy. I was happy myself.

Was Sibille clutching at her past, the high-born forebears and the baronial halls (conservatory in Victorian Gothic, causing a frightful run on the central heating: when Arthur asked about her childhood she said 'we were all permanently blue with cold')? I'll leave that to the shrinks. The point about the new castle was that it was in the Midi. But it is no difficult transition from Piranesi to 'This castle hath a pleasant seat'.

What was it put Macbeth in mind? She is Scotch, of course, and her pleasure in the slightly vulgar gallery success was a scrap indecent: 'now art thou thane of Cawdor'. She did gloat rather over the little red dots which said 'sold'. The prices were frightful. I would have liked one of those pictures but wasn't going to grovel for a discount.

My curiosity was whetted about the castle. I suppose that is a hideously stale metaphor – still, the scythe . . . I was in that part of the world six months later, an enquiry I could have farmed out, but it's nice being in the south, still 'my home' just a little, however spoilt, at the moment when spring has not yet come to Strasbourg. The southern spring first, with the almonds in blossom, while looking forward to the late, exquisite, German spring. On the autoroute one does it in a day easily, given Arthur's devotion to Lancia cars. Still, I admit, this was all a pretext for the whetting.

There are castles aplenty in the Vosges, strictly Germanic; fragments of bandit strongholds upon impossible pinnacles, too draughty even for Dracula. One sees at a glance that there is no way these could ever be liveable. In the south, though, the 'château' is often a small simple manorhouse with something toy-soldier about it. The fortifications no more than a round tower on each corner. Owners from the Renaissance on tended to knock out the grim bits and rebuild with more of an eye towards pleasure, comfort, and prettiness. They look now as though never intended to be taken seriously, much less stand a siege. Less ugly nonsense of crenellations and arrowslits. But they need water. Years of northern living have marked me. I too now want a tree that is better than a stunted bush, a stream fuller than those dried-out rivulets.

However, Sibille's was a nice castle, even stuck up on the edge of the arid Causse. Rather a barrack: I suppose its bigness made it cheap. But a painter once fashionable need never dread an impoverished old age.

A fine view from the terrace in front, and a pretty 'perched' village behind. The grey limestone had a Scotch look. One could see how it would appeal to Sibille. She was much enjoying her châtelaine existence.

Everything I say about her sounds malicious. I must correct this. I liked her before and I liked her now. The twinges of envy sometimes make me feel like Saint Sebastian (she was wearing beautifully cut trousers with a high waist). She didn't show off. She was genuinely glad to see me and was delighted when I liked the house. The towers were only good for bathrooms but Guy had a lovely studio at the back. She was full of laughter, begged me to stay the night, and cooked a splendid dinner. Guy acted very relaxed and comfortable, but I thought he had a strained, harassed look. That is a worthless piece of hearsay supposition. I promised to keep this factual. But it isn't entirely imaginary. I had a strong feeling that things were not quite well between them. There were some snappish exchanges. Business was good, he said. Exhibition coming up in Köln, said Sibille, and plans for Paris and London: she was full of this. He seemed strangely sulky at her shop-glibness.

She had certainly recreated her childhood. Her big livingroom was full of that anglosaxon litter that Arthur loves, the shabby cretonne sofas whose cushions are always covered in dog-hair. Binoculars and a bird book, lots of china and glass and magazines and newspapers. I am much too French, and long to tidy it all up. Painful I thought too, to Guy's meticulous eye. I wondered whether he was really enjoying all this. And no garden! Not that he was likely to run short! 'Far more work than I can handle.' As for the house, did one detect detachment, amusement? That is guessing: one does not 'detect' anything of the sort, and people who say they do are being vain while thinking themselves perspicacious. One can only say 'that day; in front of me' Guy showed a polite indifference. My wife's house. Well, if she enjoys it. I want her to be happy.

There was no doubt at all about Sibille's being happy. The natives of southern France, and I am after all one of them, aren't on the whole a bad lot. Ignorant and superstitious and given over to every imaginable chicanery, and who could blame them?

They are poor, and they've always been plundered. Piracy has been endemic round here since the beginnings of time, and practically in our day whenever it wasn't Arabs ('the Saracens') it was the Spanish, the English, or the awful kings of France. Nearly all the land is worthless, and everything it does produce is of mediocre quality. Small wonder that they have taken to the barbarian horde of sunworshippers with such enthusiasm. At last a fertile source of revenue! Loonies who'll pay a fortune for some wretched shack not worth fourpence. My only wonder is that on the whole their piracies are quite amiably conducted.

And the barbarians? Again, one can only be surprised that they too are mostly quiet and kindly folk. Of course there are the frightful ones: Arthur gets very cross because they bring shame upon him. And there are good ones, pacifists and tree-planters who try to battle against greed and despoliation; and there are all the artists, hardly any of them worth a glance but if there were no bad artists there would be no good ones either.

Sibille gets on well with them all. She has plenty of money and likes people to drop in. Lots of people. She piles into her car and runs about the countryside. She speaks fluent French to the natives and will hobnob as gaily with Dutch teenagers as with Brit colonels.

But something was wrong. I didn't know what. I still don't know what. I came back from that trip obscurely disquieted. And something now is wronger. Sibille has disappeared. I cannot swallow this. It is exactly the sort of thing which causes a momentary ripple among one's acquaintance. A scrap of gossip. Oh dear! Who'd have thought it! And then it slips out of one's mind. It hasn't.

For ten years now I have been dealing professionally in human failure. It struck me, you see, that there were huge holes in the network existing for people in trouble. This is why there has grown up everywhere a hundred specific organisations for the purpose. Everyone nowadays knows about AA or Amnesty. There's an OverEaters Anonymous too; I don't think it has reached France yet. No bad idea if it did. These little clubs of people in the same boat and showing solidarity take the load off a good few backs. There are still many holes left, and ten years ago in France hardly anything existed to help the battered wives or people released from prison. The police, the doctor, the lawyer . . . the overworked and underequipped 'social assistant'. Outside that – well, there's always the Sally Army. I tried to put myself to work. Bewilderment and despair brought many to my door. How do you cope with spiteful neighbours? What does the young woman do, sexually blackmailed by her boss at work? The same over and over.

'Granny is senile and my husband says put her in a home.'

'I have this skin disease and no doctor seems able to . . .'

'My auntie died and left us a house but my sister refuses to . . .'

'We haven't the space, we haven't the time, we haven't the energy and we haven't the money.' I suppose the tide of 'my-son's-on-drugs-my-daughter's-pregnant' has slackened a bit; as other tides mount. Noise, for example; the huge tin radio and the hopped-up motorbike. 'The police do nothing.'

I began to understand. I used to be married to a cop, so that the professional habit came easily to me. Most people think that the matter with cops is corruption. There's a good deal. I have myself been offered money I hadn't earned and wasn't likely to, and as for 'favours' – the free this and that, the fifty-per-cent-off, the I-can-put-you-in-the-way-of. I have felt the pressures of power: the dosage of promise and threat, the warning off. But even worse perhaps is the anaesthesia and brutalisation. One slides so quickly into the routine cliché answer. The smooth path, the easy greasy way out. I grasped that true professionalism is the task of Sisyphus; to bring some freshness to every dirty day.

Of course I know that if I were to go to the police, and tell them something has happened to Sibille, a dullard one would just look at me. A better one might just take the trouble to explain. The police, Madame, get more done by knowing when to leave things alone than by Doing anything.

I don't need any goddamn warnings about busybody old ladies. Or against professional excess of zeal either.

But something has happened to Sibille.

I have made up my mind. I am myself going to seek professional advice. I know an old gentleman who is pretty smart. He is retired and lives in the Basque country. That's a long way away. But Arthur is talking about 'needing a break' and the students aren't due back for another fortnight. He should not need much persuading to spend a few days on the Atlantic coast. He likes to walk upon the beach and ask 'What are the wild waves saying?' They say things like Eat More Fish, and Take More Exercise. They might ask how the rugby club is doing, or suggest a day in Spain. 'Do I look like a terrorist? Do I look like the political-police? Worst of all, do I look like a tourist?'

ADRIEN RICHARD . . .

If there's one thing that annoys me it is to be reminded that I was a police officer. I'm a little old man. In France, once retired you become 'un petit vieux'. Even supposing you played basketball. No use saying that you might have shrunk a bit but still measure two metres.

I have dealings now and then with the administration; cheap transport or whatever for what they call the Third Age. A careful anonymity with all those cheeky girls. When I pop off I will ensure there are none of those lengthy obituary notices in the local paper; a particularly ludicrous type of boasting.

> Fallen Asleep in the Peace of the Lord.
> Former Past President (a pleonasm or two is welcome)
> of the Intersyndical Committee
> for the Recuperation of Used Beer Cans
> Deeply regretted, Profoundly mourned.
> No flowers, but contributions to the local bordel
> Will be welcomed.

The less said about me, alive or dead, the better I like it.

I was glad to see Arlette. I am fond of this woman. Her former man was a cop who got shot. There are cops who deserve this, but to them it rarely happens. The preposterous sociology professor, to whose dossier, as I gather, I am now contributing, is more likely to be stoned. He has asked me to recall a conversation. Unlike all the old men I know I do not embellish my imaginary memoirs with a post-prandial literary gift. Perhaps on this account I can still reproduce a conversation. It won't be exact but it will be honest.

"I have an unshakeable conviction."

"People do. I'll shake it for you. Since that obviously is what you've come for. To wit?"

"The man killed his wife."

"And you've no evidence? Very well, what's your terminus a quo? Last seen."

"They left together, in the car. Ad quem is his arrival in the evening, slightly shaken, with a tale that she's left him."

"Why shouldn't it be true?"

"Quite out of character. I know her well enough to be sure of that."

"Nonsense. Man drives, woman nags. He says get out and walk, and blimey, she does."

"Certainly. It's happened to me. One takes the train and reappears, behaving as though nothing had happened."

"Or one decides that the moment is as good as another. One takes the train, to Mum, to Paris, to Vancouver Island. Bank account? Credit card?"

"Held in common. I can't check it, obviously, but he wouldn't lie about it, because it can be checked."

"She's fifty you tell me, a good-looking woman, competent and independent. Good moment to start a new life."

"Adrien, it just isn't so. A woman of simple, strong ideas. Like me."

"A conviction, you mean, of always being right."

"Touchée. But I have some training in objectivity. I'm telling you this. She might go off in a rage but she wouldn't desert a husband, any more than I would. My peasant, huguenot, cathar forebears. It's been six months."

"What were they, yours?"

"Petty wine growers, in the Var."

"Six months later, what have you done about it?"

"All the usual. The friend anxious to get in touch, the piece of unfinished business, the debt-recovery service, all the usual private eye stuff. Lefebvre himself. He's a friend of mine too . . ."

"Very well, what is your hypothesis?"

"I can't see any plotting. A flash of temper, a loss of control. He hit her, say, harder than he meant."

"And isn't he then the sort of person who would turn himself in? Does he live with that, for six months?"

"I wouldn't have thought so."

"Artist, you say. Romantic temperament, impulsive? A dependent character. He wouldn't last a week. He'd see Banquo's ghost."

"Adrien, I've thought of all this. He has found, somewhere, some justification. Telling him it was unavoidable. Even that it was right."

"You mean that he couldn't help himself? That it was all Lady Macbeth's fault?"

"Adrien, I know it sounds silly, but I think she was Lady Macbeth."

"What you think, my dear, is not enough for a judge. What's his present situation? How locked in is he?"

"He's at a stage in his career when he finds himself a big success. Largely her doing, be it said. But he's the indispensable one. He can let it snowball."

"And how safe does he feel himself?"

"Very, I should think. He has only to repeat that she left him, it's her affair, he doesn't want to know. Who is to ask questions?"

"Her family."

"There are two sisters, both in England. They tell me they're worried, that she would never allow this time to pass without being in touch. Wherever she was. But what can one do, in another country? Get on to consulates and the like. Who make soothing noises. As long as it's not terrorists . . . World's big, people get lost in it. Takes years before you can presume death."

"What did he do with the body – in your imagination?"

"In the Vosges? Full of forests? Huge stretches where you don't see a soul."

"Stopping at the ironmongers to buy a spade. Have you any idea how much work is involved in getting rid of a body?"

"Adrien, the whole point is that Guy is an expert, a professional gardener. He always has tools in the back of the car. He knows about terrain, and undergrowth, and everything. And he knows all that district."

"I see that the fact serves as an excellent starting point to your scenario. Which I must tell you has no sound base. She left him. It happens. She then went to stay with friends we don't know about. They shelter her, and they keep quiet about it. She decides to make the break a clean one, and hey ho, for Mexico. Want a new passport? Remarry. What's a bigamy or two, these days? I repeat, it happens."

"And Myra Hindley was parked by the side of the road while Brady was burying a body. A cop came along and asked what she was doing. She said the carburettor flooded and she was waiting for the plugs to dry. Perfectly reasonable, cop saluted and left. That happens too."

"Arlette, I think I know why you came here. Ostensibly to ask my advice because you are in a quandary. Like everyone else, when you get it you are disgruntled and prefer not to listen. You have fallen in love with a theory, which makes for bad police work. Correct me if I am mistaken: did you have a notion that I could somehow initiate some official enquiry – maybe?"

"I'd have to be honest and admit that something of the sort did cross my mind."

"And I'd have to tell you there was nothing whatever I could do."

"Oh bullshit, I know how a word in the right quarter works."

"If I could I wouldn't. At my age one starts a lot of things one isn't going to finish. Not this. If your friend had some considerable advantage to gain – insurance, inheritance – if you had, even, some evidence . . . In the circumstances there's no way any official will move on it."

"Adrien, what percentage of crime becomes known to the police? Arbitrary, isn't it? Nobody knows so that any figure can be put forward. But in your experience – thirty, forty?"

"Student argument. Silly one if I may say so. Keep it nice and low is the cop's prayer."

"I've heard this before and I'd still rather be silly than cynical."

"Rubbish. We know mankind to be a fairly nasty animal, destructive and autodestructive. We don't really know a great deal more. Even at our most arrogant we don't do better than the medieval mind with concepts like original sin. A cop with any sense is going to say 'Make way for the justice of God' pretty often. Because if he fails to do so he's liable to start thinking himself an instrument of justice, and opening fire. The vengeance-is-mine syndrome. Start with your decent outlaw, Robin Hood being kindly to the poor and small children, continue all the way to the mad bomber. You'll find the same sentimental fallacy in them all, from Achilles to Dirty Harry."

She stayed to supper. Nice woman. And a lot of fun. I remember thinking later that the good woman, who spreads good around her, sails perilously close to just about the worst – as I see it – of crimes; that committed in the name of God. There's no worse villain than your born-again moralist. The Bible Belt Senator, the hardcore ayatollah, zapping people under the banner of Truth. Inquisition all over again, building a bonfire round the baddies. The words *auto da fé* mean Act of Faith. God told them to set a match to the wicked.

I asked Judith later how much trouble it would be burying me – to the accomplished gardener. She thought about it. Dragging me about would be the hard part. For the rest . . . a nice magnolia on top – her eyes began to gleam.

ARLETTE DAVIDSON . . .

Why didn't I listen to that sensible voice? In at one ear and out at the other. I remember saying to myself that I'd made a mistake, that an old cop is always an old bastard.

I didn't, of course, tell Richard that I was not going to give up. He'd only have shrugged and said 'Women!' in exactly the same tone he uses to say 'Polizei!' I haven't frequented the police all these years without knowing why they view the law with cynicism. The whole apparatus of courtrooms and clerks, pleaders and judges, reeks of bourgeois values. The 'fine points', the quillets they so relish; debated for hours while the human being has been minced fine and set out to dry. Carelessness in a date, a clerk's laziness – or a judge's caprice – can set a year's police work at naught. No wonder that the public views the Court with bewilderment and fear. One is surprised when a good judgment is made, as it often is, after a year or more of bandying about.

And I say 'However bad they are they're all we've got!' The best we can do, and it's not very good. During my childhood the big city meant Marseille. Paris was too far away to be real. The gang war years, which still go on. Nearly every day some ruffian was left on the pavement in his blood. And occasionally it would be an elderly party, of weight and substance, in a well-cut suit and the hat known to Arthur as an Anthony-Eden. Enjoying his lunchtime apéritif, thinking of getting his hair cut, as his languid eye swims along the columns of the newspaper; surprised by twenty machine-gun bullets. 'One less,' said my father cheerfully; the commissaire of police added the classic tag, 'Doing our work for us.' But while the small fry were forever in and out of jail, against the seigneurial sharks there was somehow never sufficient evidence. One learned the legal jargon. 'The public action extinguishes itself.' Not to speak of 'invalidated by an error of procedure'.

As a schoolgirl I used to think 'Who needs evidence?' Put a bullet in the bugger; his blood on the deck is all the evidence we need. But one grows up, and out of the Bulldog-Drummond years.

When later I started advice work I often got dragged in to law courts. For when the poor come for help, it is often to ask why they cannot get justice. Their causes are in general simple and selfevident: they are dragged to court by some administration acting with the most tortuous chicanery, in flagrant bad faith. How can they distinguish equity from law?

I read *Bleak House* as a student and have not forgotten the impression it left. The symbols of slow torment, Miss Flite and the Man from Shropshire, are nowise faded. I have seen them both on the benches provided for the public. They are in many a condemned cell across the breadth of the United States. Prisons and lawcourts – 'it is the fire of heaven must change this place'. Why did I not think of all this? I did not think that I might come to look like Miss Flite, waiting for a Day of Judgment.

What did Lady Macbeth look like?

GUY LEVEBVRE . . .

Ed. Note: A handwritten 'prison diary'. Some irrelevant material has been cut, and the tendency towards introspective rambling, to be expected in the circumstances, tightened up a little.

'I am not much of a reader' as gets said in that self-deprecating tone, meaning not at all. So the phrase is inaccurate. Of course I read, but not widely or thoroughly. I'm not really an educated person and what I suppose I should have said is 'I'm not much of a writer'. I don't express myself clearly or with exactitude. It doesn't much matter, nobody's ever likely to read this. It's my effort to understand. Some people write diaries. Are these intended for their children, or what? I haven't any. Or is the idea to read it oneself years later, interested in what one was doing at the time and what the weather was like? Sounds pretty narcissistic to me. I mean, as opposed to the dates and appointments of a business-diary, or the bald factual record of a logbook. A psychiatrist would have answers to all this. My chief reason is that I have plenty of time on my hands and nothing else to do!

My life – up to now – has been a busy one, I mean filled with dead-ordinary hard work. Physically. Once the student days were passed, in all the growing months I've been out there, rain or shine. I suppose that is why I find myself so disconcerted now, indoors (within a door shut and bolted), idle. A garden is demanding. There is no slackening of effort while daylight lasts. Why not, since I am healthy.

I know an old farmer who is close to eighty. He got a letter which I translated for him – the officialese being to him Greek. It was about retirement rights. Agriculture was the last category of workers left in France to get them. He laughed. 'What difference will it make?' he said. 'Who's going to do the work?' He has children, and grandchildren. None interested in breaking their back on the lousy smallholding which he has worked for seventy years. To no purpose? He does not regard his life as wasted, and there's metaphysics for you. The work which is yours, is that useless? Selfrespect, is that worthless? The economists cannot understand. Money is all they know.

Sibille did not understand. That's a sort of tragedy, I suppose. Since she thought I was sabotaging her deliberately.

In the winter when the freeze stops work – that's right, I am a man of the north, and I'm proud of it – I do my drawings. In the oldfashioned architecture faculties of my youth we learned to set out a perspective, compose an elevation, harmonise proportions. We got the basics of column and pediment hammered in. Doric, Ionic or Corinthian, they were to me from the very beginning trees. The Mediterranean lands had trees once, and water. I should have loved it then. I do not forget that it was from the north that they came to pirate it all. Man the maker and breaker. Well, I have tried to pay something back. I must shoulder my share of the destruction. When the trees were cut the soil eroded and the land dried. I was taught to answer for my actions. I will. In fact I do.

Architecture now is all math math math. Students grumble if made to draw: why can't the computer do it? Does do it, so much better than us. Cameras have better lenses than our eyes, seeing so much further. The Bushmen also drew, and painted, better than us. I should like to draw animals, but don't know how. I do believe, though, I can draw a tree.

I was never good at the engineering: the weights and stresses, the piping and ducting. Take out the sweat and the shit, it didn't thrill me. Space and movement does not interest today's students, who are taught about rentability. Per cubic metre. Of course, there's no better engineering than in a Wren church: one cannot separate the functions: I had sense enough to see that I was going about it the wrong way. A tree is good at engineering too.

I express myself badly, but writing is not my profession. I suspect, anyhow, that one cannot, by definition, put metaphysics into words.

Who am I? There is no very easy answer to this. The judge of instruction asked me the question, and to do him credit he is thoughtful, and very conscientious. He spent much time, effort, patience on this. But he has a legal mind. One concentrates upon facts. Column, load-bearing element. But the space in between – which is what it is all about? – disregarded altogether. Stick to the facts, they say; the figures.

Women are better at this than men. Perhaps this is why so few men have any understanding at all of women.

I'll give an example: I'll try to make it brief. One day in a bookshop I picked up *The Two Towers*, a title to attract an architect. It was of course part of Professor Tolkien's well-known book. It interested me because he had understood a lot about trees, but his elves and goblins struck me as a failure. Their womenfolk were either inexistent or singularly unconvincing. I conclude that women did not interest him.

Perhaps I have made the same mistake? And am suffering for it? But all right; the facts first.

Lefebvre. Commonplace in France, and in England by no means unheard of. A name to be proud of. Huguenot, my father claimed. Snobbery, like going to Massachusetts in the *Mayflower*, but justifiable. The piece of history is well known. Louis XIV repealed the Edict of Nantes according tolerance to Protestants: rather than play false to their beliefs they emigrated, to Germany, Flanders, England. And it was France's loss: they were not only sober and hardworking, honest and high-principled: they were craftsmen. There are historians who date the decline of France from this moment.

Whether all this be true or false, I have felt it as a great burden.

I was thus and am English, since several generations. My father was proud of this; very Brit, boastful. That isolationist, little-islander mentality seemed to me after my schooldays merely stupid. Shakespeare has a lot to answer for. That purple passage about the gem-set-in-the-silver-sea; clever politics at a moment of frenzied chauvinism. He was a smart bugger. I was happy to go back to France. I had roots there.

HENRI CASTANG . . .

Yes, I do get ideas, now and again. Most of them come from the daily paper. I agree; that's a mine anyone can work. It is published in Paris every afternoon, reaches me by post next morning, when the Autocrat of the Breakfast Table is still quick of wit. After I reach the office, reading time gets snipped into thinnish segments. It was well into mid-morning – cloudy, dullish – before I reached Our Medical Correspondent, lurking somewhere round page thirty. But then I lunged for the telephone.

"Madame Metz!" Loud, executive. "Get me this week's duty quack." Our local jail, known as the House of Arrest, is modest, doesn't boast a resident medical officer. Like most penal institutions it dates from around 1880, a time of bright ideas all round. State primary education and such.

So the town's general practitioners take it in turn to be jail doc, police surgeon – that's right, looking suspects over for signs of police brutality. A thankless job which nobody wants. Consisting in the main of dishing out tranquillisers and constipation remedies. And there's the odd suicide attempt, by hanging mostly. But the detainees (that's what they're called, administratively) will go far in efforts to alleviate boredom. This is the one moment when they're keen to visit the dentist. There are those who will break whatever's breakable, and swallow the pieces. Always imagining they're the first to have thought of this.

"Come on Metz, what are we waiting for?"

"Line's engaged." She has the squeaky voice that goes with forever eating surreptitious biscuits.

This rotation of a lousy job means that with the best will in the world medical supervision of a detainee is of poor quality. How could it be otherwise when there's no continuity. 'What did he give you last week? And you mean to say you *still* haven't been?' A young, good, and conscientious doctor will get into bad habits. Some inspectors of police are all three too. Like Varennes, a good girl, and also a consummate bitch. Or me.

"Oh there you are at last. Commissaire Pee Jay here."

"And consulting hour, here." Short and vexed. Amongst the local bourgeoisie, the PJ commissaire is a big wheel? Don't you believe it. Not unless there's a favour he can do. There's a greasiness in the voice, then, you get to recognise. He's a handful of mouseshit, otherwise.

"Elena. Spanish waitress. Polish name which escapes me. You've seen her in jug. Come come man, sharpen your wits. She's on a homicide charge, you've given her a complete physical, because you jolly well have to."

"Yes. Uh." A patient in the consulting-room; he's going to be

49

guarded. Respect anonymity. As well as laconic, succinct; whatever they call being bored and in a hurry. "It's a normal clinical picture. Nothing to worry about – I mean uh, as regards capacity to support uh, the changed circumstances: uh, constraints inherent in the present condition." He means not over-excited so no big sedation.

The alliterative euphemisms also mean there's no good reason why she shouldn't sit in jail for six months, knitting, or twiddling her thumbs or masturbating (among the occupations available).

"One aspect of what you call the clinical picture could be of particular interest."

"What's that? Try and be brief, Commissaire, there's a waiting room here of sneezers all infecting one another."

"I'd like to know how far she is off her period."

"Come, that would come under the area of uh, confidentiality."

"Kiss me – I'm coming too." The police are low, I agree. Vulgar. Gawd help us, I've been a cop on Paris streets. I've had my hands in all the human condition there is. "Just tell me mate, is she menstruating?" He got on his high horse. But he's the one in a hurry. Bibi has lots of time.

"I fail to see how or why the detail should interest a – " watch it, the patient's ears are flapping – "a disinterested observer."

"Make it easy for me; is she or isn't she?"

"And I am far from convinced that it's a legitimate subject of interest." And the fucker banged his phone down: I was back to him in the time it takes to dial.

"Is it going to be abortion, euthanasia, or just a fiscal enquiry into your tax declaration? Now laugh . . . D'you think I'd ring you just to waste your time?" I heard him say 'excuse me a moment'. He coughed to gain time and then politely,

"Will you try and convince me of that?"

"I learn that in the two days before a period all women are under stress. Recent research shows" – and that would get under his skin; he'd hate to be thought out of date – "that ten per cent give or take can be said to feel severe stress. That this can make for a strong factor of disturbance in their behaviour. That at this moment they may give way to severely traumatic experiences. That this fact has been held to have criminological and penological significance." Had to stop for breath after that cannonade.

"Broadly – loosely – there's something in what you say." A patronising medical tone. Commissaire Sweetlips could now come out languidly with his ace.

"This indisputable fact has been accepted as an attenuating circumstance in a murder trial. By an English court of assize. A French court can do as much and the likelihood is right now."

"Who's your authority for all this?" Our Medical Correspondent has in fact a splendid double-barrelled name. But she had been doing her professional homework.

"*The Lancet*," I said, extremely bland.

"I see. Now that's all very well," shaken, but obstinate, "but professional discretion . . . I mean a court is one thing but the police have no right to confidential disclosures."

The French are forever behaving like this. Squeamishness about genital functions is not helping our campaign against shared syringes, and the french-letter, known to us as an english-overcoat, has much trouble acquiring an official countenance.

"Dear doctor, the privacy of your subject will be shared only with her defending counsel, and it might mean the difference of a few years' penal servitude. That's quite a lot, for the mother of small children. Was she or wasn't she?"

"I will hold you responsible for anything said to be a breach of medical ethics. The answer is yes."

"Be ready to repeat that in court, Doctor."

"Listen, Ca – "

"Yes yes, Caca, I know, I'm a turd. But I don't want to see that woman go to jug longer than she has to."

There's another journalist on the paper who does a little satiric-comment feature. Fond of saying, 'I'm old, I'm ugly, I've red hair, I'm Jewish, and I'm a woman – boy, am I in the dog-kennel.'

* * *

"Varennes!"

"Yes? I'm Liss-sening," singsong. She's a cheeky girl.

'In the days when you went to school . . .'"

"Can I remember that far back, I wonder?" She was 'bright' though you wouldn't think so to look at her. Dropped out after two or three years at the university, saying that even the Police was more interesting than that.

"Did you ever get *Macbeth* as an English text?"

"I seem vaguely to remember witches."

"I'm serious." Her ear tells her when she has gone far enough.

"Pretty confusing story but some lovely poetry lets him get away with it." This is the point about Varennes. Her crude behaviour is to disguise the fact that she likes a bit of poetry from time to time.

"Elena. You know, the waitress at the Russian Tea Room. She couldn't get the blood off."

"Yes." Now well switched-on. "I thought you didn't have any problems with that."

"No more I do, or so I hope. What's the point about Lady Macbeth? She'll knife you, and if needed her own husband, given strong enough motivation, right?"

"Or crime-passionnel wouldn't exist as an argument. I really am listening, go on."

"You don't know anything about it because it isn't our district and doesn't even concern us. It got put to me by a friend as a case of conscience. So follow me, a moment."

I told her about Guy Lefebvre. And Sibille. Because I'm damned if I know what to believe. I could 'put it to Vera'. I have, but I don't get a very straight answer. Vera after all is an artist. Guy Lefebvre, after his fashion, is also an artist. They don't behave like other people, which confuses things. She's too quick to see his point of view.

Véronique has not much experience. But she's a hardheaded girl. She might be quicker to understand Sibille. The trouble with Sibille is I don't know enough about her.

"Sounds like a lot of cock to me," said VV: sensibly, on the whole.

"Sounds yes, I agree, but is it?"

"Look, kiddo." This is one of her acts. Her cheeky act covers an affection; call it simply by its name. A respect, too. She is fond of me; I am fond of her. The reader ought to realise that this has nothing to do with sex, if he's not a perfect fool. "Even if that Polish woman – no, she's Spanish, isn't she? – is a bit Lady Macbeth you aren't going to go seeking parallels in stuff like this. I don't get the connection, anyhow."

"Now sharpen your wits, Varennes. Macbeth didn't want to kill the king, witches or no witches. He found excellent reasons against doing so. He's my king, he said, and I owe him my loyalty. He's a thoroughly decent man, who has behaved generously towards me. And strongest of all, he's a guest in my house: sacred. And then the woman worked on his weak brains, weak nerves, and weak resolution.

"Now lookit. She's all these things to him and more, she's his wife . . . Now suppose she commits some treachery, not some pissy little adultery but hitting him really deep in his innermost fears and insecurities. He's got far more motive to put the knife into her subclavian artery than into any king."

"Gaw," said Véronique. "Gah. Yes and no and perhaps and maybe. What are you going to do? She disappeared somewhere in the Vosges, you tell me. I've never been there. Miles and miles of stinking maquis, I can just see it. The gendarmerie aren't going to go digging there. You proposing to toddle off that way with your little bucket and spade? Don't count on me, that's all."

"No, obviously that's not the way to go about it. One might find a pretext for tickling this chap Lefebvre a little, that's all. After all, the story might be true."

"Castang, if you want a pretext, then knowing you you'll find one. No use trying to sublimate your viler instincts through me. I'm virgo intacta mate, and staying that way. Whoever Lady Macbeth may be it isn't Bibi." Slapping her powerful chest.

Turning around and hitching her skirt to mid-powerful-thigh. "Look look, no knives hidden anywhere." A good girl.

"Higher," I said, nastily.

. . . sorry, can't stop coughing this morning. Just as well I don't jog or I'd be dead by now. Sorry, unwarranted interjection.

I have to go back to the moment when I first met Arlette Davidson – yes, sorry, that's your wife. I was divisional inspector then, in a PJ service headed by an old cop called Richard, whose sense of irony used to get us both into trouble. Your wife came in about a sharpie who was dodging alimony payments to his ex. A frequent situation. Court orders get made but there's not much done to enforce them. Arlette was enquiring whether he hadn't bent the law in some other direction, which might give some leverage on the twister.

As it happened we knew about him but we didn't have ground for any criminal charge. And she didn't want him sent to prison. You don't earn enough there for the support of your ex and the children: it's a common enigma.

I put it to Richard, who found a characteristic solution and said 'Scare the living daylights out of him.' Which we did; we sent a tough inspector called Orthez, dressed up as Mafia. Call this illegal and immoral. It's well within your experience that the police is both. One doesn't of course admit it.

I can't be sure but I think this led to the idea of a move against Lefebvre, who was in an untouchable situation. As you know, the Police Judiciaire hasn't the time or energy to go running after cases of this sort. We are quite a human collection, and we check out anonymous letters and denunciations. But nebulous suppositions that So-and-so might have killed his wife because he's acting funny – they don't get followed up much.

One can debate, and probably you do, about our Code of Criminal Procedure. We have to jog along with it. In practice it's as good and as bad as any other system, including the English. You agree that its strength, the impartial enquiry by the judge of instruction, is also its weakness, because that gent has too much power. The police are answerable to him for all they do, and when he gets in the expert reports, technical or psychiatric or whatever, he alone decides. And he can commit a man or woman to prison until the trial comes up, which can take a year. On mere suspicion.

All right, judges of instruction are of much better quality than formerly. But they vary a lot. The worse ones clap people into jug for no more than administrative convenience. In prison, you're filed; immediately available for reference.

And a defending counsel doesn't have an automatic right to habeas corpus. He has to argue for the liberty of his client, and against the tide. You see, judges make great play with that goddamn word Prudence. Like the Parole Board in California, never at a loss for arguments in favour of the deepfreeze. Nightmares about the customer skipping over a frontier, destroying or falsifying evidence, tampering with witnesses. Be it understood, we're talking about the bad ones. There are good ones too.

I'm trying to say that I have some sympathy with judges of instruction. It is not easy to pursue someone, in the legal sense, while maintaining the presumption of innocence. The judge, as a rule, makes up his mind pretty quickly. Even though he's in no sense a prosecutor he tends to bias that way. I had better say that this particular judge has shown himself scrupulous. But he had this antiquated notion that a bit of jail is like medicine. The nastier it is the more likely to do you good. Quite often they use it as leverage, you know. A suspect who's obstinate, obstructive, or what they see as cheeky, they'll often think 'A week or so in jug will change your tune, my lad.' And it's true, alas, that prison will cause a personality change. If the judge were honest with himself he'd see it as the modern equivalent of take-him-down-to-the-basement.

I'm sorry to be prolix. It's your wife! You may know better how she went about it. It's theoretically possible for the citizenry to write a letter to the Procureur, saying there's hankypank going on and what is he going to do about it. Pretty rare for him to do much. Arlette knew this, of course.

As you know, I refused to do anything. My wife kept on at me, and later . . . but that comes later. I felt sure that Arlette would simmer down. I like the way she makes a case of conscience. She has all the qualities that make her a good professional in this business of supporting the downtrodden. She knows of course that neither cop nor citizen can constitute himself an instrument of justice, and that personal acquaintance disqualifies a magistrate. And she knows that these rules get bent. Dislocated is the word I'm looking for. I don't blame her for an instant. A man would say that she got possessed by the thought of this woman Sibille, and identified with her. I don't say that. Women do not think in the way we do.

I leave it to your judgment whether you had better warn her that if a defence counsel gets wind of this carry-on she may be in trouble.

I do not know, and I don't want to know, what view the judge of instruction now takes of Lefebvre. It probably depends on nobody but himself. He'd need to make a confession, bring them to where he hid the body, and you'd look for evidence *there*, and nowhere else, that things happened the way he said they did. Speaking as a cop. Quite likely he did kill his wife. But the burden of proof is on him.

Arlette came, I think, to this conclusion. He's the key to it all.

As I understand it she has played on his nerves, to the extent that he himself asked for an enquiry, and once a Proc is persuaded that a case exists, it's like the *Titanic*, difficult to stop. Not my district, thank heaven, and not my pigeon. If they don't discover a body, I think the affair will peter out; get written off to the domino effect: one mental aberration leads to another. In the unlikely event of it coming to trial: prosecutors, and Assize Court presidents, simply hate this kind of case.

CHARLES-GABRIEL ERLANGER
Procureur de la République . . .

Yes, I know, you want to ask about that case. It came into my mind because the instructing judge there takes a view based upon a severely traditional Christian ethic. Whereas a lawyerly viewpoint, properly speaking . . . Did you ever read the Stevenson novel – unfinished, alas – about the hanging judge? Weir, Weir, Hermiston that's right. There you've got it, very well done. Not that I'd look for examples in literature. Comic strips do it better; there's a lot to be said for them! There would be a balloon drawn over my head, with a trail of little bubbles, containing the one word 'Thinking'. The rest is unnecessary. Literature! Four hundred and fifty pages of complications. That's not a lawyerly view.

Talking like this over a pipe – you've got me 'unbuttoned'. Still, whatever you've got on that machine of yours, you'll give me a written transcript, and I'll read it over with my robe on.

Because wording is important. 'It has not been shown that the defendant's right to undisputed enjoyment of the premises which he occupies, and for which he pays, can properly be held to extend . . .' If I write an opinion, if the President of the tribunal writes a judgment, it is incumbent upon us to do so in lucid phrasing. Not free of jargon, I agree. But clouded language makes for clouded judgments. If only it could be in monosyllables. 'The plaintiff has sought to show a need and the Court sees no such need.' The art of drafting a marginal minute: there's a lost cause for you.

To return to this case which interests you, there was precious little law and a deal too much theology. I looked up my notes on it this afternoon.

A young woman – well, she's fifty – claimed to have collected elements amounting to a criminal act. By observation, so please you. She has some scraps of flimsy circumstance; nothing we'd call evidence. No affordable credence there.

However, she produced a reference, quite a good one, written by a PJ commissaire. Plenty of years there of criminal brigade experience so that it counts in her favour. Stating baldly that she'd sought advice, that it was no business of his, that he had – quite rightly – dissuaded her. But that upon such observation as acquaintance affords, he could regard her as a credible witness and thought it thus his duty to bring this fact – and no other – to my notice. Quite proper, correct behaviour.

It's my duty, Davidson, to look into such things. I had the woman looked into. And I got confirmation of this opinion. Widow of a police officer, I forget where, killed on duty. Remarried to some senior functionary in the Council of Europe. Quite a good background thus. Moreover she has experience of social work: can lay claim to a certain training in analysis, grasp of psychological motivation. All in all, one could form a favourable opinion.

Less so, when one heard of her doings. She had formed an intimate conviction of guilt, in no lawyerly sense, but she had sense enough not to make her imputations public. She went, boldly enough, direct to the man. She is or was on friendly terms with him. Neighbourly relations. She put the query to him, bald: had he or had he not made away with his wife? That particular type of female mind works in ways at once intensely convoluted and extremely simple. You are right in thinking of this as a theological approach. A man in such circumstances often does feel the need to unburden himself through confession. There were no witnesses to the interview. The parties agree that it took place in an amicable – one could say sociable – frame. She appears to have believed that in awakening his conscience she could lead him to initiate or at least consent to procedures which would result in legal enquiry. She claims to have been aware throughout that I was the proper person to take such steps.

Naturally enough the man denied the imputation. By their common account he warned her of the dangers inherent in holding suspicions. If he felt pressures, he said, brought upon him by such means he would put the matter on an official footing. This he appears to have done, in confused fashion. Instead of consulting an adviser he went to the gendarmerie. Who took his statement, properly enough, asked her to give an account of herself and cautioned her as to the results; and in some perplexity forwarded the papers to my office.

The lawyerly viewpoint was to see for myself. Summon her, to explain herself, in my office. No clerk, no advocate is called for in such circumstances. No charge has been laid, or had been contemplated. I would demonstrate a simple legal maxim. 'The plaintiff's enjoyment of civic rights is not held to extend to his criticising the view from his windows.'

So I had her in. I often smoke a cigar on such occasions. Makes for an informal atmosphere. Not that she was intimidated by my title or function. She made a tolerably good impression. A woman of good address and appearance, with intellectual capacity. Held her tongue while questions were put and then answered with care. A grasp of the rules of evidence. She was aware that a mere assemblage of suppositions carries no weight. She was not slipshod and did not show malice. The mere fact of finding themselves before a high legal power is enough to deflate people with damaging tales, repeating and polishing them, coming to believe in them. With my experience of witnesses one becomes fairly adept, you know. They no longer distinguish the line between fact and fiction, and when led into contradiction they become obstinate, flouting reason. There is the hypocrite, who insinuates while feigning to place an innocent construction upon a harmless fact. You have a phrase in English about butter melting in the mouth. There are the over-explainers, the over-glib. The sly, the sullen – there is no substitute for years of trial experience. She was no talebearer. However little fact there might be, I did not feel inclined to dismiss her hypothesis as mere mischiefmaking.

The next step, of an interview with the man, followed. He had gone to Germany upon his business, and stayed there some weeks. No sinister construction could be placed upon that. A loose cosmopolitanism is a pattern with such people. However, a simple verification showed that he had taken a year's lease of a flat hereabouts. There was nothing evasive about his movements.

I had made up my mind to put the matter in Boislevant's hands. He is the senior judge of instruction in this jurisdiction, a man of experience.

But we come back to your point about theology. Boislevant – his chief characteristic, professionally speaking, is thoroughness, application. His exactitude and integrity are beyond question. Fortified, I'd go as far as to say illuminated, by the strongest possible Christian beliefs. In Lent, you know, he eats no meat and goes daily to Mass. Takes a fortnight off each year, to go into retreat at a Benedictine monastery. These traditional ways have their handicaps. To give an example, he's an unshakeable believer in the death penalty. One would feel a little uneasy, from time to time, having him on the bench. But as you know, a judge of instruction is not a trial judge: the separation of powers sees to that.

This strongly theological approach struck me as appropriate to the matter in hand. And he's a sound lawyer.

HENRI CASTANG . . .

You were annoyed with me for not putting a stop to your wife. As you point out, Richard tried to. If I had done the same there would have been an end to the matter. Probably you will find my explanations unconvincing.

I reviewed the alternatives briefly. Not answering. Retreating into the official image behind a brief formal letter. All too easy.

Mrs Davidson let fall that you were addicted to the 'electronic notebook'. I'll adopt the method.

The wasps' nest metaphor applies. Don't stir it up. Anyone who's ever lived in the country knows that much. Particularly, you could say, commissaires of police in country districts. Great

believers all in treading softly. And if anybody is foolish enough
to step in one, then apply as thick and asphyxiating a smoke-
screen as you can whip up at short notice. They are like human
beings; irritable creatures who resent interference with their
domestic comforts, and react violently.

You'll have noticed that it's difficult to persuade a child or a
woman – some men, too – that even one isolated wasp, going
placidly about its business, is not per se aggressive. One can
remove it without an uproar. Aggressivity begins with fear.
Women will insist on chasing them. One then gets angry with the
woman.

There is little point in complaining about this. Men have silly
habits too. Women are irritated by our ridiculous obsessions
with titties and knickers, or our tendency to play with toys. Cars
and computers are two obvious examples. Why are we so
immature? Women's logic is often better than ours, though that's
not obvious, and we curse when they stir up wasps.

In the PJ I work with them all I can, and we don't have nearly
enough. They feel at a disadvantage, and they tend to copy the
men: they do better when they're very feminine. They're good
at private areas. Not just perennial nuisances like flashers or
child molesters. The whole sex thing, I don't need to tell you,
fertile ground. Men are bad at this because it's their deep place
of vulnerability. Many's the competent and efficient cop; one has
no complaint of his work; and at home . . . Brutality, incest,
torture – the police are badly equipped at private crime.

And one of the most troubling statistics is the one that's
missing. The grey area, the fact that we just don't know about
the old women who become troublesome, the old men whose
heirs get impatient, the baby who cries, the child who wets its
bed, the impotent men and the frightened wives.

I don't like what I can guess at. I had very little idea of the
amount of pornography circulating now that it's unrestricted. I
tried the newspaper shop of a tiny country town in my area:
some fifteen hundred souls. I counted twentythree magazines of
pussy on parade, straightforward lumpen-cunt. Totted up to over

five hundred and fifty francs. The shopgirl was embarrassed. A steady sale. So there's an unknown but large number of men masturbating themselves silly: nothing much wrong with that but just how badly skewed is the man–woman relation; how sour is it, how deep does it go?

Frankly, women like Arlette, irritating us by chasing wasps, there aren't enough.

Sibille Lefebvre – she might be the praying mantis for all I know. She might be Lady Macbeth. We're not likely to find out. One might find out something about her husband. It looks like a bad idea and might be a good one. Very often, my instinct is to leave things alone. Back to the wasps' nest.

I think of the Woody Allen line: you recall – 'Doc, my brother's crazy, thinks he's a chicken' – 'Well, why don't you have him seen to?' – 'Yes but I need the eggs': most of us keep going because we need the eggs. Most of us have forgotten how to sing, and we nearly all run the risk of forgetting how to laugh. Judging from my brief meetings with Arlette, she's really no more tiresome than my own wife.

GUY LEFEBVRE . . .

I'm in jail! This has its comic side. I do have some sense of humour. I seem to lose it rather often. One can't put that down to Sibille's 'influence' even though she was a rather humourless person and really throughout the years it is the one reproach I make of her. One doesn't influence people that way – or can one? She certainly influenced me a great deal, but her character was stronger than mine. That much is evident, anyhow.

I see perfectly clearly that if I had done nothing, nothing would have been done. I allowed myself to be panicked by the Davidson woman, and thought I should get some protection from 'the law'. An awfully stupid mistake because I should have known that when in doubt they send on even their negative reports to the office of the Procureur. I should have realised too that he, good man, was being harried by the woman. One forgets that in a bureaucracy there actually is a Man behind the 'office'. I had reckoned that if she went anywhere it would be to the gendarmerie, and thought that I would get in first. I underestimated her, and I overdid my own reaction. Is that the psychology of a criminal? The judge who is 'instructing' me plainly thinks it is. But of that, and of him – more anon, as is said. I have plenty of time. The good Maître Silberstein, my admirable defending lawyer, keeps reassuring me that there is no case, that they're bound to let this nonsense drop, but that the judge is obstinate. So I am doing what I suppose everyone does do in jail, writing the memoirs . . .

Simply, one has nothing else to do. I am quiet, nobody is horrible and while one hears dreadful tales this jail at least is quite clean and sanitary, and I don't mind a bit of austerity. I've had plenty. It has often been said that anyone who went to an English public school never thereafter suffers any discomfort. One is shut in. So were we, for three months at a time, and Silberstein tells me it won't take that long.

An error of judgment. The country gendarmerie must get a great many denunciations and do nothing about most. Also, France being what it is, there is such a colossal quantity of regulations – laws, decrees, instructions, texts upon every aspect of human activity – that absence of zeal is more than a way of life. Do nothing and then obstruct, that is of course the motto of all officialdom. Natural enough; they live in mortal terror of being found at fault. I suppose I counted too much on this.

I have no resentment towards the Davidson woman. I told Silberstein as much. He attacked her pretty roughly, which is no more than his job. Her attitude is simple – that people should take responsibility for what they do. I have no quarrel with that. If she had some axe to grind – but then nobody would have listened to her; neither the Procureur nor, I must give him credit, the examining magistrate: he's a tremendous stickler. He went after her like a tiger, not just looking for malice (I know all this through Silberstein) but for financial interest. Sil – his name is

Serge – is a great crime-fiction addict. Comic on the subject of Travis McGee, a mercifully fictional figure of fun who gets interested in injustice when there's money involved. He has to support a playboy life-style, not to speak of more women than James Bond. And they never come back to pester him!

Mrs Davidson does not bestir herself in matters when they promise pickings. Nor does she do indecent things under a pretence of favours to old friends. She does not suffer from the Robin Hood syndrome, painfully prevalent as Serge remarks, that it's quite all right being shitty in a Good Cause.

She did not really harass me. She did not seek to persecute or entrap me. If I'm in this trouble, I must have the honesty to say it was through my own doing.

But a meddlesome pest of a woman? D'you know, one can't even say that. Between them, Serge and the judge stripped her naked. She was the widow of a police officer in Holland, a decent man, who got assassinated for showing too close an interest in the means crooks adopt to clothe themselves in respectability. And that was many years ago. One cannot question her courage. When it looked as though apathy and timidity would stifle the official enquiry she waded straight in, and got to the bottom of it.*

And she remarried a sociology professor. That is how I got to know her. They had a country cottage in the Vosges, and were neighbours of ours when we lived there. He – again – is interested in the ways of statistics. Once more, appearances of respectability. As he says with justice, figures are used as sticking-plasters on top of cancers.

The difference between appearance and reality has been the fibre of this woman's life: no, one cannot dismiss her as a meddling gossip.

She did not pry. She did question neighbours, but only after they had themselves volunteered disquieting – damaging? – information.

* See *A Long Silence* by Nicolas Freeling; published in the US under the title *Auprès de ma Blonde*.

And she came to me openly. She asked bluntly 'Where is Sibille?' and said – candid – that my explanation did not satisfy her, and that I could not expect it to. Fair enough! Serge has of course pressed me to sue for malicious slander. I have refused. He has, intelligent sharp Jewish mind, agreed that I'm in a stronger position if I don't. She shows no malice; neither should I.

I told her that I would disregard her intervention into my private life, being 'charitably disposed', that I proposed to go about my business in Germany. It was, I must admit, somewhat out of bravado that I took the little studio apartment here for a year. As though daring her to do her worst. But it was sensible too. I have more German business than I know what to do with, and the 'castle' is far away in the south. I could just as easily have hired a flat in Karlsruhe or Stuttgart. But I have no secretary now, and do not want complications with German income-tax. I am a highly candid person. Sibille was forever cooking up schemes involving Swiss bank accounts.

I have since found out that Mrs Davidson asked advice of two senior police officials; acquaintances of hers. One, retired, told her to drop it. Simple; an elderly man, with no wish to be bothered himself, he has no wish to bother anybody else. She saw it as cynicism: maybe it is.

The other, still active, told her that she was a nuisance. Which she is. But that perhaps she was a necessary nuisance. Which is debatable. He refused to intervene, but gave her – as Serge tells me – what in England we would call a chitty, to the legal authorities: that undoubtedly helped her. A typically French, and complicated compromise, which set her free to act.

What is more, he followed it up. He wrote to me: asking me to come and see him, trickily saying that it was 'a long way away' and that I was under 'no obligation'. I fear this man somewhat.

I wonder whether, in the long run, I may not end up feeling grateful towards him. I did not feel so at the time. Serge takes him seriously; says 'Get him on our side'. Hm . . .

In a way I admire Mrs Davidson. Stubbornly she worked her

way through to a senior legal official, the Procureur de la République for this jurisdiction. I believe that what influenced him was her detachment. Absence of interest, in the sense of advantage: so much in contrast to Travis McGee and all those stinking private eyes. She has nothing to gain in the affair but grief.

HENRI CASTANG . . .

I had been congratulating myself. Very foolish thing to do.

We like things simple, and we don't get them. I like homicides because they nearly always are simple. Especially crimes-of-passion. Those are as simple as you can get. My Spanish waitress, who knocked off her Polish man for getting into bed with other women – that's really open and shut. Compare that to all this rubbish I'm hearing about Lady Macbeth. Judges, lawyers, police authorities – everyone contented. Except Elena, maybe, but in this general handout of flowers to all concerned she has been forgotten.

I have just been reminded.

I'm in my office now, in thought. I have told Madame Metz, my heavy-footstepped and slightly-moustached secretary, to see that I am not disturbed.

Geoffrey would like this situation. Very English; he's a connoisseur in irony. Dawson; he's a CID inspector in Dorset and his wife – lovely girl – says 'Who d'you think you are then, Thomas Hardy?'

Haven't seen him for some time. He must be a Chief Inspector by now; seniority about the same as mine. He'd be a Superintendent just for being bright, but hierarchies in both countries share the same outlook. No way is being bright a key to promotion. They prefer you to be sound, and there's a firmly-held tenet that you can't be bright and sound together. Geoffrey overdoes the irony.

I'd been thinking of him this morning. Among his complaints

about their English system is inordinate amounts of time spent by criminal brigade officers in prosecuting legal cases. He howls. 'Our job is supposed to be prevention of crime . . .' He's jealous that here we turn over the legal preparation to the judge of instruction.

Little do you know! He does know, of course, that a fusspot judge can make a cop's life a perfect misery. Fine, it's that already: then more so.

Cops don't theorise much about crime. We leave that to the professors; they've the time for it. Few criminals are fundamental shits. And they've all got loose screws somewhere. Exactly the same applies to us. Geoffrey, it's true a bit pissed at the time, was heard to say that the osmosis between cops and crooks is such that there's no real difference. 'Interpenetration. Sodomites one and all.' But I hadn't thought to find myself buggered by Elena!

I had likewise congratulated myself upon the judge of instruction in this case. We don't have many in a place this size. We could have double the number, and they'd still be overworked. The administration, a favourite trick, leaves posts unfilled, for economy. And judges go on holiday or get bronchitis like the rest of us. I leave you to guess why justice is s l o w.

Elena has one of the best judges I've known; a large number, and of great variety. A funny little woman, still young; like Geoffrey rather too bright. Of what is called working-class-origin. Furthermore of Spanish origin – so much the better for Elena. Unmarried, and not many women say plump-out that a family as well as a job means that your mind is not properly upon either. Miss Alice Jimenez is a good judge.

Severe. She stands no nonsense from anyone and that includes me. In fact Monsieur le Commissaire is often regarded as an obstruction to justice. Alice is also a punctuality fiend; I tell her she should be a dentist. Her clerk, prettier but just as frightful as Madame Metz, takes pleasure in ringing up to say that Madame le Juge wants me at the Palais at ten, and that means sharp. And did just that this morning.

In our major cities, even largish towns – which by French standards this is – the lawcourts and offices are grouped in a large pompous building called the Palace of Justice. These can be palatial, much pillared portico and rusticated stonework, if dirt-encrusted. The insides mostly dingy, if in recent years money has been spent on the dignity of justice: painted up for the circus it's still a very old horse.

A gallery contains the judges of instruction, a row of offices with their names on the door. One used simply to knock and walk in. Then there was an epidemic of bystanders slipping guns to toughs brought from jail to get instructed: there were even instances of judges held to hostage, so now there's a turnstile to pass, like before getting on a plane, with a cop on duty to shake you down and rummage in your briefcase. The lawyers got very high and mighty about *their* dignity, until a few of them got held up too.

Alice was as usual bolt upright behind her desk. Her clothes are dowdy but she has presence. She's maybe thirty; wouldn't be called a goodlooking woman. Nice-looking; she could make herself attractive if she wished. The fiendish clerk was sitting to the side at her typewriter desk: big untidy mop of hair, big evil grin at seeing me.

"G'morning, ladies."

"Good morning, Commissaire." No smiles coming my way from Alice and the tone of voice, at best neutral, was not encouraging. "Please sit down. I have asked you to come in order to verify a number of points in the context of this Krasniewski affair. Does that surprise you?"

"Mildly." An unusually pompous exordium.

"You appeared startled."

"I thought it was that business with the train. My mistake. Krasniewski, good. Some time ago. Let me gather the wits."

"I'd be grateful if you would." The tone now definitely nasty, and I couldn't think why. "I was also surprised," she went on, "so much so, in fact, that we'd better have this formal. To put a name to it, this is an interrogation." And from being surprised I was now astonied.

"For the record, please state your name, age, address, and present function . . . You are married? . . . With children? . . . Very well. Now this place, the Russian Tea Room. This is one of your haunts, am I right?"

"I'd hardly say that. I might pop in, once a month or so."

One recognises the technique of hostile advocacy. A word like 'haunt' is plainly designed to irritate. All cross-examiners do this but I can't recall when a magistrate last talked to me this way. Still, I've been read off in my time, and by rougher than Jimenez. She has also the nasty habit of saying 'Thank you' after each answer. I use the technique myself. Pepper up my bum, just the same.

"You are well noted in your profession?"

"Tolerably."

"Your attitude towards professional obligations – your superiors find this correct? In general?"

"There have been exceptions."

"Have there indeed?" As though she wouldn't have had to give the same answer! The air of pretended surprise created a chilly draught. "Your attitude, for example, towards the conduct of enquiries – let me narrow that for you. We'll hypothesise an enquiry. You are satisfied of the identity of a criminal but legal proof is lacking. How then?"

"In the case of known criminals. there is a basis of understanding and even sympathy, as your own experience will have shown." Sarcasms were a mistake; her eyes showed me that.

"Most of your work does not involve professional criminals, you'll agree?"

"It's a generalised criminal brigade."

"Answer for the record please."

"Violent crime or financial fraud would in general be dealt with by the specialised brigades based in Lille. It follows that most of my work is of a routine nature. Observation and verification."

"The case under discussion – an incidental infraction of the criminal code. Albeit grave, almost accidental – you'd agree?" I shrugged. "My clerk cannot record facial expression."

"I'll agree."

"You would feel understanding, and sympathy."

"My feelings are irrelevant to my work." I am an officer of judicial police. Of some seniority. This young woman is a magistrate. My legal superior. In the context of an enquiry – a matter determined by herself – she has the right to interrogate whomsoever she pleases.

"There is no point in denying that methods are often used which are technically illegal, but tolerated for the results they bring?"

"I have no reply to make to that."

"You admit to awareness that such methods exist?" But this is ridiculous!

"With respect, Madame le Juge, the purpose of these questions escapes me."

"Make yourself easy about that, Commissaire; it doesn't escape me. I am quite serious, and I listen for your answer."

"It's obvious."

"You wouldn't deny that you have used such methods?" When one gets this shit in court, from an advocate, the President will as a rule intervene.

"What methods?" I was getting fed up, because every cop is forever skirting the law, as every examining magistrate perfectly well knows.

"Very well, Commissaire. You have upon occasion made promises of favourable treatment in exchange for an avowal?"

"Yagh, I'll take the Fifth Amendment on that one."

"Pressure upon a witness? Do me a favour and I'll do one for you?" This was impossible.

"You have in mind some point you want to make for the record. I don't know what it is. I'm not going to tag along after you blindfold. If you've a point, then make it."

"Thank you. Specifically, have you at any time used the inducement of lax or indulgent treatment towards a suspect?"

"My understanding, Madame, is that you interrogate me, as is your agreed right, in the context of your instruction of this woman Krasniewski. Have I held out inducements to her? Of course not; don't be ridiculous."

"Disregard the insolent phrase," to the clerk who was typing away as though her sane and happy sex life depended on it. "Question – in this or any other judicial enquiry, have you promised or hinted indulgent treatment towards a witness in return for sexual favours granted?"

"You can get a swollen lip for that, Jimenez."

"Strike out that answer. But no further chances to rephrase it, Commissaire."

"Then I refuse to give any answer whatever, and record that. Try it again and formal complaint will be made to the Director of the Police Judiciaire to be forwarded to the Minister of Justice."

"Don't give me that shit," said Alice in Spanish. I gawked at her with my mouth wide open.

"Such a complaint has been made to me, Monsieur Castang, and I seek to know what weight to attach to it."

"You mean you've got a witness?"

"Indeed I do, Commissaire. Indeed I have."

GUY LEFEBVRE . . .

Rather to my surprise the magistrate has 'inculpated' me. Surprised, that is, in a technical sense, since he has precious little evidence and of course no shadow of a 'proof'. Astonished I am not.

My advocate, the admirable Serge, made a show of astoundment and stupefaction, habitual vehicles of French rhetoric to which neither the judge nor I paid any attention. As soon as we were in private he hastened to tell me what I knew already: this is a sort of legal fiction. The judge need not, does not feel or even profess the 'intimate conviction' that they make much of. It is, they claim, a security measure. In reality an administrative convenience. By pronouncing, with some pomp, that in his opinion there are elements which warrant inculpation, he has a handle to put me in jug. He surrounds the word with reservations enough to make it meaningless; and he can – will – withdraw it.

Serge tells me this particular judge is a great believer in jug; termed preventive detention. I have understood, of course, that they cook customers this way by simmering them in the pot.

I must not discourage zeal in Serge. I pay him enough for showing it. The fact is that I do not really care a great deal. I am relieved that the press shows no interest in me: the story is in no way juicy and I am not a conspicuous person. It does not even greatly harm my livelihood. The press, unhampered by any real sub-judice rule (and setting up a great scream about censorship at any mention of same) can be very damaging indeed, but I am 'only a foreigner'; my customers would be unmoved by this sort of thing. In fact it might well make me more interesting in their eyes. The bourgeoisie as a rule are not much interested in tales of made-away-with-his-wife: they've mostly done worse themselves, and malversation by a banker would worry them more.

My technique with the judge – do I flatter myself? – is adequate. I am polite, low-voiced, bland. I tell him with respect that his suggestions are nonsensical. He is adept, to be sure, in phrasing designed to make me lose my temper, and I do sometimes, but the invaluable Serge has learned to listen for the rise in those dread ringing-English-tones, and interrupts with protests and stage-effects until I recapture selfcontrol.

I quite like this judge. He can be vicious, and is well known, tells Serge, for a fierce hanging countenance. Boislevant – 'Sang devant': the local bar makes numerous jokes. Crusty is an oldfashioned word and an outworn cliché. A nasty tongue on occasion and a hostile manner, but he is polite, in, again, the oldfashioned sense. Silberstein, a man of my age, regales one with tales of old blood-drinking judges of instruction dead or long retired, who struck terror into the beholder – pointing with a cigar to intimidate.

Boislevant is old, and fairly chalky. Serge says he's a figure of fun, and does a good imitation of him exhorting malefactors to repentance. Apparently he embarrasses everyone with hellfire, though I have not seen this yet. But as Serge warns me, even if now embarrassing to his own reactionary cronies he's still in the saddle; and if he does think I made away with my wife he will be obstinately determined to have-it-out-of-me.

It is time to speak of Sibille.

I am obliged to go back to early days. People write screeds about their childhood, the minute details of which give them exquisite pleasure while boring all their readers. Lucky that I have no such temptations. I am not looking for a public, my childhood was dull and mostly nasty, and my interest is only to identify the salient influences: I don't know what else to call them. Self-discovery? I am still discovering 'her'. I think about her a lot. Well, if it helps me to know more about myself . . .

I was brought up in an important house (it was called 'Montreux' which tells one pretty nearly everything one needs to know about it, together with Professor Pevsner's remark that you can get the English to live in absolutely anything as long as it has bow windows). This stood, in a largish garden, on a broad avenue with a lot of trees, in a posh district of a large city in the North of England, which had a very high opinion of itself.

The house was of red brick, itself very nice, of excellent quality. It had a turret. Also a conservatory, a detail I have since come to like. The garden was full of laurels and laburnums and boring flowers of the type then liked; roses and stuff (I've never much liked roses since, and as for begonias and salvias . . .) There was a tennis court and a kitchen-garden. The gate was painted white with black letters and was of course of wood. The house next door was called 'Normandie' and had a black gate with white letters. On the other side of the avenue was a park. The trees in my memory are lindens, though I think they were more probably planes (I love both). Trams ran up and down.

Where their masts touched the cables they sparked furiously, splendidly, in wet weather. The trams were doubledecked. They swayed and rattled and the hard leather upholstery, of a blackish green, smelt good. No other kind of public transport has ever pleased me half so well. These details are from the mid-nineteen-thirties. It is important to have lived before the war, which so absorbs the English.

The inside of the house interested me little. I recall a wide shallow staircase, very well built, much oak painted white, comfortable chintzy furniture. Plainly all in that characteristic English style; excellent craftsmanship and no design. My mother swayed about, not much interested in me? I remember oddly little about her. I am ashamed to say that I have not much interest in other people. She had no other children. I should imagine that I was a dull and tiresome child. Later she disappeared. A pious legend was put about that she had gone for treatment to some sanatorium for an unnamed malady. I found out much later that she had simply run away. This was not spoken of. She was kind, generally gentle, sometimes indulgent, with that high clear English voice. She read, a lot.

My father I saw little of. He was quite wealthy. He had a brass-founding business, small but high-class, making intricate locks and mechanisms for closing portholes and the like, of a marine nature; unlike the house of very good design as well as exceptional craftsmanship and finish. One would have seen his products on White Star liners and such triumphs of the period. He was a silent man who liked country pursuits; shooting and fishing (he was good at both) and dogs. It was only when with my mother that one heard his voice raised. He looked after his business with total devotion, the first there in the morning and the last to leave. Undoubtedly he was very fond of me, in undemonstrative ways. I was a fearful disappointment in I am sure every way imaginable. I have a feeling, now, for that lovely metalwork (all melted down since and gone into things like cartridgecases). I once found a piece of his on an old old sailing boat with 'Lefebvre' in block letters and his 'puma' stamp almost obliterated by fifty years of polishing.

I was eleven and the war just starting. 1928, a splendid year for claret. I remember few of my father's jokes, though he made better than that. He was killed in the air raid which destroyed the foundry. 'Montreux' was wiped off the map the same night. But I was at school.

I simply cannot imagine why I should not have been sent to the admirable local grammarschool. I should have been far happier, I would have learned a great deal – my life would have taken different directions. More fruitful? Happier? Every man's thinking about the past must be filled with the word 'If'. My father had much respect for intellect, and no insecurity, I mean no social snobbery. Oh well . . . this too was a 'famous' school (especially for rugby). There is no point in complaint or denigration. It was a good school of its kind no doubt, even then oldfashioned. Livy and bits of Ovid. Caesar and Virgil. Greek in the upper classes and Horace. French but of course no German, nor any other language. Arithmetic-algebra-and-geometry. The rules of English grammar. Eng. Lit. Eng. Hist. and partial (in every sense of the word) European hist. Geography of an imperial sort. A lot of religion of a biblical anglican nature. I seem to remember vague classes from time to time in drawing, in carpentry, in music – for those gifted which I wasn't, though it was mostly pianopractice and a notorious 'skive'. And that seems to be all! Surely a terribly impoverished curriculum even for wartime? I can discover in retrospect no physical sciences whatever – not even elementary botany or biology. Maybe there were some, but for the 'less bright'. I was thought of as scholarship material and there was talk of Cambridge.

It could have been done. Why not? I don't really know. The chief trustee of my father's affairs, a surgeon, seems to have had other things to think about: I scarcely even met him. The other trustee had domestic preoccupations. Everyone was wrapped up in the war. The headmaster loathed me and really small blame to him. Everything was botched and I added much adolescent sabotage of the usual sort, making a more or less deliberate hash of the scholarship examination. I was told I'd 'missed it by a fraction' adding that to a very long list of grievances; together with the information that I'd only escaped expulsion out of charity. But why add to all this now?

It is so boringly classic: a clumsy, insecure child, and physically ill-coordinated, useless at all games and thus by the standards of this sort of school a useless object full-stop. Nothing could have been more English than my parents but I was known as 'Frenchy' by the Bells and Bartons, Townsends and Cartwrights by whom I was surrounded. They didn't like me, I didn't like them. The masters were, it would seem, a hearty and insensitive lot. I was always getting punished and always it appeared to me over-severely; I was passed over for prefectship when all my contemporaries were given honours and responsibilities and even juniors had authority over me: I laughed and was soured. It is the archfamiliar tale to anyone with an inkling of adolescent psychology, and it set a pattern of failure that handicapped me badly for many years – up to today?

It is of course a defence mechanism against dislike, a forestall-ing of contempt. Rather than find oneself last in the race one walks out on it. This has to be publicised, made to look deliberate, in dramatic poses of languid eccentricity and insol-ence to cover the lack of confidence.

I do not want to linger on those years. It is painful, naturally, to recall the series of bad choices, the wrong, the silly, the arrogant. The egoism too is insufferable; the deadening, weari-some I, I, I. It is not interesting. But I am the principal, perhaps the only witness. If this is the reef upon which Sibille ran aground and was wrecked, then I am obliged to take the measurements of the reef, plot its situation and map the hidden dangers.

A word in passing: even as a schoolboy I was antagonised and repelled by the homosexuals. And only those of my age and situation – I mean the well-brought-up boy of bourgeois condi-tion and timid nature in a large city – can recall how difficult it was to make any sort of contact with a girl. The pathetic, yes, but much more laughable figure of Young Woodley is now meaningless. I went into the army on national service as a private. The war was over and only comic drillsergeants remained. Weekend leave in London was the first opportunity of getting rid of this absurd and odious virginity, which I promptly did to a West End prostitute and a very nice girl she was, a thin blonde with a splendid cockney accent, smelling slightly of disinfectant: she was kind and gentle with me and I remember her – clearly – with grateful affection. With longer leave, and some money, I went to Paris and was luckier still: I had drunk too much and had a fiasco, and the young girl I had picked up behind the Palais Royal was not only spotlessly clean and still able to laugh but had the wisdom of bonté (goodness does not translate this word). She cuddled me, reassured me until I was able to laugh, and laughed with me. I cannot remember either of their names, and am ashamed of that. On the verge of my twentyfirst birthday my guardian-surgeon made for the first and last time a fuss, inviting me to dine at his club and giving me much good advice, of which I did take the central material item, which was to enroll myself at a university, a thing then quite easy for anyone with a matriculation from a well-known school. The choice of the School of Architecture seemed arbitrary, like the later interest in botany. But I was obeying deeper instincts.

Words interest me. If I manage, now, to give a fairly coherent account of myself perhaps it is because the exactitude of words, and their meanings, is important to me. A little of the schooling has stuck to me: there must have been one or two good teachers, here or there. It has helped me, in a nomadic life. Already at school I learned that the native territory, the habitat clearly described and understood, is important to mankind. So comforting and reassuring are these known, familiar backgrounds. The nomad, lacking this, seeks the more reassurance about his identity, and purpose; can only get it from human relationships, and this throws an extra weight upon the partner. Both need a greater sense of responsibility, and less selfishness. Lesson:

hesitate before you take a person out of their 'home' background. As I did Sibille.

I have the time to think about this. I never before gave myself time. Serge tells me that it can take six weeks to persuade an obstinate judge to sign a release order. He has an armoury of legal tactics. He talks about these. I have – obviously – some interest. Not all that much! One is not really human in an advocate's eye; more a succession of fine points, shades of meaning. How hard to push the threat to sue for wrongful imprisonment? – pleaders delight in such arguments. I surprise myself, by feeling more indifference than I allow to show.

It was one of my very earliest jobs. I should explain that my father left money enough to get me through the university, and even to finance a start in life. Though there was nowhere near as much as I thought there would be. I understood little of this, and was taken into no one's confidence. The plant was wrecked, the house knocked flat. Sums were owed to suppliers, compensations must be paid to employees – and a lot of people interested in getting their investments back, with 'interest' . . . Banks and people saw to it that they were well covered. I don't suppose for a moment that the eminent surgeon was dishonest, but he could not be bothered, as I imagine, to try very hard. What should, certainly, have been a substantial amount had somehow melted away down endless rat- and mouseholes before I got my hands on anything. Yes yes, provision had had to be made . . . a bland and courteous bankmanager droned on at great length.

From the accumulated débris a certain sum had been found, and this had been Prudently Invested. I don't doubt that they were indeed good investments: I did not, and do not, have any real comprehension of that stock-exchange jargon. But I discovered that the certain sum was one of those awkward lumps of capital the income from which is not enough to live on. To meet the bills at the end of the month or term one is obliged to 'sell out another hundred' all the time, and this seemingly effortless process accelerates, firstly because there is less income each time, secondly because it is so easy to slide down the primrose path. Kept very tight during student years I inclined to extravagance. The trips to Paris became stays in Venice or Vienna. I told myself that there was plenty of capital left for the start-in-life. So there was, if it had not been handled both recklessly and wastefully.

I notice that I am putting off the account of my first meeting with Sibille.

Jobs were hard to get. In those years fewer people than I thought were interested in landscape architecture or willing to spend money on garden design. Most who were went to elderly gentlemen who had been practising for years. The rich seemed oddly indifferent to my enthusiasm and talent.

I thought it a marvellous opening. A big job – at least, on a large scale. I took it very seriously, giving all my time and effort. A bit more experience, or just worldly-wisdom, would have told me it was a bluff, a fantasy of the owner, that he had no real money to put into his grandiose vision and that probably even a consultancy fee would be paid with reluctance after much delay. Such types are often met with. But I was so green . . . I was dazzled by his asking me to stay, treating me as a guest, a friend. Naturally, this was a manoeuvre. To do him justice he was probably barely conscious of the fact that he was manipulating me: that a young inexperienced man had a head easily turned by flattery. As well as being cheap. His daughter saw it easily enough. She started, I feel sure, by being sorry for me, though in all these years she never admitted as much.

But what do you do, when you are young and eager, and a distinguished elderly gentleman from the landowning aristocracy asks you to stay? A smallscale Balmoral, an ugly manorial barrack with fake castellations and crenellations. The inside shabby, to me convincing because shabbiness is an affectation of this class. It had not struck me that one can own a big house and a lot of moorland and still be poor. There was stained glass in the hall, incompetent central heating and a shortage of bathrooms, the usual smell of wet dogs and gumboots as well as the litter of tweed hats and croquet mallets: the caricature is well-known and all too often unforced reality. Three grandfather clocks and three pretty daughters all six telling a different time.

Friendly girls. They set me at ease. Sibille, the middle one, was quieter, more reserved. It is a highly conventional story. The father was straight out of *Field*, with that sad dewlappy look of an elderly setter; the slim handsome figure that looks good in a kilt. There was a painting of him in black velvet and silver buttons, of perfect academic nullity, lace jabot and row of miniature medals: he always looked exactly like it. The mother was a kind woman, with what seemed always to be the same blouse, and absent-minded about where she'd left her cardigan. Gardening did not interest her, save that this kind of woman feels it her duty to be on her knees putting in bulbs. The girls were openly bored. Pa affected learning, discoursed upon the natures (both robust and fragile) of the Himalayan deodar as against the Lebanon cedar.

I did my first drawings in – outside – that house; decidedly flattering perspective of baronial chimneypots. They thought it was nice having an artist around.

I was a susceptible young man. Not to be wondered at. Where could one take a girl in those days? In all the student lodgings gimlet landladies came pouncing out of the basement at the barest breath of female presence. One could go to the pictures, into the park . . . no wonder there were all those jokes about love in a cold climate. Ludicrous as it appears now it was an excitement simply being under the same roof as three nubile young women.

The other two were flirtatious in a jolly game-of-sardines way. Girls of that class . . . They'd been given a 'good education' at some eminently respectable High School. Even if they'd been unusually bright or showed ambition to go on to the university Papa would doubtless have said he couldn't afford it. They had no professional training, nor enthusiasm for anything their parents would have thought 'suitable'. Their experience seemed limited to stays with aunts in London. Papa was the sort of man who says 'I hate abroad'. Their horizons were narrow past belief.

They had nothing to do but hang around waiting for marriageable young men in the neighbourhood: some hope.

The youngest and most talkative – Faith – held out much promise which evaporated at closer quarters. Eleanor the prettiest, a tall blonde (her mother must have looked like that twentyfive years earlier which was a sobering thought), I once cornered in that house full of corners; or she cornered me because she certainly thought out the experiment. I am afraid I went too fast for her and she did not repeat the moment. Sibille's dignity and reserve made a – sounder? – basis of attraction. And when she made up her mind it stayed made up. Her parents made oddly little fuss. Pa produced the usual blither about money and prospects. Ma showed an unexpected warmth towards me. I suppose she realised that her daughters were not getting younger, and that this quite nicemannered young man was perhaps less of a mirage than those young army officers still running about places like Cyprus and Malaya.

I am of course not going to write about 'married life'. I am not a writer. What to put in? What, rather, to leave out?

Sex, for instance. The judge does not dwell unduly. 'And were you faithful to your wife, Monsieur? Hm . . . And was she faithful to you?' And probably there isn't much more that needs saying on this burning subject. Of course the French bourgeoisie, be it Catholic or Huguenot, is obsessively prudish, more so to my mind now than the English were then. Serge says cheerfully that some of the younger judges of instruction would be painfully outspoken – or cheerfully curious. Not this one!

I'm glad to say that it wouldn't worry me. I sympathise with the legendary duchess who said about love, 'I make it often but never never talk about it'; but if I were questioned there would be nothing to tie me in knots.

Sibille was 'a good wife' in every sense. She was of course a virgin when I met her, and despite much siegework remained obstinately so till marriage. Yes, she had inhibitions. I think it might be fairer to say she had a strong sense of modesty, and that's no bad thing. She had been scuffled at no doubt by heavy-breathing young men. A few burst buttons or grappled suspenders, but nobody ever got her knickers down and that's flat. Then or since; something I'll put my hand in the fire for. I will do myself the justice of saying that I had at least sufficient experience by then to behave properly towards her, with patience and at least some sensitivity. She was a completely normal woman, like any other looser after a few drinks; neither unpleasantly cold nor fearsomely hot. Just – modest. Always rather coy about being undressed, uneasy at having her skirt lifted in odd moments or places, fussy about locked doors and drawn curtains. But one must be fair. There was nothing abnormal about her. She remained childless. This was and is a thing to be un-happy about.

Question me as sharply as you like. Yes, in early years I had two or three escapades. Only one beyond the most fragmentary: a woman who was my mistress for six months and who gave me a baby. She was herself married so that my responsibilities in this matter were limited. She covered the matter with skill, and we took the greatest pains to avoid scandal or pain. Sibille certainly suspected, but suspicions do not avail against stout denial; not when there is no evidence. The truth of all this is that we have been married thirty years, and only in – round it out and say the first ten – did I deceive Sibille. She was a good wife. I would have felt filthy, and I would have felt a traitor, and I had better not be a hypocrite, either: Sibille was also a singularly wide-awake and sharp-eyed wife.

No, questions along those lines would be barking up a very wrong tree. Frustrations there were: they were of a different kind. One could not call Sibille the ideal sexual partner: she lacked humour, and was not gifted for the little charades which make sex into a delightful entertainment. But within my experience few women are.

She had a kind of aridity. I recall an Indian student who had a flat in the basement when we were on the first floor (we were still in England). He had a dismayingly vulgar mistress and when one day at a party he was reproached with this he said, much

astonished – 'But she's very clean, and very economical.' Everyone burst out laughing – except Sibille.

We didn't stay long in England. To me it was always a
humiliating struggle. With the scrapings of my 'capital' (we
didn't get much out of Papa) we made the jump. I was beginning
to feel more and more that France was the country I belonged
to, although I have never identified myself with France either: I
do not feel French . . . We had two, nearly three years in
Touraine, of poverty and happiness. We found work then, in
Germany, and were able to buy the little house in the Vosges. I
ought to pay a tribute to the way she coped with English
schoolgirl French: she got on marvellously with the local people.

It might sound like a Scotch caricature – I don't know; I've
not known any other Scotch women. Certainly she was frugal
and careful. She never outran the housekeeping money – saved
up change in jamjars. Unimaginative if you like: not a 'good
cook'. But she always had a meal and it was always eatable.
Rather dowdy – she had no clothes sense either. But is one to
prefer a sloppy, slapdash wife who has spent the rent money on
shoes? And worked like a horse, uncomplaining, tireless in
ferreting out work. She used to go and canvass at big houses.
We'd never have survived . . .

A sentimentalised picture of the devoted helpmeet always
patient and sweet won't do either. She had no taste at all. She
would think that the mere fact of being female made her better
qualified to arrange a bowl of flowers but she had no feeling for
the work. All those years she would go on stubbornly arguing
with me about proportion or distance, convinced that her own
eye was as good.

(*A day or so later*) It really does seem preposterous that an
examining magistrate could be so divorced from reality. To hear
him talk you'd think prison was the answer to the world's evils!
An austere withdrawal from follies, where the unruly flesh can
be sanctified. Poverty, obedience and chastity. I suppose it's a

half-truth, like so many things. I have been told that the contemplative monasteries are doing a roaring trade. Yes, people are fatigued, worn down by the unending petty treacheries and revolted by the cheap, tinsel attractions. But I wonder how many stay. Idle speculation. They can walk out when they choose. However . . . Live from day to day, as Serge advises, and 'We'll soon get you out'. Sometimes I get impatient. At others I don't even remember what day it is. There is a tiresome inconstancy about the judge's doings. Day after day I am called for escorting to the Palace of Justice (two or three of us generally, handcuffed together and hustled into a van) and kept there all day while he goes relentlessly over and over the same set of details. But there are odd gaps – ten days passed without a word.

Still, I am well treated. The French have respect for an 'intellectual', and I am privileged. Also I am quiet and well-behaved: polite too, and I talk to the guards, who are only doing their job. They like this. They would be quick to detect hypocrisy or currying, but they enjoy a little chat. I ask about their children, I show interest in their working conditions and overtime scale, their housing and pastimes. They appreciate it that I am not impatient or irritable or eaten up with grievances: they like little jokes. They get few enough, poor devils.

Important too that in a French jail, and I suppose indeed in any other, one can do a lot with money. There are many here who 'outside' had plenty, but since most of their crimes have to do with money they are deprived: the rule that suspect sources of income are blocked pending trial. Judges of instruction regard everything as a reward of peculations and malversations: very likely it is true. Since most of the 'intellectuals' are embezzlers I am set apart: being furthermore under suspicion of a 'crime of blood' gives me a certain prestige. A feeling that they would all gladly do away with their wives, once they thought about it . . . I am admired, as it were, for having found a good method.

I can draw freely on a bank account. A variety of little comforts on the canteen list. Not only food but camping equipment! Chocolate, cigarettes, Nescafé are powerful items of commerce, replacing sordid currency. I could get almost anything I wished, including servants. One starts to notice the value of things to which one had never paid much heed; soap or lavatory paper and a shower when one feels like it. The régime for the poor is adequate but harsh: the food is that of the army. Since nearly all the detainees are addicted to tranquillisers, which the administration hands out lavishly as the answer to most problems, they are all constipated, but I eat no pills and plenty of fruit. Generosity with my canteen articles gets me all I want, including several items officially forbidden.

All I want? What more do I want? A woman?

I am left in pleasant solitude, with no cellmate. I mend tattered library books with scotch tape. For pen and paper I have only to ask. What more should I want?

I don't know what the hell I have to boast about. What do I suppose I'm doing? Is this the famous examination of my conscience that the judge so earnestly recommends to me – peeling off layers of dead skin to get at the real man within? Perhaps it would be like an onion: one could go right to the centre and then find nothing there.

Yes, I miss Sibille; more than I can say.

A physical need? Everybody in jail masturbates as a matter of course, and some seem to do little else. I do too. There is a brisk trade in porno matter, and many complicated homosexual relationships: these do not interest me. Odd how much propaganda there is, inside or out – and how many people are anxious to believe it – that a woman is nothing but a toy, an agreeable face and figure, a sweet scent and amusing clothes, to be taken off either quick or slow for the joys of tit and bum beneath. For the rest, we are led to believe, she is an imbecile; ready, indeed longing to be thrown into ecstasies by his new aftershave, her new washing-powder. (I could have a television set if I wanted one: I do not.) Sibille did not resemble these idiotic dolls.

Well, what was she like? I had better face it.

That man Castang started this. In fact he started the whole

process. But for him, I think, I would have paid no further attention to Mrs Davidson's imaginings. He asked me politely to come and see him.

He dropped a phrase on that occasion. I have not been able to get rid of it. Like something in one's teeth. Or those splinters which get under the skin; one picks away with a needle, getting nowhere and probably infecting it (Sibille was skilled with such minor miseries).

Castang only asked, 'Was she like Lady Macbeth?' It is out of a book by Chandler: a typical joke. We learn at the end what we had been suspecting, that this mouse in rimless glasses is a multiple murderess. 'Nobody ever looked less like . . .' – but what *did* Lady Macbeth look like? Like Simone Signoret, or Mrs Danvers in *Rebecca*? An Edwardian actress like Ellen Terry, in a glory of brilliant oriental stuffs and barbaric jewellery? Red braids down to the waist and an iron crown on top? 'My dear, where *does* she buy her frocks?' Or did she look like the Little Sister? Is she tremendously sexy?

Producers, in depths of despair, have tried just about everything: every actress has broken her teeth on the part. Shakespeare's fault I suppose: once he starts turning the fire up, those rickety old plots fall to pieces. With those six terrible monosyllables 'The queen, my lord, is dead' the thing has come to an end.

I have been thinking of the last scene in *Casque d'Or*, when from that window on the boulevard she watches her lover guillotined. Some producer who had seen that cast the actress, Simone Signoret, as Lady M. Her talent as well as the axe-chopped looks and ashtray voice made her a good choice. The woman should be there, to see the destruction she has brought about.

Well, what did Sibille look like? Hard for me to answer, because I saw her first in the fire of youth and with a romantic imagination. And this was the way I continued to see her. Thirty years later. She wore well. It was within, where it did not show, that the balance wore down, distorting her.

Scotch – I suppose that there were conventional elements to her looks: she was tall with reddish fair hair. Upright springy carriage. Finely-modelled features. Her nose was too long and too sharp and her mouth too wide, but a classic cast. Fine grey eyes, a little too small. I can assemble all this, but it doesn't add up. She had great dignity. No, nothing that I say can – I am too insensitive. The artist is alert to much that most people miss; but he is too much of an egotist. Arrogance, complacence, sheer stupidity. I made too many mistakes with Sibille. She was exquisitely, cruelly sensitive.

She did not show it, being a terrifying bottler-up of all emotion. One would have sworn she had the hide of a rhinoceros, but it was the animal of the Just-So story, with cake-crumbs and blackened currants under the skin. The smallest injury, the most trivial snub was never forgotten and rankled evermore. She was a mass of scars. Too late now I learn that there must have been a terrifying accumulation of hurts and humiliations. Hate, what is hate? Silly melodramatic word – 'I hated Rebecca.' What did Rebecca feel? I think I know, now, that Sibille must have suffered much. I have myself. We loved one another.

I am trying to recall whether Lady Macbeth was childless. I do not remember mention of any offspring. How long, I wonder, had she been married?

Edited Transcripts: Interrogation of Lefebvre

These are excerpts from the 'verbal process'; interrogations by the instructing judge, taken down direct by his clerk-stenographer. She omits inessentials and parentheses, depending on her skill and experience: this one, like the judge, was rather literal in method. Since the judge tended also to be exhaustive the transcripts formed a voluminous pile and I have only used the few relevant to present purposes. In the legal sense they are accepted as a true-and-faithful-account of oral proceedings and countersigned as such by all parties. – A.D.

" . . . Very good, Monsieur Lefebvre, your status at this moment is that of 'interpellé' – d'you understand this? You are not inculpated and still less are you accused. Imputations exist against you: explanations are required of you. Your advocate is present in an advisory capacity. This has been made clear to you? (D'you wish to add anything, Maître?)"

"Quite clear, Monsieur le Juge."

"We know something now of you. We'd like now to know something of your wife. A picture, to situate her, of the relations between you. In your own words."

"Am I the right witness? As far as I can make out I'm supposed to have done away with her: won't I be thought prejudiced?"

"You must let me be the judge of that."

"I know her better than anyone in some senses. Worse, in others. I mean that I'm not objective, am I?"

"One of the difficulties in the case of a death – thank you, Maître, a death hypothesised – she is not there to speak for herself. We cannot hear her voice. Consider this metaphor: we make transparencies; we superpose them. A composite portrait. There will be other witnesses. From the very beginning. A first marriage for you both? Have you children?"

"No."

"That was important? A deprivation to you both?"

"Yes."

"Describe the manner of your life together."

"She took an active share in my work. I am often away. Planning and building is a lengthy job. Delicate too. The client's tastes and wishes are often violently unsuitable."

"You have to get him to agree?"

"Get him to see why it is he's hiring me. Lot of tact needed. My wife was an active helper, a great support. Notes, photographs, measurements; research; looking up sources – titles, permissions. I mean, you don't go to a lot of expense, and then find a roadwidening scheme just at the garden gate."

"She was a partner thus?"

"Well, qualify that a little. More a sort of glorified secretary."

"Why should you qualify it?"

"You're asking for exactitude of detail. She had no technical knowledge. Soil chemistry or plant biology. Or a gift for aesthetics – I don't know why; matter of taste, one has it or one doesn't."

"You imply a disagreement."

"Yes, of course."

"Is that a source of conflict?"

"What are you seeking to imply?"

"Make no such suggestion: I establish. Within your marriage, a shared work interest. Hers, inevitably, was a subordinate rôle?"

"All right, I understand. That this was a source of frustration? Yes, she could never really enter my world. That's commonplace in any artistic pursuit. It is by definition solitary."

"And that she accepted?"

"Let's get this clear. She was an intelligent woman of great strength of character. I think it was always a source of embitterment and I've already said, we had disagreements. Especially in recent years."

("Surely this is a commonplace in all marriages. 'Il y a toujours un qui baise et l'autre qui tend la joue.'")

"I accept that, Maître. This is your client's view."

"I think so, yes. Looking back, I think she got increasingly restless. She went on a lot about living her own life. I must take blame for much. I feel I must have appeared often as overbearing and tyrannical."

("Our whole position, Monsieur le Juge, is that Madame Lefebvre came to the conclusion that she would be happier leading her own life, and that a dispute more or less acid brought this to a head.")

"Yes, we've heard about that. And the subject of this dispute?"

"She wanted me to concentrate on painting: more money in that. I wasn't prepared to agree."

"Your reading of the matter is thus on both sides an obstinate sense of independence leading to a clash?"

"Yes I suppose, if you insist."

"Leaving that aside for the moment: your shared life otherwise was happy?"

"Like most people's, I imagine; placid. Very happy moments, yes, as well as stormy passages. She was no doormat."

"Your wife has thus vanished. You accept that as definite?"

"Knowing her, I can't see her reappearing now. Strong sense of pride."

"I am given to understand that your property is held in common and your bank account shared?"

"That is correct."

"She could thus have paid for a voyage or flight. She did not do so. Did this strike you as strange?"

"No."

"You wanted her to come back?"

"Certainly."

"You still wish it?"

"At times. It isn't easy to know how I feel in this ludicrous situation."

"To sum up; you would describe yourself as of a quiet disposition, but easily roused to anger?"

"Yes, that's fair."

"The same would apply upon occasion to her?"

"Oh yes, she could be a right fishwife."

"There were moments when you would both do or say things you would afterwards regret?"

"That's just the point. I thought she'd be back within a day."

"You didn't go back to search for her?"

"I have pride too."

"Did it occur to you that she might have met with an accident?"

"It doesn't seem very likely. Prudent woman, knew how to look after herself. Quiet country district. One would know, anyhow. She was carrying identity papers."

("As an Englishwoman abroad, Monsieur le Juge, she was in the habit of carrying her passport.")

"Quite so. And the other possibility? That she had met with violence?"

"Never entered my mind."

"What worries us, Monsieur Lefebvre, as you see, is that at the moment of this altercation, you drove off, in an access of anger, wounded pride – do you wish to qualify that?"

"No, that's fair."

"You left her standing in the road, with her overnight bag."

"Correct."

"You expected her to return once tempers had cooled?"

"Yes, of course."

"What would she have done – to your mind?"

"Well, there are a number of possibilities. As I recall there is a village not very far away. I'd expect her to walk or get a lift if someone came along, and then look for a taxi."

"It is remarkable that we can find no trace of anything of the sort."

"I don't know how to account for it."

("You are bearing in mind that when this fuss was made by a former neighbour my client went at once to the gendarmerie to urge an enquiry?")

"It is not disputed, Maître. My experience of village life is that a stranger and a striking-looking woman in the circumstances would not have passed unnoticed."

"She could have got a lift from somebody passing through. A travelling salesman or whatever. Improbable perhaps but not impossible."

"Is it not still more improbable that nobody, not even her own family, should have received word from her since?"

"I've no suggestions to make, I'm afraid."

"Very well, Monsieur Lefebvre. I may want to see you again. You intend as I understand to remain here for some time? I ask you to hold yourself at my disposal, on terms your advocate will explain to you. Is that clear?"

HENRI CASTANG . . .

Quite a lot of time passed, you realise. Arlette poking about had stirred something up but it bogged down again. Bureaucratic channels . . . Vera said, 'Do something.' To my reasonable remark that there was nothing legal I could do she replied, 'Well do something illegal.' Oh yes? Drop a stone into these murky waters and see whether anything happens.

A letter, I thought. Apart from the perennial temptation, familiar to yourself, to write to *Le Monde* reminding them that the plural of the French word 'medium' is not 'medias' and that 'graffiti' is not a singular, I don't write many letters. Or not out of the office. We have a number of printed forms, handy. 'Please present yourself immediately upon reception of the present advice at the Commissariat upon subject concerning you taking pains to furnish yourself with your identity papers as well as this advice.' Rude, ungrammatical and of course tautological.

But this wasn't official business, or not officially so. I had to make it quite colourless. Not easy – one always says too much. Typing it myself on plain paper I produced this: Dear Monsieur Lefebvre, I'd be grateful if you could make it convenient to pay me a call within the next fortnight, yours faithfully. In passing, why is a fortnight in France fifteen and not fourteen days? I don't think much either of our ingrained habit of assuring everyone that we entertain distinguished considerations towards them.

He'd either react or he wouldn't: the second likeliest and that would be the end of it. He must know that any enquiry was not in this jurisdiction, that I had no official standing and no hold upon him.

But if he did? It would show that he was uneasy. We do sometimes drop hints of this sort, in the quite frequent cases where there is no evidence (you might recall the fisherman who did or didn't take two tourist girls for a ride in his boat – the

92

bodies were never found). It is not always pointless to let them
know that we are not duped, and that we keep some files open a
long time. The women worry about their scruples, asking themselves 'Are we really convinced that So-and-so killed her own
child?' The police mind does not work this way. Start with that
and I'd get no work done. But if faced with a concrete question,
our duty is to look for an answer. To say 'it's outside my district'
is an evasion.

And he did! I was surprised. And I was alerted. I had nothing
to go on still, but a cop is never at a loss for bullshit. I have a
secretarial biddy, a great pest she is but a screen from the
importune. A Monsieur Lefebvre is asking to see you. Well,
well.

He had himself created a pretext for coming; significant.

"Some nurserymen I had to see. This was anyhow on my way.
No trouble to pop in just to see what it was about."

"To be sure." There is a cop technique of pretending to have
forgotten what it was about. Refresh the mem with knitted brow
over some meaningless paper. The ploy can be useful with the
self-important and their carefully prepared openings, but don't
make a habit of it. "I recall very well. You were thought to have
helped your wife out of this world."

He raised his eyebrow a bit.

"The rumour seems to have got around."

"Oh, you know, we're highly computerised nowadays. Is it
only rumour?"

"But aren't you rather far away, to feel concerned?"

"I'm acquainted with aspects of the affair." The eyes opened.

"What? I ask the gendarmerie to enquire into the whereabouts
of my wife, and the police up in the North are taking an
interest?" This was sticky ground.

"Rogatory commissions fly around," I said vaguely. "Fail to
pay your television licence and you will receive a reminder from
an obscure bureau in Poitiers." Quite true as it happens. "A
judge of instruction delegates a law-enforcement agency to do
spadework. The gendarmerie, the Police Judiciaire. Can on
occasion be both."

Also true, but I forebore to say that there is much friction and hideous jealousies on this account. The system is complicated past belief. I should be embarrassed trying to explain it. I'm embarrassed applying it. As you probably know, gendarmes are military types – War Ministry. We are civilian functionaries – Ministry of the Interior. Mutual distrust is a distinct understatement. Now tell me why the government likes it this way.

I did the look-at-him-suddenly while lighting a cigarette.

"Did you kill her?" There are people who have answered yes. One does not ever know. Some retract, later.

"But you must tell me why that isn't impertinent as well as insulting."

It was raining so I said "Is it raining?" and got up to look out of the window. I was getting curious about the chap. If he'd come all this way, under no real compulsion, it was to find out what I knew. This meant that there was something to know.

I turned round to look at him.

"I'm not sure that it's either. But is it irrelevant?"

"Exactly. I fail to see the point."

"People do kill their wives. Sometimes a very small thing is enough. As the man said, 'Because she was evil and wouldn't give me any.' It's a common error to believe there must be an important explanation. If you told me, 'Because it was raining,' I shouldn't be surprised."

It didn't wash. He kept his level tone, midway between irony and sarcasm.

"Aren't you begging the question? You seem to me to fall into a commonplace heresy, Monsieur le Commissaire. Looking for complications. Who says she's dead? Why? Who says I killed her?"

"Tell me the story, for me to see how simple."

"There isn't any story."

"Good. Then we have only to be patient."

"I don't follow."

"People who vanish will sooner or later unvanish. You will get a message."

"I'd like to feel convinced of that."

"We have experience. When you get such a sign, Monsieur Lefebvre, perhaps you'd be good enough to let us know. Missing people bother us."

"There are so many?"

"Most come to light." That as you know is shading the truth: too many don't. But it was best to keep to the light friendly tone. "In a case like yours," fussing with my papers, "it's a legal thing, a financial thing. Suppose you wished to remarry. Suppose you wished to dispose of property. You propose divorce on grounds of desertion. Did she desert you? One would like to know. Quite reasonable, don't you think?" He said nothing, leaving me high and dry.

"Thank you for coming in. I apologise for putting you to the trouble. But I'd have been unhappy if you hadn't." He nodded. There were things he thought of saying, and he thought better of them. He gave me a curious look, picking up his hat. One had better not read too much into curious looks and twice-thinking. They can be quite meaningless. One can also not read enough.

Just as well that there was nobody there to ask me for an opinion, because I didn't have any. People do indeed decide suddenly to make a clean break and go to Mexico. But there is somebody they will inform, sooner or later. A sister would be a likely candidate. Or a lawyer.

It could happen that they are never heard of again. Perhaps they got caught in an earthquake and remained unidentified. That is fairly rare nowadays. I could see that a judge would be slow to make his mind up.

I think of something that Commissaire Richard, for many years my professor in police practice, used often to impress upon me. When you meet an unorthodox situation, handle it in an unorthodox way.

Edited Transcripts: Interrogation of Lefebvre
Arrangements were made (date and time added) for judicial transport to districts in Vosges area, for purposes of verification.

*In the presence of the Instructing magistrate, his clerk under-
signed, M. Guy Lefebvre as free agent interrogated, Me. Serge
Silberstein advocate. Notes by roadside (coordinates given).*

"Somewhere along here but I can't really feel sure."

"The purpose of the outing is to refresh memory."

("Stopping for a pee, Monsieur le Juge, isn't an immortal
occasion. He wasn't certain of his road.")

"You are by your own account familiar with the countryside
in which you resided a number of years."

"Yes, but one says that loosely. Large area. Acquainted rather
than familiar, this far. Hills, woods, roads, all looking much the
same and a great many of them. I thought at the time that this
was a short cut and got muddled. I didn't have a map."

("You might recall too that he'd driven a long way and by late
afternoon one is naturally wearied.")

"Certainly. The roads are, however, well signposted, compared with most places."

"Yes, I was aiming at a village and missed a turning
somewhere."

"Start from the known; a landmark you can recognise now
and did then." . . .

"I feel sure of this: I remember thinking those shutters were a
frightful colour. Now herealong one can choose between the
pass and the valley. I thought the pass would be shorter and it
was a mistake. I'd lost the way once already. We were both tired
and short-tempered."

"The circumstances are familiar. Your wife was abusive?"

"To be fair, I'd have been the same, had she been driving."

"Endeavour now to be extremely precise."

"Somewhere along here."

"Better than that."

"I wasn't counting footsteps, you know."

"Control your irritation. You would not stop on a bend."

"One is the same as another."

"Stop here. Repeat your movements."

"Like that. Slammed on the brake and pulled in. I sat for a moment because I was boiling over. I got out and walked a few steps. My head was going round."

"How far?"

"I don't know, twenty, thirty. I stopped to empty my bladder. I realised I'd been driving dangerously. When I turned round she'd got out and taken her bag."

"Did you speak? Did she?"

"No. I just thought spitefully, 'Walk then; it'll do you good.'"

"And then?"

"Nothing. I just got back in the car. I didn't have any reaction beyond, Well all right then, that'll stop the nagging anyhow."

"Nagging about your dangerous driving?"

"That and this argument which had been going on, and anything else that occurred to her."

"We agree thus? You were fatigued, irritable, violent."

"You might say that."

"You felt provoked, exasperated. When she got out of the car, you found that a further provocation?"

"On the contrary, it seemed a good solution."

"Continue. Do as you did then."

"I remember only glancing in the mirror as I drove off. Walking away in that stiff, obstinate fashion."

("That's vivid. I find that quite coherent.")

"Yes. Carrying a bag; would you describe the bag?"

"Airline sort of thing on a shoulder sling. The usual sort, for overnight."

"And the next thing you remember?"

"Down here at the bottom, there's a turning and a signpost. Oh good, that brings me back on the right road after all."

"I notice that this is the junction of the road you spoke of as going through the valley."

"That's right. Longer way round, but easier."

"During the time we have spoken of, did any other car pass you in either direction?"

"Not that I remember."

"That accords with my observation. We have seen no one."

"Most people take the other road, I suppose."

"Why didn't you?"

"Don't know really: vague notion that the pass was shorter and a prettier road. One wants to relieve the monotony."

("The pass is marked on a tourist map as presenting a striking view.")

"I've taken it before, I think, going the other way. I'd forgotten how much it twisted."

"You would be aware that in general it is deserted?"

"Woodcutters I suppose. Tourists in summer."

("As you'll agree the choice is not eccentric in the light of his personality.")

"Possibly, Maître. Very well, go back the way we came." . . .

Ed. Note. *This continues: I abbreviate since the judge was exhaustive. He developed the hypothesis that in an admitted highly irritable state of nervous fatigue Lefebvre had struck his wife. L's reaction to this was quite calm: he shrugged and said he could agree it wasn't preposterous but it hadn't happened. Overriding protest from Silberstein the judge questioned him quite sharply. We know now that what he had in mind was the detail of the spade which L. was in the habit of carrying in the car. L's words and behaviour read coherently, and are convincing. One could call it a piece of legal bluff. The judge would hardly have thought of asking the gendarmerie to go hunting about and digging over a downhill passage ten kilometres long! I've gone over it myself; a typical Vosges 'shoelace' descent, and it's perfectly true that it all looks the same.*

In conversation with me, Silberstein said it was preposterous; that L. could well have clonked his wife (who could be maddening; I agree from my knowledge of her and my wife concurs) but that the reading of L's psychology is all wrong: if he had injured her at all badly he would have driven her at once to a hospital. I agree: he loved her dearly and was quite dependent on her. I give weight too to S's opinion: he observed his client closely and is extremely shrewd.

In private argument with the judge, Silberstein made much of the argument that she could well have been assassinated, and perhaps buried somewhere, waving the spectre of alcoholic peasantry, offering a lift and fancying a bit of slap-and-tickle.

This to my mind is quite sound, meaning more convincing than the judge's hypothesis though equally unprovable. The local people are indeed a pretty dotty lot. The woodcutters work in gangs of three or four, which militates against, but are secretive and tortuous.

I believe we could say with fair certainty that the gendarmerie skated lightly over their enquiries. They would have been nervous of getting burned as they had over the 'Villemin' case, which happened close by in both time and place and created an inextricable legal imbroglio.

One could argue also that the judge's reaction was also influenced by this 'cause célèbre'. In reaction: the instructing judge of the Villemin affair was young and inexperienced, and it was widely held that with the best intentions he had made a mess of it. This judge was both old and experienced, and might well have developed the notion that 'he knew better' despite the insufficiency of evidence. It seems plain that he chose to inculpate Lefebvre out of obstinacy, upon amazingly slight and supposititious grounds. It is equally plain that he was a tremendous believer in locking people up. That there are still magistrates like this, if mercifully fewer, will only astonish those unacquainted with the feudal beliefs of the right-wing bourgeoisie, whose mentality is as backward, as devious, as incestuous as that of any woodcutter . . . Silberstein was perfectly clear that it would never come to trial – as in fact it did not – but that the judge must be given his head since there is in fact no legal brake upon him, bar an appeal to the tribunal, which like all legal processes everywhere is a dilatory mix of prudence and inertia. S., a crafty old legal fox himself, was farseeing enough to rope in all sorts of loose ends – even including our by-now old friend Commissaire Castang.

My wife, being thoroughly feminine, was much aghast at this raising from vasty deeps of spirits which came and then refused to go away. Prisons are like nuclear power stations: nobody civilised can ever feel happy with them. And she was relearning the lesson she should not have forgotten; what kittle cattle witnesses are.

Edited Transcripts: Interrogation of neighbours

" . . . Now then, Dr Dorp. Forgive me, we seem to be having some trouble with these preliminaries. Would you be so kind as to spell it?" (Ed. Note: *hilarious but longwinded. One could hardly find a name more English and really more commonplace than Thorpe, or more unpronounceable to a French mouth. Was it hard or soft? Oh dear, like an English* the, *or a Spanish* c? *Monsieur Boislevant was determined to get it right; falling again headlong at the given name Ian.)* "And you are both of English nationality?" *(Poles? Magyars?)* "Madame? Oh . . . M a í r e." *(Tones of voice, expressions of incredulity, are unfortunately unavailable in clerical transcripts. No, no further facetious interjections but the interview got off to a sticky start.)* "A pure formality, Madame. Je vous en prie . . .

"Now you were for some years neighbours of Monsieur Lefebvre. A certain intimacy? Quite so, we – certain shared factors, might we perhaps say? Nationality. Background and origin? Some intellectual tastes. Artistic? Well well, a certain similarity. I am attempting to get the precise picture. Yes, Dr Thorpe? – no no, je vous en prie."

"Doctor only in physical sciences: I'm a uh, physicist at the research establishment: my wife does uh, librarian work. I'm acquainted with Professor Davidson. We were both at Cambridge but not uh, contemporary. Arlette is a friend. I wouldn't quite uh, call Guy a friend."

"You need be in no way afraid of compromising yourselves. A disappearance of this abrupt nature calls for enquiry. No accusations have been made."

"I don't want to compromise anybody."

"Nor need you be afraid of doing so."

"No, there's a misunderstanding, I only meant friendship's like class, there are nuances. Call him a friend then, why not? We were on dropping-in terms. Oh dear. He was very kind at the start about helping and advising over the garden and we sort of went on from there. Dropping in isn't a very French thing, is it?"

"And Madame Lefebvre who is the object of our interest?"

"Sibille, yes. Funny woman, rather."

"Describe her personality."

"Easier said than done. Like quarks with different flavours. Sorry, I only meant personalities are complex. She could be very simple and forthcoming, and you'd suddenly strike secretiveness and reserve. We got on well enough as a rule; you never knew quite where you were with her. Intellectual interests? – well, she wasn't really very bright, you know."

(Mrs T.) "I rather liked her. She put on an act of being distant and rather haughty; shyness as much as anything perhaps, but I always found her friendly. Opinions aplenty, very decided ones, never hesitated to voice them. A bit sharpedged in company. When we were alone we always got on well. Very pretty."

(Dr T.) "Not a bit pretty."

(Mrs T.) "My husband's being excessively cautious, as you gather he wasn't particularly keen, but we used to tease him; she was very attractive."

"Attractive to men in general?"

"Don't get me wrong, she wasn't at all flirtatious."

"Did she confide in you, at times?"

"Never. In nobody, I should think; emotions kept severely in check. And very principled, if anything rather puritanical."

"You scout thus the hypothesis that she left with another man?"

"I thought we'd come to that: I'd describe it as out of the question. But it's a couple of years since we saw her, you know; they moved down to the south."

"Based on your knowledge of her, at that time, your expression implies some certainty."

"I only meant that she shied away from personal or emotional things and was rather prim. Most of our conversations were dull and domestic, knitting and cooking. She was what you call femme d'intérieur. She didn't want a job and wasn't trained for any but she did Guy's accountancy and stuff. She was his secretary really. She had an interest in houses, kept her own beautifully, I always felt a sad slut alongside. Meticulous, rather rigid. If one said something she disapproved of she put on a face . . ."

"I understand but we can't write that down."

"Yes, well, perhaps she didn't have very much sense of humour."

(Dr T.) "Didn't have any at all. Made things difficult. One would make a joke and she'd take it literally. And she'd lay down the law, highly dogmatic, tiresome lecturing manner."

(Mrs T.) "Rather an oldfashioned feminist. I felt it was a pity she didn't have children. Pretty frustrated about that I think. What? Yes, two, but they're at home, at boarding-school. Sorry? Home, I mean, a way of talking. This is only a job, we won't be here for ever. Sibille – all that polishing of her house – I wonder."

"Will you explain?"

"Two sorts of English people. Like us, here on business and live here but don't really put down roots. And the ones who go native – sorry, I don't mean that pejoratively, but bring their children up here, settle down permanently."

"And Madame Lefebvre?"

"One didn't feel that she belonged. Loyalty, yes, where my man goes, and all that. Guy now, he is English, yes, but he was quite at home here and one would never feel he had a problem."

"In this light, you think it probable that she would feel the need to return to her country? Postulating a violent dispute or an emotional disturbance?"

"Yes, I think so. Yes, that's what we assumed when we heard she'd left."

(Dr T.) "Guy's a bit of a clinging vine. She could have made a clean break, in order to peel him off."

"Ah. You have psychiatric training, Dr Thorpe?"

"Good heavens no. Simple common sense."

"This seems the most plausible explanation to you?"

"Yes. Why not?"

(Mrs T.) "I'm not sure I altogether agree. She didn't believe in divorce. I'd accept that she'd work herself up to a violent effort, and separate, with a clean chop, no messing."

"You see her as the stronger character of the two?"

"Oh yes, definitely./ Yes indeed; I agree."

"Did he show sign of resentment?"

"I don't think one could go that far."

(Mrs T.) "Better not exaggerate. He wasn't a sort of comedy henpecked husband."

"Very well. We'll come to the episode of his arrival on the day she is said to have left. Can you try to outline the salient details of the occasion. Of anything that struck you at the time?"

"Well, he was plainly distraught."

"One moment. His arrival was unexpected?"

"No, not altogether. He had phoned a day or so before, I think."

(Mrs T.) "Along the lines of he had to see German customers, and what about dropping by. All quite ordinary. I said delighted. I mean, they were friends we hadn't seen for some time."

"The indication was that both were to be expected?"

"Oh yes. My husband misunderstood; it was Sibille who phoned."

"The point has importance; that she planned to come. You are sure of that?"

"Oh yes, because we were taken aback when he came in alone."

"Think back carefully: it is crucial that you be exact."

"Let's see. I'd got home around the usual time. Say six or a little after."

"I'd cooked a casseroley thing, the sort that can keep without spoiling."

"Must have been about seven, or not much later because we weren't starving, or ready to give them up."

"Was it dark, when he came?"

"Getting dark, I think."

"Raining?"

"That I don't recall."

"The forecast for the area on that day was for cloud and intermittent showers."

"It generally is. Hazy on that. What I do remember is that he came in alone and when we asked where's Sibille he just said – "

"With as much precision as you can."

"'She's left me' or 'She walked out on me'. You can't expect me to be more exact than that."

"But you remember this phrase."

"Well, wouldn't you? Quite a startling piece of information. And a bit embarrassing. One covers up. Come on in, you must be tired, I'm sure you're starving, come and have a drink."

"Describe his appearance."

(Mrs T.) "Did somebody say distraught? I remember dishevelled. Shocked is the right word, I suppose. He took pains to be quiet and composed and not to make a drama. Natural in the circumstances."

"What do you mean by dishevelled? Wet? Dirty?"

"Not as I recall. Hair all over the place. Eyes a bit odd, sort of staring."

(Dr T.) "Better be careful. One's always a bit travel-stained after a long drive, and one's eyes are tired. I would automatically have said something like wouldn't you like a wash. In any case once he'd had a drink he was perfectly all right. After that it was just a conventional evening. Out of ordinary social tact one wasn't going to harp on the matter."

(Mrs T.) "Might have been better if we had; get it over with."

(Dr T.) "He was plainly tired and nervous, didn't stay late and we didn't press him."

"We have a record of a hotel booking in the town. Anything to add, Madame?"

"No. He was a friend after all."

"Was?"

"Is. I don't see any occasion to pay heed to illnatured gossip, and as far as I'm concerned that's all it is."

"That does you credit. You are however aware that a sentiment of loyalty cannot allow you to conceal any fact that it would be in the interests of justice to make known. Even if it appeared prejudicial."

"I don't see why there should be anything to conceal."

"Gently then, Monsieur, there is no suggestion that you do. I place upon record that I find you careful and painstaking. I thank you both and hope to see no occasion to trouble you further."

Letter. Maître Serge Frédéric Silberstein, Advocate at the Bar. To Commissaire Henri Castang, PJ

In reference to our phone conversation of yesterday, I confirm that I find a meeting desirable at the date you suggest, bearing on the facts known to you.

The instructing magistrate has seen fit to pronounce an inculpation, which in the state of known evidence is preposterous but which allows me access to the dossier. I add that Madame Davidson has expressed herself as much shocked by this decision, which explains her intervention.

Private detectives are looked upon with little favour by anyone likely to be concerned in this matter. I would approve any enquiry that you accept to undertake upon a vacationary basis, and can arrange payment for the expenses of same. Madame Davidson has energetically represented her faith in your agreement to correct any miscarriage of judicial process. This course is possible, since no rogatory commission has been addressed to the Police Judiciaire. I therefore suggest that it can form the basis for discussion between us.

HENRI CASTANG . . .

'Vacation' is one of those funny words like 'pathetic' which are the same in the two languages but have different meanings. It has in French a specific technical connotation to a commissaire of police, meaning a particular job for which he is allowed to receive payment. It is in fact a 'perk' because he's well paid: probably the best-known is 'constatation of adultery' made for cuckolded but vengeful husbands. This idea of Silberstein was unorthodox but rather smart: I liked it on both grounds. In fact I prefer this to being asked to go catch women in adultery, however much I get paid.

VERA CASTANG . . .

Henri came home early: asked why (he's conscientious about this), said it was to Take me in adultery; serves me right for a silly question.

It exists still. In theory, anyhow. Catch a woman in flagrant délit, with a proper legal official as witness – and a commissaire of police will do nicely – you can have her punished by three months' imprisonment: it's in the Code to this day. You'd even find a judge here or there ready to pass sentence. Nothing happens to the man, of course.

I don't know whether anyone ever asked Henri to do this. Now they have, he says. A fortnight of Detective Work; he hasn't done any of that for a long time. Not perhaps lurking about in the street beneath lashing rain at three in the morning, but strenuous activity. Generous expense account: great added inducement.

"I'm stale, too. And you'll be pleased to see my back." Yes. I'd rather like to go away myself on expenses. Lavish promises have been made to this effect.

"And there isn't a lot doing in the office. Rather too sedentary lately."

What's the real reason? I asked bluntly, and he went and got us both a drink, sign that he was in a conversational mood.

Yes, well, since the judge of instruction had got this bee in his bonnet . . . that meant Mr Lefebvre got dug into, and pretty deeply too, but in a foreseeably narrow, tramline sort of way. His powers were great, but. Rather like those geological survey people looking for oil or uranium, who can go down three thousand feet and bring up a carrot. Looking for something specific which will be exciting and commercially viable.

Whereas he – it would be a superficial look but broader. Sometimes if one gets the light at a certain angle it shows things up one didn't know existed: prehistoric remains or whatever.

I suppose I made faces at these metaphors, but I could see that he wanted to do it, was pleased with the opening given, and nothing I said would change his mind. Still . . .

Was it worth while, all this effort? The Davidson woman dramatising things. She made it appear interesting but *is* it?

He looked at me then with the big reproachful eyes. I was vaguely vexed. I didn't really know why. I was jealous, maybe. I stumped about on leaden feet, getting the supper ready. He sat over the Paris paper, grumbling, giving occasional maniac laughs (the antics I suppose, as usual, of the Minister of the Interior, saying 'Know that I am God' to policemen), while things filtered slowly through my dim wits. Being female I tend to disagree violently with any given viewpoint, and then come round to it bit by bit: he knows this, damn him.

Guy Lefebvre is an interesting enough man as people go. Or so he sounds; I haven't met him. Not the sort of man to kill his wife, one would think. Or if he did, while drunk or on uppers or downers or whatever they're called, or what is most likely in some idiotic and really accidental way, then he'd have gone straight to give himself up.

This is all the domain of the judge. Means–motive–opportunity. And if faced with one of those deaths that seem too stupid to be accidental, like fiddling with electrical apparatus while standing in the bath, the judge starts looking narrowly at premeditation. Article 296 of the Penal Code. Oh yes, I've got to know quite a few of them by heart too. 'Murder committed with premeditation or ambush is .termed assassination.' You won't get a lot of extenuating circumstances allowed thereabouts. The judge would go boring like a whole colony of termites into state-of-mind. Such a load of balls. The judge would commit Guy, and one is already starting to feel sorry for him, to psychiatric examination practically first-thing. Any defence advocate, abolishing this result as prejudiced even if it isn't, roars for a second opinion, chopchop. Hell, chopchop takes twelve months, and the third, so-called independent expert with which the judge counters to 'hold the balance', means eighteen. Pity the poor bastard who isn't even properly accused yet. He's 'prévenu'. Just for curiosity I looked this up in 'Robert', who gives the game away with characteristic lucidity: there's not much cant in Robert. '*Prévenu*: he who has strong suppositions either for or against him' is the primary meaning. A deadly secondary: 'he who is considered to be guilty'. A tertiary quite as bad: 'inculpated'.

But psychiatric opinions, even when they don't all cancel each other out, are not of great evidential value. It's a matter of 'likely: unlikely' – what's the technical, police evidence?

Isn't any. No corpse, no corpus delicti. Since all this is desperately boring, one can see why it bores Henri.

For there's a pretty good rule in police procedure, sounding first paradoxical and then disillusioned, like Parkinson or Murphy. To 'Whatever can go wrong, will' and 'Work expands to fill the time allotted' add 'Serious crime is the victim's fault'. In criminal psychiatry this has a pompous appellation; catastrophe theory or something of the sort.

I have bellowed about this on numerous occasions, getting extremely emotional about girls raped on suburban trains or families in cars massacred by autoroute cowboys, to the accompaniment of police chuckles (But of course, dearest girl – isn't she sweet!). I do see the point. If something drastic happened to Sibille, shouldn't we look at Sibille? Order *her* a psychiatric examination.

So I went back and gave Henri, so to speak, my blessing.

HENRI CASTANG . . .

Patience in public, and with the public, is an essential for a cop, even under great provocation: what a big hollow clonking truism. It's not at all easy. The meanness, the avarice, the cowardice, the squalid self-interest of the Pubalick . . . the interminable chicanery of all one's dealings with same. Oh well.

Even some meek little man like Guy Lefebvre. There come times when one has such a colossal wish to give him an unmerciful clout over the earhole.

And if I were an examining magistrate – a thing I thank God daily I am not – there are people one has in the office, and how do you stop yourself jumping up and landing them one in the chops. Come to that if I were Guy (thank God, etcetera) I daresay I'd jump up and land the magistrate one (there's mostly a cop present, for just such occasions). I've been in this situation! And had to be my own cop!

I have a shortish fuse, I agree. Adrien Richard, my superior for several years, had many qualities to admire – and many like deviousness to unadmire – and among the first his selfcontrol. His troops could commit unmeasurable imbecilities (myself foremost) for which he would be answerable, and he still didn't raise his voice.

I govern my rages ill. They are brief, I grant, and sudden, and forgotten – at least by me – quickly. It throws a lot of strain upon Vera. My subordinates are supposed to be disciplined. But when, as once happened, I lost my temper with a judge of instruction . . . She was a friend luckily, and a woman, and handled it well.

Mademoiselle Alice Jimenez charged me openly with tampering with a witness in a criminal affair. A female witness. When I say tamper the word has another and familiar meaning . . .

She kept her head when I bawled at her. Slamming the door is a figure of speech. The doors in the Palace of Justice don't slam; they have pressure closers. And they're soundproofed, padded because people quite often scream in there. Jimenez handled it well. She did not go yacking to the Proc nor yet to Commissaire Sabatier to have me suspended. If she pushed me harder, and more unfairly, than she would a witness, I am a professional. I interrogate people; I know how it is done. If I were guilty of malpractice, I deserved to get a sniff of my skin when scorched, for an hour.

I did not go back to the office after simmering down. The phones there are not secure. I went home instead, and called her from there.

"I think I had better apologise."

"I'm pleased to hear that." A light, dry voice, unemotional. "Do you think you could call me again, in an hour's time?" While the jury is 'out' the prisoner plays cards with his guardians. Connoisseurs of the courtroom, they offer friendly and expert forecasting of the 'right score': it's a football match, when all is said. I read the newspaper, right down to the stock-exchange quotations. Had my shares gone down?

"All right now, you can talk; I've sent her to lunch."

"I meant what I said."

"You should, you know. Calling the instructing judge a Spanish cunt may be a factual description but in front of her clerk it's outrage to a magistrate. And I also will apologise, for the rough passage. It was essential, you know, that you should not take it lightly."

"Jimenez, it is impossible that you should believe this."

"There has been no solid suspension of disbelief; as yet. I'll be seeing Miss Olga again this afternoon."

"I don't think she can have done it on purpose. I've been booby-trapped, agreed. The notion wouldn't have occurred to her. It smells of a lawyer, catching a stray straw and gleefully building a brick."

"I differ in my reading," she said coolly. "From what I know of Olga she would be much shocked at such a suggestion from outside, and would instinctively reject it. But she might come to believe in it from within. It becomes then a truth. On the assumption naturally that it is not objective truth."

"Alice, you have to accept that it isn't."

"I don't have to accept anything of the sort," still more coolly. "But since I give weight also to my reading of your character, since you have the right to a presumption initially favourable, and since the friendship even of a judge is elastic, I require stronger proofs of guilt. Apart from your outburst of rage, I take it you have no direct evidence."

"One so seldom has." It's the biggest truism in the book that circumstantial evidence of innocence is impossible to produce, while anything can be used to make you look a villain. Vera, whose eyes across the room had been getting progressively bigger, padded across to listen to the phone extension. "You could have a confrontation."

"I don't see that as particularly useful. Olga is a simple soul, and you are skilled in the arts of subterfuge."

"So what do you propose to do?"

"Don't fly off your handle: Miss Olga must expect to be exposed to professional disbelief like anyone else."

"But if you leave this on the file it's at the very best a damaging innuendo against me."

"I'll take the decision in due course," unyielding. "You have a point. You deserve no bad mark on account of a stupid imprudence, or even a coarse joke. Leave Olga to me." And slapped the phone down.

There are no answers to the unspoken queries in a wife's eyes. Explanations are always futile. When a judge *orders* you to explain – why, childish remarks ensue. 'Pretty mean of Alice.' We're back in the girls' boarding school.

"This one," I said heavily, "is sillier than most." Tja, Vera,

Alice, Olga. Three women. Tough odds, even for big macho cop.

It's a Polish story. Traffic in secondhand cars . . . The Commissaire inherited a new 'company car'; a police vehicle. He then wished to swop his own car, a stationwagon suitable for very small children when there are prams and stuff to shove in the back, against a smaller car suitable for Vera, whose leg is not brilliant and likes an automatic gearbox. Just the sort of subject that gets hassled over the coffeecups, and Olga had overheard enough to make her ears prick.

Her husband, she said, was in the market for a bigger wagon, and was in preliminary discussion with a chap at the motel-outside-town; you know, by the autoroute junction . . . A complicated, three-way deal began to take shape. I picked up Olga one evening after work, and trundled her out there, and gave her a lift home afterwards. I didn't much like the chap's car, and had suspicions of the gearbox. He was far too emphatic about the brakes being new. Now from here on, a number of facts exist. Like Olga is a remarkably pretty girl. Why refuse to admit that yes, I do find her attractive? The fact isn't important. It wouldn't – and didn't – make the price of a car better. I agree, naturally, that my joke about assignations at roadside motels was vulgar, coarse, and unfunny.

What I did not know – one of my inspectors told me later; it had been 'before my time' – was that the motel manager had been in trouble on a charge of procuring. Nothing surprising in that since motels and casual prostitution are not mutually exclusive concepts, but it had been the one thing too many: he took my remarks as an unnecessarily crude reminder that there was a file on him, and worse – that a cop would use the fact as pressure to cheapen a car deal.

The rest is Olga's character. A fiercely loyal girl. To her own man, and any waitress who happens to be pretty is vulnerable, and sensitive, to remarks from customers. It wouldn't have been important but for her loyalty to her workmate. To see Elena picked up by me on a charge Olga found ridiculous merely exasperated her existing certainty that all cops are hypocrites. She could find no means of defending Elena, but she could find a way of discrediting a stinking cop. And the motel man was ready to hand as a witness, needing no suborning; he had his own grievance.

Laugh it off, if you like. Most cops would laugh. Come to that, they'd laugh brassily, and press a perjury charge into the bargain. I cannot manage to feel much indignation at Alice Jimenez finding nothing improbable in a tale like this. Her experience shows most men to be pretty grimy objects.

And Vera? Most police wives adopt the attitude of whether it's true or not, and it well may be, they don't want to know. Because if you let a thing like that threaten your marriage, then you're better off divorcing now, and be done with it. But Vera is no believer in taking the easy way out. Any more than Alice. Oddly similar, those two women. They are both 'absolute'.

Really schtoopid, huh?

ARTHUR DAVIDSON (witnessed direct) . . .

Monsieur le Commissaire, after a fruitful conspiracy with Maître Silberstein, appeared upon our doorstep in nice time for lunch.

"Oh good, good," Arlette cried archly, adding 'Good' in case one should mistake her meaning. "Stay to lunch."

Never having met the chap, I was now exposed to the penetrating police eye. What he sees is a tall bony type with large feet and that awful English hair which falls about in odd directions. Pipe, picked up, put down, one can never remember where: the time and energy spent searching is better spent than that of those prissy people who've given-it-up. Tendency to noiseless powerful laughter, causing the glasses to fall down on his nose and having to be pushed up again: it is a bore having to explain the beastliness of bifocals.

What I saw was a spare, indeed enviably slim physique, light on the feet as well as minus-bow-window: I am aware that I walk like two men carrying a ladder. Stiffish dark hair, the sort that goes grey prematurely. Face made of several pieces of leather amateurishly stitched together. I am enough of a cop myself to look at ears and hands: both well-shaped and clean. Clothes oddly those of a retired jockey; shoes splendidly indeed obsessively polished. I tell him about Ludwig Bemelmans' dog, called Hitler and trained to piss on over-polished boots: he is entertained. He has nice candid eyes, which cease abruptly to be candid and become most malicious, and disappear altogether when he laughs. Viewed in the context of the Polizei-in-general this is all reassuring. It strikes me belatedly that it's supposed to be reassuring.

"I suppose it isn't the first time in history that a criminal brigade cop is pressed into service as character witness for the defence. Must be fairly rare though, and Sonnenschein an imaginative fellow."

"Silberstein," said Arlette who was fussing about with drinks. "Don't be antisemitic." I do sometimes get people's names wrong on purpose but this was flagrant injustice: still, Castang is used to that.

"A good tactic," he agrees ambiguously, appreciating malt whisky. "I can't see how they're ever going to get it to court. Suppose he killed her: then he buried her. Need to dig up half the bloody Vosges. Nice long spell in jug, thinks the judge, will cause our chap to be duly overcome by Christian remorse."

"Did you see him? – the judge, I mean."

"Oh yes, I had to. I can't do anything undercover, what's that English phrase?"

"Hole 'n corner."

"I'm not technically under his orders but he has authority over me. He got into a slight flounce. 'Hold you bound to communicate any findings whatsoever without delay, concealment or omission.'"

"Could he in point of fact forbid you to poke about?"

"Could if he tried. Using PJ resources or personnel, certainly. No rogatory commission. In this narrow context, disputable."

"And you yourself – is this interesting?" At this time, remember, I was myself interested chiefly because alarmed at zeal leading my dear wife into a wasps' nest. She has been involved in criminal cases before now, and had some narrow squeaks in consequence – these can be frightening. As for the police . . . they move in a devious world: it makes devious people of them.

Castang thought, while playing with his drink. His voice is low, quiet. In ways he is very much cop, and French into the bargain. Plenty of experience in being devious. Now that I know him better I am impressed. He does not allow his professionalism to possess him. He is not closed to new ideas; he forces his own mind out of routine patterns. It gives him a freshness, an openness met with rarely among officialdom in France. Many have sharp intelligence, much wit, immense sophistication, can make one rock with laughter; and remain oddly hidebound. They can be very narrow, amazingly conventional in their lives and beliefs. One wants to touch them up a bit, introduce a grittier element into these over-smoothed-out spheres. I was about to learn how he did this.

"Interesting?" Moving the word around, rearranging it to make the light fall differently. "To a cop? – no. On the contrary, run a mile instinctively. As Richard told your wife. This sort of judicial blind alley . . .

"As a man yes, he's interesting. Recall, I've hardly met him. Quarter of an hour in my office. So I was being official, so was he. Haven't seen him here, don't know that I want to. Be a handicap to us both, perhaps. Silberstein made him this offer, that I do some work. Neither yes nor no; said he'd think about it. Wrote a letter saying yes, next day, and he'd pay all expenses. As though he'd thought about it, in a detached way.

"I don't have any presumptions – guilt, innocence. Allows me some scope. There are psychiatric reports: they aren't in yet: if they were I don't think I'd want to see them. Mostly they're like statistics, can be read the way you want to read them. Same as economics: inflation is down, unemployment figures are up; what d'you read into that?

"He's English. He may have a French name, remote French origins but he's shaped and formed by several generations of English life and thinking. Comes back here to work, brings an English, sorry, Scotch wife with him. This is a factor, I don't now what it means but it's there.

"Take you. You're a sophisticated international sort of person but you're English. Living here, having a French wife, it will exaggerate certain areas of your personality, diminish others, I don't know how.

"Take myself. I'm French. Not maybe as French as all that, since some instinct pushed me to ask a Czech girl to marry me. Why? Am I trying to be less French? It can be a big handicap marrying across a frontier. There are all sorts of little blockages, incomprehensions, irritations. One uses this, or tries to.

"English people are very different. Oughtn't to be, close neighbours as they are, but they make a cult of their island. Those faces, knobbly and shapeless like a potato, insisting upon driving on the wrong side; proud of it."

I suppose I was grinning. Arlette certainly was. He wasn't.

"So just his being here interests me. Bringing the Scotch wife, next. Does that togetherness in the foreign country bring them closer together, as man and wife? Being without children – I was, for some years. Was thought my wife couldn't have any, or shouldn't try. In this case, is it deliberate, accidental, and if so on whose side?

"I have a small professional interest," drawling it, "as well. I don't come into this for your wife's beautiful eyes. I put myself to a little bit," drawling it, "of trouble, because there's a principle at stake.

"A socialist Minister of Justice was abused by the reactionaries and the antisemites because he didn't like it that a judge can still clap people into jug on such flimsy grounds. I agree. This judge is an honest man, but there needs to be a better filter. The Minister wanted there to be three judges, for a decision of this gravity, but where d'you find them, who pays for them? Fine in

116

theory, but the mechanism is too slow and too complex already. Want less law, more bloody equity.

"I like the English system of magistrates. Not judges, not lawyers, not even paid, who look at things a bit commonsensical and say, No, we won't send the chap to jug. Bad side of that is that the police have too much power, prepare the case themselves – that's bad, bad. That's the strong point of our system; we are controlled by the judge; believe me, he does.

"Sure, the law is ridiculous in any country. Look at all that nonsense about barristers and solicitors. Then come back to us. It is outrageous that a commissaire of police can be paid to burst into a woman's bedroom and roar 'He's hidden in the wardrobe' just because some cocufied prick of a husband can hire him."

I was of course filled with vivid delight. I could catch Adulterous Arlette in her nighty.

"Seriously," said Castang, "if the judge stays obstinate because he has feelings about yer-man being guilty, then Silberstein can ask the Chamber of Accusation for a ruling, but meantime the guy is in jug for three months.

"My last reason for taking this on is that there's no press interest. This isn't anything glamorous. The Polizei hates things which are glamorous. And he could of course be guilty: good reason to try and prove him innocent."

I nodded.

"Arlette now doesn't want to think him guilty because she feels guilty herself. The number of times she's wanted to assassinate me."

"Dinner," said the lady, poking her head in. She's too slapdash to be a good cook, but she's not the world's worst either.

"Vera being Czech," said Castang eating her fish soup, which is good, "is better at cabbage soup than anything else."

117

HENRI CASTANG . . .

I do not know this part of the world well. I have been here a few times, in pursuit of complicated doings: rogatory commissions on behalf of other judges of instruction. I have a recollection, rather too vivid, of being here with Divisional-Commissaire Richard, in a conspiracy I shudder thinking about, to kidnap a woman from across the border in Germany. A thing incredibly reckless. Profoundly immoral. Cops aren't worried by illegality. They're illegal every day of the week.

Arlette Davidson lives in a pleasant apartment, the second floor of a solid, generously proportioned house of the early nineteenth century, in the middle of the university quarter, about which Arthur Davidson perambulates upon an antique Dutch bicycle much like the house. One of those southern women with fair hair and a Greek nose, or is it Phoenician? They are tall, have a splendid carriage and fine eyes; they age well. She's a better cook than Vera.

She drove me afterwards to the airport in quite an oh-I-say Lancia, great change from police vehicles.

Montpellier isn't very exciting either. It was nice to have, for once, no business with the regional service of the PJ, and I wasn't anxious to arouse their curiosity. I got a hire car and set off on the Alès road. Department of the Gard.

The thump and throb of a refrigerator motor was so loud in the stillness that it startled me. Chilly too on an April night. I could think myself still in the North and was glad of my leather jacket. Raining hard outside and a booming wind. One would be glad of a fire in that big baronial hearth. These stone houses, cool in summer, are in winter small joy. Monsieur Gaillac, clattering about with keys, turned on the electricity mains and hung about until I sent him back to his own cosy fireside; nice and stuffy in front of the television set.

Silberstein had got me a note from Lefebvre. Show the bearer

118

anything he wants to see and tell him whatever he wants to know. I was not going to declare myself a cop. Village people do not take kindly to the Policía. Suspicion and sulkiness would have clung to every step I took. Monsieur Gaillac had been devoured with curiosity as it was. Elderly man needing a shave, in a greasy old hat and a leather jacket like my own, a small farmer, which means a winegrower in this part of the world because there's nothing else. Vines on this stony upland soil give plentifully: in fact there's far too much and they look with fear towards Spain and Italy. This huge ocean of Languedoc plonk washing up and down all the way to Béziers isn't nowadays rich pickings. Little extras are welcome. Every tumbledown shack on the mountainside has been sold to sun-hungry northerners. The natives can make more from a bit of masonry and plumbing on the side, arranging little difficulties for a small commission. Nice, friendly people, but it doesn't do to play the snob or the city gent.

"Not thinking of selling, is he?" Monsieur Gaillac caretakes and his daughters help out with a bit of cleaning while the German or Belgian owners are away.

"Not that I know of." He was fishing, but so was I. "Some papers I'm seeing to for him. Asked me to look around since he'll be away some time."

"I look after the place."

"Sure, but after the winter – one's always a bit worried about the roof." Which was safe enough; one always is. "And Madame away too." His eyes got smaller; he was wondering how much I knew. I bought him a drink. One can't hurry these old boys.

A steep-pitched village perched on the scarp of the mountain massif that is nowhere far from the sea. Eastward from the fleshpots of the Rhone valley you are among the harsh peeled rocks of Cézanne country, the Monts de Provence stretching into the Maritime Alps all the way to Italy and north to Switzerland. Turn west and you skirt the big sombre plateau of the Massif Central. Little rivers have carved steep narrow gorges in the limestone: you find sheltered secret nooks lush with greenery.

But in the harsh uplands there is nothing but stunted scrubby ilex and spiky thorn: the 'garrigue' of austere and fragile beauty, the 'causses' which will only support sheep. Down in the hot marshy coastal strip they grow vegetables and fruit. The old towns have still a Saracen, Visigothic look. In the foothills there are only the vines. The little orchards of olive and almond are abandoned.

The village houses are massive, ancient structures in fortress style, narrow windows in their thick stone walls and much dim vaulted cellarage in their bowels, and on many a defensible spur there is a crumbling castle with memories of troubled times. Saracen pirates ravaged the coastlands and out of the north came ardent defenders of the holy catholic faith, to batter this obstinate land out of its vile and wicked ways. Languedoc is protestant country, huguenot country, cathar country. Had Guy atavistic notions of return to his remote roots? Or was it Sibille with baronial memories? I was not going to mention her disappearance. Monsieur Gaillac would come round to that in his own good time.

The usual story. Impoverished, improvident petty aristocracy clung on, selling off land to meet the end of the month, until an old woman died and nobody wanted it any more. Uncomfortable, unheatable, half ruinous, primitive in sanitation, far too big and awkward for any buyer but a wholehearted romantic. Sibille had got it cheap. What kind of echo had she found here of a damper, draughtier tower in the North?

Guy, said Monsieur Gaillac, getting confidential after three or four glasses, had never been much interested. Great big warren round the courtyard and no garden. But she was delighted with the challenge. What to let go, what to make of the bits you decide to keep and work on? It would be a bottomless pit of good and bad money alike, engulfing millions with nothing to show for them, unless one had the right combination of skill, intelligence, character to match the obstinacy of these dour stones. Sibille had. This was her house. She loved it.

But she's gone? – the way I heard it . . .

120

Gone, gone, who knows? Where has she gone? Went off with Monsieur on a business trip. That was as usual. Hadn't come back and yes, there'd been rumours. The gendarmerie had come asking about. What was one to tell them? She was liked, around here. So was he liked: he didn't mess about with anybody; respected people. Gossip there would always be. Little place like this. But nothing in it. They had tiffs. Who didn't? Madame liked her way. He knew a few more women the same. She loved this place. If, that is to say – well, least said. Meantime, he looked after the place. Nothing wrong with that. Monsieur was always perfectly correct. Sent money. He could account for it. Every penny.

He knew a lot more, to be sure, but wasn't giving out, not for a whole evening of free drinks and I had no desire to sit there pumping. He opened up the house for me, and I could prowl around.

Guy would have been seduced, at first. He had reached a crest of reputation as a garden architect, a good income and money too from painting. He had tackled projects of this sort before. Nothing is prettier than a fortified manor converted into a pleasaunce. In the North there are many such, with towers and moats around them. But here? The steep slope, the absence of water, the piles of ruinous stone. Nothing but a walled terrace to the south, jutting out over the village vineyards. Discouraging. After the initial determination to tussle with the difficulties and find satisfaction in them, he could quickly have grown bored. Sibille, narrower tougher nature, would be the more stimulated.

Comfort is a stupid word, perhaps. It has a lazy, materialistic sound, like an old dog on the sofa cushions. But success is a normal kind of human ambition, like security. One sees the 'business men' fight frenziedly for trivial and childish badges of prosperity which they can wear on their lapel like their little plastic nameplates. The gold credit card and the good table, the big cigar and the seat on the company plane, the vintage wine and the expense-account callgirl. Somebody said you mustn't grudge them these pleasures because look at the filthy work they do. One could go further than that: they are treated like dirt and their lives are full of fear. If they were deprived of these inducements and attractions how would they ever cope with the humiliation? Guy, who is not a man to be interested in slicing the salami .thinner, is not perhaps much excited by election to the country club. But Sibille? A woman wants 'her house' to be a fine one, where she can be hostess, socialise and entertain, and enjoy the reflected glow of success.

The front façade, with its two flanking turrets, was impressive. A salon opened on to the terrace, with a diningroom behind and a big, lovely kitchen. A – library would you call it? No, it was a work room, with a draughtsman's table in a good light and Guy's botanical literature. I could make no guess whether the collection were valuable but flower books, I know, are very expensive. On the other side was the woman's domain, a sort of morning-room and office combined, where she did her books and the shelving was full of files.

The turrets were too small for real rooms, had been made sensibly into bathrooms. A fine staircase of smooth beautiful stone led to the upper rooms. There was a wonderful gallery here, the whole breadth of the house, with a slate floor I guessed to be original. Marvellous place to hang pictures, and Guy had here some of his big garden perspectives as well as a few of his imaginary jungles. I wondered what Vera would make of these. I liked them greatly but I am no judge. One was of a sort of glade, full of sinister tropical growth, banyans and lianas and Spanish moss, with in the middle a patch of innocent, very European grass. On this stood an ugly, comfortable Victorian armchair. There was nobody there – he had just left. On the chair was a crumpled copy of *The Times* and on that lay a pair of horn-rimmed glasses. I wondered what a psychiatrist would make of that, and decided I didn't care.

They had separate bedrooms. I didn't see much in that, for a couple married twenty years. Maybe he snored. Maybe she did. Nothing especially feminine about Sibille's sleeping quarters. There were some framed photographs, unmistakeably parents and family, a childhood group among them, posed and formal, of three pretty little girls. A shelf of books and maps concerning Scotland betokened devotion – perhaps ancestor worship? Everything was extremely neat and tidy.

There were a couple of guest-rooms, conventionally furnished, looking as though nobody had ever slept there. Lefebvre's bedroom, along the passage, was anything but neat. Tidiness was the farmer's daughter; the bed straightened out and a hasty sweep round. Bookshelves of paperbacks; a man who reads in bed, and crime-novels at that. Plenty of objects, the sort that get given as presents which one neither needs nor wants but is reluctant to throw away lest feelings be hurt: an electric razor still new: ostentatious things of brass and leather in trad English style. But the room of a man at ease with himself. Sure of his identity? We say in French 'comfortable in his skin'.

The bathroom at the end was 'his'. No cosmetics beyond plain talcum-powder; the 'pharmacy' half-empty boxes of remedies for minor injuries and passing ailments: the kind everybody has and never manages to throw away. A quick search showed no stimulants nor soporifics.

Hers was back at the other end. Unless she had packed everything, which did not seem likely, she was not a great user of perfumery. A few jars of standard beauty-products: expensive quality and the large-economy-size. I looked at her clothes. There seemed a lot but most were old. Perhaps she was one of those women who cannot bear to throw anything away. Good plain stuff. She didn't go in for frilly finery. No personal vanity whatever her other vices were. Everybody has some. But I was tired. Tomorrow is another day, I say quite as often as Scarlett O'Hara.

The kitchen was very nice, plainly the original, a big lovely room with a vaulted ceiling and beautifully-laid flagstones. Some up-to-date apparatus. A big iron stove from the north was pleasingly familiar; Godin from Saint Quentin. I sat in a wooden armchair and stared at it. It would heat this big chilly room even in bitter weather: these were plainly the winter quarters. 'Eignes

Herd ist goldes wert' – I have a store of such folklore aphorisms, culled from Vera. Nothing like your own hearth.

Magnificent house. Fine to start with, and a lot of money spent since. Much was dilapidated still – one could spend a lot more. Most of the furniture was worn and even tatty. But a tremendous potential. Isn't that an abiding, a tremendous delight; hankering for things, doing them bit by bit, as money comes in?

I live now again in a rented flat, with no house of my own; it bothers me. Familiar police problem; one gets posted about like a letter by the administration. They care nothing about one's home life. They pay me well and that to them is the end of the matter. It's a good flat, large and comfortable, fitted up in almost luxurious fashion. Every modern convenience, quoi. I can still, in even more senior rank, get sent hither or yon at the caprice of the hierarchy: wives and children are of small account. I have two – children I mean. I am rambling, rather; I am tired.

In my last post, where I stayed many years, we had a house of our own, bought pretty cheap; an old cottage much dilapidated. Like this on a humble scale. We did it up, put a lot of work in. It was a wrench leaving, even though we sold it at a good price. I want again a house of my own. So do most people, as I imagine. Pretty deep-rooted instinct.

Guy Lefebvre has not been back to this splendid house of his, and seems uninterested in it. Has something horrible happened to him here?

And Sibille . . . this is 'her house'. Would she walk out on it?

Sitting in a kitchen is making me hungry. Good God, it's half past eight.

The village 'hotel' is just a country pub. A little café at one end where the owner is serving drinks to a few locals who are gazing vaguely at the television set. A diningroom in the middle where there are only two other customers. Half a dozen bedrooms above. The owner cooks, with an eye on his bar through the serving hatch. It's only April. When tourists start appearing he'll hire help in the village.

He made me a good dinner. Arlette Davidson, solid southern

woman, had given me a tagine, lovely Algerian stew with prunes
in it, and here I got seiches, the white octopus which is so good
with américaine sauce and rice. So no potatoes; I am forever
telling Vera we eat too many potatoes. Don't ever marry a
Czech wife. Eat coarsegrain semolina like Arabs to keep the
belly light and the mind alert. Vera's mashed potatoes are
marvellous but inhibit thought: all one's energies have gone
upon digestion. Those businessmen one sees in towns, bacon-
heavy at the age of thirty – they're all going to die of over-eating.
Don't think either I have the faintest sympathy with the low-
calorie-margarine brigade who think they're never going to die
at all. But I'm Arab enough to like their frugal habits. I wonder
what kind of cook Sibille was. Oh never mind: go to bed.

The locals are devoured with curiosity, and pump me a lot harder
than I'd dare try with them. I do not look all that cop but it
doesn't do to think the village thick. Woe betide the cop, in fact,
who thinks himself sophisticated. As for the gendarmerie, they
can smell police-judiciaire the way you or I nose a putrid fish; a
long way off and without pleasure. No way would they ever find
me sexy. I've no mandate, no rogatory commission, no official
standing. They unbend very slightly when I tell them it's enquiry-
on-behalf-of-the-family, which is not too far from the truth.
Rather more when they hear that the judge doesn't like me at
all. They stay mistrustful and uneasy, as parallel police forces
always are in each others' company. It's rather like persuading a
small child to eat the dinner it decidedly doesn't want; cold,
messed about, and quite disgusting in the first place. Learn
patience. Leggy after leggy, the doggy went to Dover. When he
came to a stile – Hop, another spoonful – he went over . . .

To their mind, there is no clear conclusion. French phrase –
'c'est pas évident'. That ol' judge can think what he likes; that's
nothing to them either way. No evidence for homicide. The
woman took off, period. They've looked at the house and seen

the same things I have, thought the same thoughts, but people do the unexpected, verdad?

No physical evidence. Monsieur Lefebvre went on a business trip and she went with him. She always did. Secretarial and to wash his socks and this is a pattern. Three or four times a year since we've known him.

Sure they had fights. Often and quite violent. Made no bones about it. High words, yelling, unconcealed. Plenty of temper there and no hard feelings after. But it's the quiet ones you want to know about. Pas vrai, Commissaire? Rancours behind closed shutters. Nice clean façade but shit swept under the carpet.

Foreigners – well, we could wish we'd more like that. We did of course a neighbourhood enquiry. Lefebvre doesn't get mixed in any clans or cliques, a friendly word to everyone and buy them a drink; neither liked nor disliked because he never got under anyone's skin. Except the mayor, but everybody's under *his* skin. No politics; as far as was known, no opinions. No funny frequentations.

Madame, yes, blew with a high wind. Temperamental, could be quarrelsome, but not malice-bearing. Would have a barney with anybody, but would likely ring up an hour later to say she was sorry.

So what's to conclude? She went off in a paddy; she'll come back. Even if that was six months ago. She was a goodlooking woman: she'll have found another man. Yes, it is odd that she seems to have passed unnoticed up there in Lorraine but there, we don't have a spy satellite do we? We can't take photos of every tourist passing through. We've maybe three hundred houses in this district owned by foreigners. People among them nobody's seen for three years on end. Haven't we got troubles enough without worrying about where they've got to? One day they're there again, calling in for the milk as though they'd never been away. People lend their places to friends, don't even tell us. We leave them alone.

It seemed sensible to me. But the judge didn't like it. His

attitude, at least as conveyed by Silberstein, was that the whole of this tale was just too damned fundamentally improbable. Too much out of character, as Arlette Davidson had thought it.

Need more witnesses.

The first I got, everyone steered me to and one saw at once why: a one-man local entertainment-industry. The English are eccentric only on their home ground? It stopped, together with the Empire? You have to go to California now to find them? Don't you believe it. If retired admirals of the Royal Navy are preposterous figures, our own is no less ludicrous: known as La Royale because they've never quite accepted the revolution of 1796. They've always lived in a completely unreal world, protecting Kerguelen or Ascension Island from invasion by the Swiss. This one told me that during the colonial wars St Lucia changed hands between the English and the French fourteen times. No wonder nobody has ever been able to take them seriously. Even nowadays, when they take themselves far too seriously, creeping about under the pack ice with their appalling missiles, one can only hope and pray that there is enough dottiness aboard to keep them in balance.

He was gardening, of course. I must have a word with Guy Lefebvre about the English genius for gardens. Does it go along with poetry? I had been expecting the conventional figure-of-fun with shapeless tweed hat and enormous moustache but he was a thin old boy in elegant tropical clothes suitable to St Lucia, and the only sign of eccentricity was a baseball cap with two peaks, and 'Dolphins are AIDS Carriers' written on it. The English in France are very garrulous, and possessive, hideously knowledge-able about phylloxera and Bordeaux vintages back to the Black Prince, or the smaller, uglier alpine flowers; but apart from a resounding 'Bonjour l'Enfoiré' he was calm enough until I told him I was from an insurance company in Zürich and he concluded that I was at war with the French.

"Bidets, what do they want with bidets, toothpaste is what they need. A people claiming to possess technical skills and can't even understand the mechanics of a sash window. You see, my dear boy, the French simply do not know how to build houses, make their windows opening inward, now I had to change all these round to open outward, magic casements, perilous seas forlorn.

"Guy Lefebvre? Hasn't been around here for months. Poncing about somewhere selling monkeypuzzle trees to benighted Krauts. Perfectly sound Englishman and because of his name pretends to be French in order to suck up to the niggers."

"It's Sibille I'm really anxious to lay hands on."

"Pronounce it Sybil, my boy, that's how she says it, however she may spell it. Sensible Scotch woman. Gone off I hear, auntie died and left her money."

"Did she?"

"Well, seems to have vanished and nobody's heard of her."

"We're beginning to wonder whether she mightn't be dead?"

"Company seeking to dodge paying out on the policy, hey? Dead, how would she be dead?"

The idea was making him thirsty. Colossal drinkers these empire-builders. The year of Victoria's Jubilee they got through nine and a half million of champagne: a robust folk.

"How should I know? Rumour to that effect. Now you who knew her well – "

"I should think we did know her well. Splendid woman. Guy's a good chap but distant you know, withdrawn, lot of don't-bother-me-I'm-thinking." After all those tightlipped years of starboard a trifle, nowadays it's port a lot. I settled down to little corrections whenever the flagship got off course.

"Mary, come here and listen to this preposterous tale." A quiet woman with an aureole of fluffy white hair like a seeding dandelion and pretty blue eyes. Practised in shooting down admirals.

"You wouldn't know anything about it at all, dear. Sibille is a very shy woman, too proud to speak her thoughts about private affairs. She isn't the confiding type." She sat down, striped cotton like a deckchair and wooden legs straight down to tennis shoes. As an afterthought she took away the bottle. "You know,

I wouldn't be surprised if she did go to Mexico without telling anyone. I always thought her a profoundly unhappy woman. Dotty too about ancient religions. Now the Mayas came from Atlantis and – "

"You'd think it was in character, would you?"

"Yes I would."

"Never heard such rubbish," said the admiral. "Ask me I'd say that sly Guy knocked her on the head and put her under a bush."

"Tom, you've no right to suggest anything so vile and irresponsible."

"Funny though," I put in. "It has been suggested."

"Then dismiss it. Nasty-minded malice."

"Don't be too sure," looking for the bottle and turning a bloodshot eye upon his spouse, "the times I'm tempted to shove you under the roses."

"Tom, you're just being embarrassing. They'd squabble, yes, and say things they'd regret afterwards."

"But you don't take it seriously?" I asked.

"Two strong personalities. Sibille goes her own way. Guy's not the henpecked doormat. His tactic is to withdraw, stroll off to commune with a lonely sequoia. They did say bitter and wounding things to each other, even before other people. Guy has a nasty sarcasm. Sibille like most women can be fiendish."

"Under the rosebushes!"

"Oh shut up!"

"You said she was profoundly unhappy, Mrs de Salis."

"Childless, you know. But temperamentally the wrong marriage. She made no confidences, so I don't break any. If I said she complained I'd be lying. But one can see. There's much bitterness in her expression sometimes. She's too much of an idealist, I think, about life and about marriage. I only mean that most of us have learned how to put the telescope to the blind eye. She set her sights too high, perhaps, and refused to lower them when reality didn't correspond."

"Have another."

"That's quite enough, Tom."

The next village had another classic of the countryside. I do not mean to be caricatural. The English abroad are, simply, a little larger than life, and the Empire goes on in ten thousand villages of every country that has a Mediterranean coastline. Nor can they ever resist sending themselves up, camping it a bit – they have phrases for this. Sibille might have given way to this tendency to overact. On Guy it might have jarred.

So one says loosely 'two old English pederasts' (antiques business, of course) and it sounds cheap. They did slip into the rôle now and again. 'Would our guest like whisky?' said John, and Ralph at once, 'A man, dear, you must give pastis.' They were sensitive, grave, devoid of malice. If 'Guy is a perfect darling' it was Admiral de Salis who advertised the screaming old queens, and they felt they had to live up to the reputation from time to time.

Sibille was also a perfect darling. But highly-coloured language doesn't necessarily imply a bad witness.

"She's a courageous and dignified woman. A fish out of water, but doesn't go flapping and gasping about it."

"Will you explain that?"

"You see, Guy's an artist, and she doesn't understand the first thing about art, and she tries very hard not to let that show. She's picked up a lot of the jargon and gasses on about a Turner watercolour, which she doesn't know the difference from a Staffordshire china dog."

"You might well ask well why the hell did she marry him then and the answer is she's a real northern romantic, really swimming in ghostly twilight. She in dreams beholds the Hebrides. Silver sands and magic seals, for all she makes such a show of her great hard-headedness in business matters. She's good at that, so survives. If it wasn't for her Guy would be ripped off blind by all and sundry, and would be wondering when his next meal would arrive."

"But when she sees the Aurora Borealis in far skies over the Orkneys she'll say at once, 'It's chilly, where's my woolly?'"

"If she'd had three brats to get her teeth into, changing nappies and smacking bottoms to get the wind up, she'd have found outlets for all these unfulfilled longings, what."

"I mean, Guy *seems* very moony standing there gazing at the swamp cypress but in fact the old computer is calculating away like mad fitting it in."

"She can be terrifically Madam showing-the-garden. Now *this* has to be a perfect *blaze*, and old Guy there biting his nails in despair. And she feels obliged to act the fearful snob about her ancestry and all, yacking on about King Malcolm the some-thingth. Mean to say, Scotch medieval history, nothing but incest and witchcraft."

"Simply pools of blood dripping off every sweaty hairy palm."

"Lovely," said Ralph, or was it John?

By this time I really was wanting a drink, and was delighted when a young woman offered me elderflower wine, which I've never had before. I exclaimed over it, a bit too much perhaps. I got a slow smile and a laconic "I keep bees." She was married to a Frenchman, plastics or something in Montpellier, a placid woman, balanced. Bees like such people. They won't thrive, I've been told, where there is envy or egotism; I can well believe it.

"Sibille? My husband dislikes her but I don't. You see, I'm Norwegian and we understand the Scotch. A French man from hereabouts, that's more difficult."

"But he understands you."

"That's because we love one another. May I have one of your cigarettes? I hardly ever smoke but I like the smell. Guy and Sibille don't love each other at all in the way I understand it. They are utterly dependent on each other which is rather different. They were in love with predetermined ideas and still are, I suppose. I'm told they've separated. Perhaps it took so long because both are so obstinate, so stupid, and it must be said so nice." The words were not harsh. The judgment sounded severe in the gentle contralto voice. An Amazon though with those wide-spaced grey eyes, the straight ashblonde hair in a long plait. She was wearing a man's check cotton shirt, jeans cut off at the knee: one would like to have seen her run. She was curled up with her legs folded under, in a big rattan armchair. She looked at me curiously, drawing on the cigarette, taking her time, and said, "I don't think you're an insurance agent."

"Confidence for confidence, I'm a cop."

"Ah. I rather thought so. PJ perhaps?"

"This is quite alarming."

"Just that you shouldn't be masquerading, really."

"Quite right; I'm a criminal brigade commissaire."

"I've never met one before but I rather thought you might be."

"The equation is simple. If you will trust me then plainly I can trust you."

"I like your equation."

"I'm not pursuing anybody. I have no judicial mandate. We do a lot of work to a formula known as In the interests of the family. Disappearances are quite common. Schoolchildren who run away from home. Or wives who go off with other men."

"Is that what Sibille did?"

"Monsieur Lefebvre is paying me to find out. That's why I'd value your opinion. Do you think it likely?"

"This is conventional cop thinking, isn't it – that it's sex?"

"I'd say that would depend on the person. Sex is in fashion. People are ruled a good deal by fashions. Terrorists are fashionable and so is lung cancer. Road accidents never are, even if they cause five times as much damage."

"Oh well, but oh dear, too; sex and northern women, Nora and Miss Julie, Bergman films: deep sigh. Southern men, we won't talk about the French, go completely mad, convinced we're all obsessed. I wonder whether the proportion really varies, south or north, catholic or calvinist. Mm, some women like sex; I do myself as it happens." It was not an invitation. Maybe I was not able to prevent an eyelid from flickering – at the corners of her eyes, a grin spread. "Oh I think I judge you accurately, saying that you won't misunderstand me. I only mention it because a good many women don't, much. I dislike the subject rather because there's so much nonsense talked about it. Put it that if I were to disappear it would be quite a legitimate inference that I'd gone with a man. I don't think that's the case with Sibille."

" 'I – hate – men. I can't abide them even now and then . . .' " She put her head back and laughed.

"That's *Kiss Me Kate*. I don't know about hate. Despise, perhaps. She hates a lot of things, including herself. She's got too large a share of that feyness and northern mysticism." I recalled Ralph-and-John with their talk of Aurora and magic seals. "I'd better only say that Sibille is a raging sea of conflict.

"Guy after all has art to fall back on; he's genuinely talented. Love gardens to that extent, you're not a barbarian. Sibille is barbaric." She was searching.

"A woman I interviewed said she was Lady Macbeth."

"But yes! You haven't mentioned it, but it must be in your mind that he might have killed her. The other way round would be more likely. A narrow fixed mind, and no humour." I waited. She wanted to do it by herself.

"She's been driven back upon her own resources, and her trouble is that she doesn't have many. A tormented woman, and perplexed. You see, her intelligence is not very great, and she has no skill at seeing herself with any objectivity. Whereas Guy has. It is a source of bitterness to her.

"I think I'd better say I'm fond of her. I'm sorry for her: I'm glad of her too. She makes me look hard at myself."

I liked this woman.

"We Norwegians, you know, didn't show up very well in that horrible war. The materialist Danes and the horrible Dutch, they did rather better. We're intolerant, antisemitic, unpleasantly fanatic. In a word rather Nazi. When I look at myself it's not a delicious vision."

"If she did decide to break away, would she then run like hell and leave no trace?"

"I don't know. I wouldn't have thought so. She had talons, and they were sunk pretty deep into him. I tell myself I'm mistaken. I'm not mistaken in this – any weird idea she does get in her skull she'll make a complete and ruthless job of it, once she has her mind made up. So maybe she did run away . . . I can give you some lunch if you can bear it being a bit vegetarian."

"I'd rather go to bed with you."

"Yes, that's what they all say. I don't have a gun, I don't have any brass knuckles, I don't know any judo or karate or anything. You could always try raping me if you think it would do you any good. You'd have to kill me, I think, or cripple me. Maybe I'd kill you afterwards. I don't think I would but one just doesn't know. People do kill one another." She looked at me queerly then. "You are a cop; you must have seen a lot of violence."

"Much too much, and still I don't understand it. We explain it afterwards. Like earthquakes or hurricanes – worse since we can't predict. But one has the same feeling of impotence."

"I do better with bees."

"And I'd do better writing out parking tickets."

I went back to the house. I'd got some bearings but where did they intersect? Celestial bearings, taken in open sea from a small boat which went up and down a good deal and no coast anywhere in sight. What I wanted was a nice faithful lighthouse some-where. I had no official right to any perquisitions, and wasn't going to let that stop me.

Sibille's workroom was that of the conscientious wife, scrupu-lously secretarial with the business papers. Shelves of cardboard folders, for every customer he'd ever had. Yearly files for the bank and the taxes and the social-security, the housekeeping accounts and the dentists' bills. But there were boxes too;

ordinary wooden wine cases stacked, carefully lined and closed with brown wrapping paper.

An archive. A family: centuries of letters and documents. Much seemed original. Photocopies too of parish registers, records of all sorts, carefully docketed. Another box held objects of piety, wrapped in tissue-paper, lovingly labelled. Much that was male and military; a spur and a sabretache from the Peninsula, a native dagger with the legend 'field of Assaye'. Feminine too. 'Honoria's fan, Court Presentation'; 'Lace Beatrice christening robe'. Sibille had become – made herself? – the repository of ancestor-worship. Many people do this. Roots. In almost any public record office you will find people copying out old entries, hunting for lost generations. A feeling of triumph when some particularly awkward gap is bridged. Well, I can understand the amateur detective. This collection would be valuable. It was bulky, heavy. I could envisage, easily enough, a man saying, Oh that junk . . . A woman does not throw things overboard.

In the bottom drawer of her writingdesk I found manuscript sheets covered with her flowery handwriting, legible and elegant. Headings, here and there beginnings for what evidently was intended to become the Book, which so many people start to write in middle age, when everything to do with the past becomes so important, and aglow with glamour. To everyone else so very dull.

And I have heard of women who can be more ruthless than any man. I've even known one who decided never to go back to an earlier life; never to speak of it. She told me an anecdote concerning Teresa of Avila. True or not, it is convincing. A woman aspirant to the Carmelite convent asked permission to bring with her a prayerbook she had had since childhood and to which she was much attached. 'If there is anything you value,' said Teresa, 'do not come here.'

There are women, and also men, whose beliefs are so strong, so intensely held, that they allow nothing to stand in their way. There are people who reject all evidence. For example, who will argue with the utmost conviction that the extermination camps of the nineteen-forties never existed. All an invention, they say, of Jewish propaganda. It is difficult to admit that this belief can be sincerely held. The fact is there.

The centre drawer held a raft of letters. I picked up the top one. It was dated about a month before the disappearance. A handwriting much like hers though more angular. Dearest Sib. Two pages of small doings, full of nicknames and abbreviations. Chatty, gossipy – why not? Your loving sister Faith. A name I had not met before. Again, why not? Spanish women have names like Esperanza. I found an addressbook with Faith in it, 'near' some village in Herefordshire, and made a note of it. There were some American addresses too.

There is nothing here I could call conclusive. The papers, the clothes, this very house; everything pointed to her coming back here unless physically prevented. Radically so. That was the conclusion of the gendarmerie: on that indeed, and the undoubted fact that she had since given no sign of life, the magistrate had based his conviction that she had met with foul play.

She had been seen 'for certain' last at lunchtime. They had stopped at a well-known staging point just off the autoroute; a great place of gastronomic pilgrimage. The waiters naturally could remember nothing: they do not look at people's faces. Attested by a credit card payment. Asked about the bill, Guy said that Sibille kept such things. Which is reasonable; went into the expenses file. Urged to scour his memory he had found details of the meal, 'memorable': the place has two stars in Michelin. How else would one remember after several months? The dish described had indeed been on their menu that day. And I don't believe he had lunch there with another woman. There was a stop for petrol too. Nobody could be expected to recall that, but again the creditcard figure fitted with the distance.

Some way further, the crossing of the Vosges makes an awkward barrier. The whole day one has whizzed effortlessly along, and here one is hampered by a succession of awkward little crossings, none of the passes high but all difficult, with numerous alternative routes and none any better: I found the story perfectly believable.

Silberstein agreed. We have had experiences of this sort. One is tired and irritable after a day of driving: losing the way makes one thoroughly scratchy. The judge hadn't liked it but Guy had been unshakeable: what I would call, and Maître Serge did call, 'just forgetful enough to be sincere'.

So 'nobody will ever know'? Write it off? As another one which increasingly resembles causes célèbres, famous in their day. Nobody knows, and nobody ever will, who killed Sir Jack Drummond and his family on a roadside in the Haute Provence in 1951. We can only be pretty certain that it *wasn't* that tough old primitive Gaston Dominici. The police work there was extremely bad; the trial a perfect farce. And I'm only glad it wasn't me. There are still families to be found in France, very like the Clan Dominici, all accusing one another and one will never find out why because they will not, cannot say.

I knew that Guy, when asked, had spoken of his wife's family; that Faith and the other sister had made statements that they had seen and heard nothing of Sibille and found it most extraordinary. I thought it might be rewarding to talk to Faith. Where was Hereford? I looked for an atlas. I'd had a couple of good witnesses here, with interesting things to say of Sibille. I had a little talk on the phone with Maître.

Planes are handy things, if you can afford them. Even little, provincial places have airports. The girl at the airline counter is not perhaps very strong on brains and into the bargain lazy, but the little computer terminal can make our existence less wearisome as well as hers. It is unexpectedly easy to get from Montpellier to either Bristol or Cardiff and I was there next day. I even had a selfdrive car. Trying harder, as they say. Aren't these English girls nice! Unwashed possibly: draped in ridiculous garments very likely: but when they have la bonne volonté and are kind, they're lovely.

My English is a little rusty. I talked it to myself along those narrow twisty little roads with the roundabout every thirty seconds. Driving on the other side helps to get the articulations supple. I have a good friend who is an English cop and a great suppler of my articulations both mental and physical, but he lives near the sea in Dorset; he would be of no help here. I trundled along at the statutory thirty an hour. I liked it here. We have both much to be ashamed of. France and England, two silly old ladies and sadly stiff in the joints whacking at each other with the umbrella. The Duke of Wellington worries me, but a good deal less than he worried William Cobbett.

There was a hold-up at one point. A large truck, denying passage to another large truck, made a mess of both. Troublesome, but nobody got killed. Bumbling along at fortyfive kilometres an hour for ever and ever is fatiguing, but one doesn't get killed. The automobile is rather less lethal than in our hands. The English sit placid in a roadblock. They even turn the motor off.

I was called, not many weeks ago, to a house where a man had died. Years in the criminal brigade but I still have not grown accustomed to it. Like Admiral Nelson, whom I do not otherwise resemble, I am sick. Being a professional I do not get sick: I just feel sick.

This is quite a dim little anecdote. But bear with me. I sat there thirty minutes on that fucking roundabout. It passed the time.

It didn't even have anything to do with the PJ. The woman phoned from England as it happened. She was having a high old time buying absurdities in Harrods (cucumbers? little dogs? an ivory piano?) while respectable banker hubby stayed home and stole money. He didn't answer the phone. She was in such a stewed-up certainty that the Arabs had broken in and assassinated him that I went to look for myself instead of just passing it to Police-Secours. I took Véronique Varennes.

The door, it is presumed, is where the undesirables are likeliest to force entry, and the door of a bourgeois stronghold is thick

138

and heavy, metal-sheathed. Electronics: three locks. No reply;
get a locksmith. Easy to *say*, as VV did not fail to remark. We
found the man in his bath, where he had been some days.
Unpleasant colours and worse smells. No need to worry about
carbon monoxide or the black mamba coming down the bellpull:
massive coronary. He had got into the bath and been subsequently in no condition to answer telephones. Never have baths,
remarked VV with feeling. Right; showers use less water too.
She went to be sick, but after she had done her work. I had
sympathy: I am often sick, even now. People talk about violent
death. To me they're all violent. A firing squad is neater: at least
the boys with the stretcher don't have stairs to climb. As a city
cop I climbed many stairs. I have not been a gendarme, so have
been spared the more ketchup-stained traffic accidents. But how
much of it is the consecrated passing-away-peacefully? People
turn blue sitting on the lavatory, and Bibi here has to kick the
door in.

If Lefebvre has really hit his wife with a shovel by the roadside
she'd had no worse a death than most, provided he hit her hard
enough. But we've cops and lawyers and judges running all over
Europe. There are twelve thousand road deaths a year in France
and the fellow with the lethal weapon has only to say 'I never
meant to'.

Faith was like her sister, and unlike. Smaller, more rounded,
fairer of hair. Prettier? – photos are misleading. A very pretty
woman. She had cows, lots of cows. Cows are wealth. Nobody,
least of all me, understands the Agricultural Policy. Farmers
were paid to acquire cows. Now that there is forty times too
much milk they are paid again, to get rid of them.

The house reflected wealth: not like a farmhouse in any sense
I understand even if there were barns and stables and a pleasant
smell. The big BMW may be spattered with mud: cowshit puts
the price up. There was no Rolls: that would have meant the vet
had come. Missis had a Mercedes coupé tucked away: the two
big shiny motorbikes were her sons'. I thought of Guy Lefebvre's
beat-up station wagon.

Chill reception. Any cop would get it but a French cop double dose. To these people Europe is a ski resort. Likely enough a holiday house in Provence, primitive but picturesque. France is restaurants, racecourses, and handbags from Hermès: the rest is frogs. Geoffrey Dawson, stout friend and stout England-lover, about Brits noticeably less enthusiastic, has thoughts I can echo: being French I like France: being French I don't care for the French much. He finds the twee Cotswolds distinctly lowering. Pressed to explain – overcosy, overcomfy, rather too Sunday-paper smart? – he grows sombre. 'Aloof. Incurious. Unthinking. God made Stow-on-the-Wold and peopled it with Us, and felt pretty pleased with Himself. I do not wish to Remember Adlestrop. There are times when I could turn all the bloody birds of Oxfordshire into pie.' Talking to Faith, I understood this better. I don't like that yellow stone all that much either. She looked at me the way Sister Heavenly did the disguised Pinky: – What you do then, fall in some blackberry juice?

I don't think it an injustice to sum it up as Sibille having made a huge mistake, the sort meaning loss of caste. Having made it you are right not to admit it. Stick to your guns, nail your colours. But you made it.

I did my best not to fence. I didn't want a clash of foil upon foil; I wanted a quiet talk. I succeeded as far as being asked into the kitchen, where the au-pair-girl made me tea. But the vet after calfcastrating or whatever gets sherry in the drawingroom. Not Bibi.

"It was a pity Sib had no children."

"Do you know why?"

"I never asked. One doesn't, you know." Pow-ow! Haughty.

"She didn't come here?"

"A couple of times. To stay, naturally. Not this time. Which puzzles me." I couldn't even rape her because of the au-pair-girl.

"You haven't been there? Her house, I mean."

"A farmer, you know, doesn't get away easily. I was hoping to, this year."

"She wrote you letters. Nothing in them to suggest to you
. . . ? You are sisters. You are close."

"Close, ye-e-s. We don't talk about personal affairs much.
And we don't lament . . . It seems very odd, you coming all this
way."

"Yes, well, nothing official. Upon Monsieur Lefebvre's
instructions I'm doing what I can to find his wife."

"Rather odd of Guy to send the police after his wife." 'Guy'
like Aye aye: I'd forgotten it was an English name, that Lefebvre
was English.

"You got on well with him?"

"Guy? – really I hardly knew him. I saw a bit of him when we
were girls: since then . . . I kept in touch with my sister."

"You could give me your opinion, quite subjectively."

"I don't really think it's called for, seeing he's employing you.
Or is that true?" Cool yes; cool both ways.

"Perfectly true; he pays the expenses. They could hardly come
out of public funds." Touch of frost. "This does not preclude my
taking an impersonal view of whatever I may see or hear."

"You think she may have come to grief, do you?"

"Grief?"

"Manner of speaking. Harm?"

"I've no reason to believe so but as long as a disappearance
remains unexplained any explanation may be the good one."

"You're a commissaire – that's the equivalent of our police
superintendent?"

"Roughly; there are grades. I'm somewhere in the middle."

"But you're a senior officer."

"True."

"Tell me – is this a criminal investigation?"

"There isn't a yes-or-no answer to that one."

"Then whatever you care to give." I had tests to pass.

"I am a CID officer, you'd call it here. I'm not engaged upon
a criminal enquiry. For that I should need authority and I have
only what I showed you."

"I see. Or I don't see, actually. A phonecall would have told

you that my sister wasn't here and that I hadn't seen her recently.
I haven't heard from her lately either, but a number of things
could account for that. What do you want of me?"

"I don't know your sister. I've spoken to friends, neighbours.
I get conflicting accounts, I'm trying to build a picture. The
clearer the picture the better my chances of making informed
guesses. What she would do, in some given situation. Better,
how she'd go about it. It's evident that you aren't a witness to
her actions, but you are a good witness to her thinking. Character, in short."

"I see. Can I offer you a glass of claret?" I had earned,
perhaps, a good mark by not smoking. I can do without upon
occasion.

This came in a decanter of such unadorned good taste as
almost to be ostentatious. England is full of traps. Was one
supposed to guess the vintage, or say 'Hey, this is plonk'? She
said, 'It's quite nice, I believe,' which might mean distinctly
beyond my station-in-life. I had to get rid of the polite
periphrases.

"I look at you, and I try to see her."

"No; we're of very different character. Perhaps I see what you
mean – that we share the same blood, had the same upbringing?
Yes, but when one marries . . . when one goes to live in another
country . . . I'm rather a down to earth person. Sib is hardheaded, a good business woman, but she's a romantic. I thought
that a dreadful marriage, and I said so. It made a chill between
us which lasted a number of years. I don't want to sound over-
critical. In fact I don't want to discuss Guy at all. He's a nice
person, with many good qualities."

"It lasted, the marriage. Not quite such a commonplace,
nowadays."

"Yes. It seems to have broken up now. In a way, this might
be the explanation. My sister is an extremely proud and also
highly secretive woman, and if she has left him, which seems to
be the case, she'd take it very hard: it might take her a long time
to get over. She'd find it – very – difficult to admit failure. It was

all her work, you know. Guy has talent, but no determination, no drive. Every scrap of his success he owes to her."

"And might he come to realise that and perhaps resent it?"

"After all these years? French enough to know damn well which way his bread was buttered."

"From all I've heard the idea of a love affair doesn't carry much weight with me."

"It shouldn't carry any," said Faith with some haughtiness. "Not with the women of this family." She had hardly had anything to drink. I couldn't imagine that it had loosened her tongue. For a moment I wondered – a philandering husband? But it was none of my business. She went on, lowering her voice, giving her glass little wrist flips to make the wine swirl around.

"I don't really see this walking-out business as permanent. A violent tiff I can understand. But not to come back . . . that's not the way we were brought up. Always give one more."

"Will you explain that?"

She thought; drained her glass; put it down abruptly, with a thump. Leaned over to pour me more: a set face.

"It's not like me, to discuss matters of belief with total strangers. Since we're this far . . . it's a straight answer after all to a straight question I myself have put.

"My – our – father was an unsatisfactory person in a number of important ways. Which does not mean that we would ever feel or show disloyalty towards him. My mother would never, never – this is all rather American, isn't it? They seem to tend to baring their hearts towards psychiatrists. We are more reticent as a rule."

"Nor am I a psychiatrist," risking a grin. "But I do have a professional habit of respecting confidences. And I think what you're about to tell me is valuable." She sat back with her hands in her lap; gave a sigh, soft but long.

"Rules made, never to be broken."

"I understand. And 'always one more'?"

"How shall I put it? – a childhood thing. Whatever you're doing, do a bit extra. Cleaning your teeth, make it another ten seconds. Sixpence for Oxfam, make it a penny over. The way we were trained. One more, for your mother or your sister. Or a friend, a neighbour. It's giving one for God, I suppose, really. I shouldn't be telling you this. It's private. I'm doing one for you now. Because one must never do it pointedly, never underline, never emphasize. Never say, never boast. But otherwise you wouldn't understand, would you?" Just a little haughty, again.

"It sounds rather like 'noblesse oblige'."

"That's very oldfashioned and corny but perhaps, in a way, yes."

"She's like that?" Nod. "And he's an artist. They wouldn't have these ways, mesquinerie, I've forgotten how you say it in English. Like suing each other for alimony."

"Pettiness, that's right. We part, and this is my spoon and that is your fork."

"So if she did walk out she'd make it a clean cut, no comeback or recrimination."

"That's right, I think. And yes, Guy too. I haven't a lot of good to say of him but I've no ill to speak either. But I really think that now . . ." polite but pointed. So I was formal too, said thank-you-for-a-nice-party like a wellbroughtup child, kissed her hand.

"Oh dear. French charm." But she said it nicely, without sarcasm.

Maître Silberstein was 'in court' that morning, but had left word that he'd be happy to see Monsieur Castang, and an invitation to lunch: the gentleman's opinion would give him an appetite for oysters.

"So now – will you have a dozen?"

"No, a half's enough. Do you put on lemon?"

"No no, as they come. If they're any good anything else spoils them. Tabasco, all that rubbish. Put it purely legally," setting to like a man who has met nothing all week more serious, "and put it at its worst. You can expect to be crossquestioned pretty closely by the judge."

"I'd be bound to say that I've seen and heard nothing allowing me to suppose criminal intent. So far we're clean. I can envisage, I can imagine, but that's not what a cop is for."

"Exactly, we're dealing with an artist, a complex sensitive being with too much imagination. I want you, as the prudent experienced officer . . ." He was eating two to my one, so that we were keeping pace nicely.

"There'd be things troubling me, but the onus of proof . . ."

"Stick to that. Now given this woman, on the basis of a judicial enquiry, within your own frame of reference . . ."

"They are nearly always financial, as you know: legal presumptions of death for an inheritance. For a legal presumption she's alive . . ."

"Exactly the fiction the wretch of a judge is sticking on." So I told him about Faith.

"Splendid, splendid, she'd go off into the blue, we don't owe each other a thing except dignity, and dignity is silence now and for ever, and we've that from her own sister; with this we mow him down. They do very good pickled salmon here, I don't know whether you're fond of it." It was a marble-topped sort of place, smelling deliciously of fish. All the eating-houses of Alsace make a great thing of fish, announcing it brazenly as the local speciality. Which really is pretty brazen, Alsace being five hundred kilometres from the sea. Oh well, poor them; nothing to eat but choucroute . . .

" . . . not before four-thirty," said Maître with his mouth full. "See you then at the Palais, shall I? I hope you've got a reasonable hotel, Guy's not a wealthy man but he's in comfortable circumstances, leave the expense account with my secretary, sorry I've no time for coffee but sit here and enjoy it."

I did. I had a cigar too.

Monsieur le Juge in an office like a bank manager, one of a row in a dingy if pompous courthouse, does not look nor sound like Hizzoner the Mayor, but his signature upon a piece of paper is more frightening. If you don't like Hizzoner's face you can always move to another city. This man – or woman – might still be in the twenties, low-voiced, informally conversational, rarely given to rhetoric or emphasis, unmajestic. But that piece of paper might fix you to a space twelve feet by ten: the door shut.

He listened to me politely.

"It cannot be called conclusive."

"Not, certainly, as far as findings are concerned. I have nothing to add to the dossier."

"On the contrary, you are to be congratulated upon important new facts. I instance this collection of family history, to which she plainly attached great importance."

"She could come back for it at any time."

"But she hasn't."

"The sister – "

"Quite so. It is disturbing – troubling – that this one person with whom she took pains to keep in touch should have heard nothing."

"I don't say the contrary." Knock-knock, who's there, Maître Silberstein all smiles and fulsome excuses, wide-eyed at the news; everyone pretending he hadn't heard it before. Made rather a thing of being horrorstruck that Lefebvre was still in jail.

"Create a most unhappy impression," luxurious air of unmasking hidden batteries, "see fit to disavow . . ."

"You're not in court now," said the judge. "Point made. You've a case for release from custody. I'm considering it. There are other decisions of weight."

"I quite agree. The case for there being no case."

"Which I'm far from ready to concede."

"But by all means bring it to court: I ask nothing better."

"Don't be trivial. You are perfectly aware that we're close to the border here. The man has a flourishing business in Germany. The surrendering of his passport – "

"Preposterous. Arrested by the Polizei on an evasion-of-justice charge, frightening all his customers into the bushes, where his whole livelihood is based on trust!"

"I have here the initial conclusions of psychiatric reports." Paying no attention to the interjection. "Interviewed by Professor Dombasle on the twentyfifth of the month . . ." The voice was a little pettish but neither bored nor perfunctory; the level tone and rapid delivery of a man who reads thousands of papers and hundreds aloud, takes his glasses off to polish them without having to search for the line. He is not a bad judge. He is not vindictive. To speak of showing bias would be silly. To show himself pliant to the insistence of an advocate would be tantamount to admission that he would be as amenable to argument from a prosecutor.

"Mm, areas of rigidity, inadequacy, insecurity. Not adjudged to be traumatic in normal circumstances. Ill at ease in personal relations. Dependence, and subsequent conflict . . . well well, I spare you."

"What a pity that we haven't the equivalent picture of the wife to set alongside."

"A psychologist, Monsieur Castang?"

"As you are, Monsieur le Juge."

"And does a person like that kill, in your view and experience?"

"I don't know, I haven't met him. Anyone can, as far as that goes. But we don't know much about her personality."

"Wasn't that the direction and purpose of your wanderings?"

"I didn't meet her, either."

"One doesn't get far with this. Observation of anyone of high intelligence brings out the contradictions. The brighter the stupider, as it were. Well, Maître? It is your undenied right to ask for a counter-expertise."

"Professor Dombasle," as though unwillingly, "is – I think I would be expressing a generally held opinion of the Bar – accepted as severe but fair, as experts go."

"I'm glad to hear you say so, though he's not wholly complimentary towards your client, regarded as selfish, demanding, inclined to use tantrums towards his ends."

"Sounds rather like any of us," smoothly. "His conclusions," more smoothly still, "militate against confinement, the utility of which is questioned."

"Castang? Your professional view can be taken into account. If, that is, you have any."

"I don't know if he's guilty or not; see no likelihood of ever knowing either, short of digging up half the Vosges." The judge seeming not to have heard shuffled his papers.

" . . . Emotive, fantasist, something of an actor . . . they all are. I'm going to sign your release order, Maître. Largely because I'm going to give the matter more thought before calling for supplementary information if I so find. It would be, I deem, an injustice to enforce custody in my present state of mind. I may tell you I'm far from satisfied, and there's no question of letting the affair drop. Release will be provisional, will be conditional upon sureties, and reversible should I see fit. He will engage himself not to leave the district and report himself to the local commissariat."

"Aren't you depriving him of the means of his living?"

"He can paint pictures: I gather he has a talent for it."

"In deferring to your ruling I must reserve the right of appeal against restrictions in the absence of fresh evidence."

"Make your application in three weeks," curtly, taking the form his clerk had filled out.

"As much as I could hope for," said Maître, climbing into a cream-coloured Jaguar, old but comfy-looking. "Largely thanks to you, Castang; I appreciate. I've got to get over to the prison; give you a lift anywhere?"

"Come with you, if I may. Quite curious to lay eyes upon your Lefebvre. Heard too much and not enough." The leather upholstery smelt nice. The dashboard was walnut. Not exactly a Hispano Suiza but I don't mind riding in it from time to time.

148

"No problem. He's a generous chap and would like to thank you personally. Bloody rush hour, hell, we're going to be late. The old schnock was reluctant to cough up. Didn't have any choice but he's a narrow old boy. Not many examining magistrates of that religious old school now. They love putting people in prison – so good for the character."

"One has to do it sometimes and in my experience it's generally disastrous and it's hard to see the alternative so let's abolish crime and give you and me the sack."

We sat in the road, Jaguar and all. Strasbourg is like any city of medieval origin: the traffic's a shambles. So put in ever more red lights and one-way streets. The obvious solution of banning the sacrosanct automobile from the centre, and giving yourself space for loose, flexible public transport would be an outrage. They'd rather dig a metro system underground. Ten times the expense and inconvenience, but nothing yields to vanity. Island republics, whose people can't afford a bicycle, are the biggest customers for Boeing.

And at the prison it was as foreseen. Duty Chief Screw, excellent man but fenced behind his Standing Orders, shook his head sadly.

"As you well know, Maître. Formalities of the lock, personal property, taking him off the ration strength – can't be done before tomorrow morning." Our little life is rounded with a sleep, and with a standing-order.

"But you can give me a parlour." The word derives from the verb to speak: a parley. Jails are like convents. A glassy picture of Our President, with upon his bosom the insignia of the Legion of Honour: the Sacred Heart. Warders are like nuns, charged with the care of handicapped children. Mad nuns, sadist nuns, they still exist but they're fewer. Recall the precepts of poverty, obedience and chastity; you'll understand prisons better.

"Sure; he'll be pleased to hear the good news. Fish out Lefebvre, Olivier. You can scratch the body search. See his supper's kept warm." The lawyer has the right to confidential terms, in the parlour. As a PJ officer, I have it too.

Success as a prisoner ('detainee') depends on being a good rôle-player. They're all actors, said the judge. Guy did it well, relaxed, joking with his guard. Slimmed by eating half the food provided, avoiding the proffered sleeping pill. Paled by the lack of fresh air and the overheated cell, but handling himself well.

"Hallo, Maître. That nasty bronchitis cleared up?"

"Absolutely. And we'll have you out of here at breakfast."

"Oh no hurry. I'm well content," shaking hands with me. "Nice to see you," without sarcasm.

"A certain amount of nonsense we have to live with for the next couple of weeks" – all lawyers are impatient with every moment that attention is diverted from themselves – "but then we'll get you an extinction-of-the-public-action, and it can all be forgotten."

"No doubt," with a pleasant irony. "I've found it a valuable experience. Gives one several new insights, to belong to the criminal class. I'll be pleased to see the end of it though. Some of the poor buggers here . . ."

"Like a hospital," I said. "Don't stay too long or you'll become really ill."

Maître talked about German contracts. He wouldn't let his client stay too long in jail. Too many bills to pay, including his own. Lefebvre listened to him with a sort of polite boredom. Silberstein would start thinking of the stable any moment; the rub down and the oats like any sensible horse. Guy gave me a look when we got up.

"Thank you, Monsieur Castang. I feel confused, as they say in polite circles." I couldn't be sure I knew what to make of the look on his face. If it was a smile you'd call it wry, you'd call it thin, and whatever it was it was crooked.

Everybody-who-is-anybody in the city of Strasbourg lives up at the North End. At the corner of the Orangerie park stands the complex of buildings which house the European Parliament, the Council of Europe (nobody knows the difference) and the Court of Human Rights. These buildings are startlingly ugly. They manage also to look both mean and silly: there are cynics who find this appropriate. The notables, meaning Silberstein, live clustered about here. Trundling along the east–west axis of the Avenue des Vosges you turn left at the United States Consulate. He dropped me here. There is a pleasant stroll along the Rue Goethe and around the Observatory garden. Slightly inferior people, like university professors, live here. There is even a tiny observatory with a dome which could open and allow a telescope to peep out and look at stars. Improbable, under the cloudy, rather dirty skies of Strasbourg. So that what they do instead is to measure earthquakes, with such minuteness that as Dr Davidson remarks one scarcely dares cough in the neighbourhood. He lives just opposite.

Seven o'clock struck: Mrs Davidson ought to be at home: she was.

"I came to cadge a drink." She sneezed; none of us know what's in the air we breathe. "Now the thing will announce a calamity in Mongolia."

"Come in. You might as well cadge a meal while you're at it. It's only spaghetti alla putanesca." Arthur Davidson was in the kitchen, in order to offer helpful comments about the composition of the putanesca.

"How's old Guy?"

"They're unlocking the door tomorrow morning."

"On the faith of your reports and things?" It was too much bother to contradict. "So he's not guilty?"

"Damned if I know. Damned if anyone else does."

"In Scotland they have a Non-Proven; sensible of them."

"And here we've a Non-Trial. Known as extinction of the public action: sensible of them too."

"You're not satisfied?"

"Why would I be anything else? – I'm getting paid. What I really came for, I'd like to hear what happened in New York." We ate the spaghetti. The putanesca is the usual tomato and basil stuff, hotted up with smashed anchovy fillets. Arlette eats it with expert dexterity, holding her fork against the spoon and winding. Inexpert I make dog's dinner. Arthur who couldn't care either way lets it hang down and slurps and gets the whory bits on his chin. We boozed away at the Soave. Panics about antifreeze and other toxic chemicals added to the plonk have had the salutary effect of making everybody's plonk that little-much purer. Rather the way boys getting shot for having-no-driving-licence makes the Policía that scrap more scrupulous.

"Sibille made a date with me in the Algonquin. It isn't the enormous sort of hotel. It's a Victorian drawingroom cluttered up with nice ugly furniture and little nookies. Sibille hove in sight with her gallery man, who looks like a banker, and Guy creeping along behind – skulking – looking mortally ashamed of himself."

"She's always like this," said Arthur, gloomily. "Women can never come to the point."

"Sibille very smart, little black frock, handbag from Hermès. Terribly entrepreneur, doing a hard sell and good at it. Guy more bored and hangdog by the second, playing with the olives and the toothpicks and horribly ashamed." She'd said this twice.

"Establish the ashamed."

"Guy always did perspectives of his houses and gardens, beautifully clean, Indian ink with wonderfully delicate colour washes, and decorated them with grasshoppers and toads and dragonflies. Instead of being flat and dull they have a weird grandeur. Pollyooly or whoever, exquisitely Florentine."

"Pollaiuolo," said Arthur, "and she means – oh, never mind, she's being elliptical again."

I was getting, I suppose, a look on my face because he rescued me.

"Artists don't mind flattery. Drink it in; often prefer incense to payment. But sitting there with salesmanship going on as though they weren't there – they writhe if exposed to this."

"I begin to see." Even though Vera is firm about describing herself as an illustrator.

"Cold technical discussion," said Arlette. "It's too big, it's too

152

small, there's too much black or there's not enough. About something they've shed blood over."

"Yes."

"He was taken aback, I think, too. Sibille all these years has been the competent secretary, good at keeping the muddle under control and paying the bills – and sending them in. He was used to thinking of her as an answer-phone. Suddenly she's showing herself queen bee, ordering drinks and arranging dinner, bullying headwaiters as to the manner born – and laying it on the line about lighting and hanging."

"This gallery – "

"There's just about nothing more blasé and cynical than a metropolitan dealer. Seen everything, right? A relentless pursuit of novelty. All right, Guy makes nice drawings, and his fields of little flowers, with a unicorn or a buffalo strolling about, these are nice." I nodded: I had seen some of these in the château. "To a training in classical draughtsmanship, to a sense of composition, he adds imagination. I don't know – I suspect this banker type had seen enough metro graffiti, amoeba forms done in acrylics. Took a sudden fancy to something less flimsy for a change."

"Odd, this," said Arthur. "I'd always thought of Guy as a flimsy character." Arlette, hitherto voluble, kept silence and ate. There was an antagonism in the air I didn't understand and didn't want.

I had got some of it, anyhow. It was a vivid little picture she had drawn, the woman with her sheaf of shiny photographs, making her presentation to the banker who might invest: the man in the middle, sullen, drinking too much, pretending he isn't even there. I wouldn't start pontificating about the psychology.

And I had seen a couple of these pictures. Now that I am helped by hindsight, I think I saw the first. An ordinary-seeming architectural perspective of the bombed church in Munich which they have left, just the way it was in May 1945, as a memorial, with its bleak graffito: *nie wieder Krieg*. Trees grow now out of the ruined dome.

I saw two more, here in Strasbourg. One of the building where Lefebvre had hired his dreary little one-room apartment. In the Esplanade quarter, a block as dull – and as flimsy – as you could wish. Guy had drawn it from across the street, covered it over in virginia creeper which had grown across and masked nearly all the mean little windows. Quite simple; scarcely even exaggerated.

The other was one of the most familiar scenes in the world, seen a thousand times on television. The railings on Pennsylvania Avenue, and two tourists (rather like heraldic beasts) gawping through, squinting their cameras at the White House beyond. The familiar portico looks quite as usual. You look again and see that it is not quite as usual. You cannot put your finger on any line that is really out of true, but unmistakeably it is about to fall down.

Davidson had made an amalgam with the comic strip thing one sees frequently, full of witches and serpents and necromancers' castles. No, not in the least. When I got home from England I tried to explain to Vera some of the things I had seen in the château. There was one of a verandah, in the neogothic railway-station style. There is nobody there. Instead there are two pots of flowers; a lily and a climbing rose. You feel the world has come to an end, that if it had a title it would be something like 'Bacteriological Warfare'. She went and got a book of medieval paintings, showed me things by Roger van der Weyden, Martin Schongauer. Yes, like that.

Recently, I tried to describe my memory of the White House one; used some such phrase as 'mad Canaletto'. 'But that's exactly what it is,' she said. 'Venice is sane: Washington isn't.'

Arthur Davidson belched, which is permissible after spaghetti. He got the putanesca off his chin, drank a big glass of bianco and went to get his pipe.

"Was he jealous perhaps? Stupid Sibille, who hasn't a clue about proportion or suitability or taste, and likes things like copper beeches and weeping ash . . . And now of a sudden she's centre stage. But I think what he hated most was her making a whore of him. An expensive one to be sure.

"Too strong? Look, I was just sitting there mesmerised: I didn't utter. I was watching though. I caught a very venomous look. I hope I never get one like that." Arthur smoked his pipe and said nothing. I've seen Vera look at me too sometimes.

"This is what made me certain, when I heard about the disappearance, that worse was to come. That worse had come."

"One hasn't the right to feel anything of the sort," said Arthur round the pipe. "He'd had a lot to drink. He was feeling uncomfortable and embarrassed. Obscurely, humiliated."

"Probably you're right," she said, sadly. "I've created all this atmosphere of suspicion. I've had occasion, since, to reproach myself bitterly. I still feel in my heart . . . if I were Sibille, I'd be dead."

"Rationalise," said Dr Davidson. He used this word often. I do myself . . . women despise the rational. They're right, of course. Especially when you see the results. Guy Lefebvre would agree, no doubt. He was painting the goddamn results.

"Do you think I haven't tried?" asked Arlette. "Sibille is or was a fiercely ambitious woman. Guy has his little success in his narrow orbit and sits in it. Makes a living, not grand but adequate. He's a good technician, a conscientious craftsman, a nice minor artist. And over the years, he has learned to fit in. Most of the clients are vulgar, pretentious, and ignorant. They want a weeping ash in the middle of the lawn, he'll put it there. They pay, after all. They want crazy pavement and a naked woman atop of the fountain: great; that's bread and butter. Once or twice he's had a free hand and done something good. Mostly it's been kept to a sheet of cartridge paper. But even there, once he's done it, it exists.

"And that's private, almost secret. His way of making up for phony rock gardens and dinky conifers.

"Making up for disappointments. Sibille was one of the big ones. I think he couldn't learn to take her as she was. He went on hammering at what he wanted her to be, the piece of real sculpture on the lovely big Bernini fountain he would never do, never be able to do. Am I making sense?"

"No," said Arthur. "Maybe."

"Oh I'll say no more. I know this though, that Sibille's ambitions were unbounded. She saw him getting the big commissions, for real money. The plush estates, the fast young millionaires. Lunging like a pike. Why shouldn't Guy be a Djinn in the desert, Capability Brown in Arizona? Whereas he – I can see him hating it. Hollywood whoredom. Hating her for pushing him.

"I'm getting blind as a bat," putting her glasses on. "Either of you want coffee? I haven't anything exciting. No fifty-year-old calvados." Wound up tight she gave herself some malt whisky. "Oh well, it's only my imagination." Sitting there, after all, is a Police Judiciaire officer. Someone with small time for fancy theories from amateurs. An atavistic sort of masochism would bring her to say 'female amateur'.

Whisky made her reckless. Or just unselfconscious.

"Why should it be so ridiculous? We go on thinking of Lady Macbeth as a great busty soprano, Salome in a red wig and oriental trappings. I think she's much more likely to be small and plain and dowdy. I don't mean stringy hair and a bad complexion. I mean an ordinary housewife whom you don't really notice much. What's Macbeth after all? – big sweaty soldier, lazy, rather dim in the wits, good at horses and pigsticking, hard drinker in the officers' mess. She wants to put some real scotch in him," suiting the action to the word.

"She's tormented by her own frustrations, and she goes too fast, and he feels trapped. He takes it out on her. He hasn't any way out.

"So she looks like Barbara Stanwyck in *Double Indemnity*? And he's honest Fred MacMurray saying he never knew murder smelt of honeysuckle? No no no no no no no. That's a nasty little suburban adultery. Sex as bait, come come." She pounced on me suddenly.

"But isn't that the way the cop mind goes? – screwing with the insurance man for a few thousand dollars? Cops understand that. But can they make head or tail of that wretched girl in Epinal? Whether or not she killed her own child is unimportant. The entire judicial apparatus tied in knots and can't understand a thing. But isn't she Lady Macbeth? There's a clan quarrel. She's determined to see her man come out on top. She'll stop at nothing to get rid of the rivals. Sure, she's just a poor illiterate peasant.

"Oh dear; are you about to put a cushion on my head and sit on it?"

"Not really," said Dr Davidson with tolerance. "You're quite entertaining when pissed."

"I'm not going to be freudian, I know nothing about her sex life and I don't want to. I don't believe Lady Macbeth would have commited adultery for all the gold of France and Navarre. Fiercely and possessively faithful to her man, but when that gets distorted it's more horrible than any stupid sex story.

"It's comic but it's unimportant Sibille being Scotch, and coming out of a castle, and scrabbling her way back to another castle, all rather secondrate. A coincidence. Or is there any such thing as coincidence?" With a sexy great wink at me, causing Arthur to guffaw. She'd had enough to drink, all right. Putting Scotch on top of Soave . . . vino veritas? In common with every cop in France and elsewhere – I should be saying every *other* cop – I'd thanked my lucky stars I didn't get stuck with that frightful job in Epinal.

I waited for him next morning, outside the prison. This sounds tactical, or it sounds sentimental. Bit of both, I dare say.

He stood there with his suitcase, the usual overnight bag stuffed with dirty laundry. When there is no one (as happens too often) to meet them, there is a moment of indecision, confusion. One has been thinking of that precious moment when the damn door will finally open, after leisurely formalities within, and the chill indifference of the world outside strikes one as bleaker still. Prison is a passive place, where decisions are made for one. A simple action like walking to the bus stop has to be relearned. It was raining, as it generally is, and the Strasbourg bus service . . . I wound the window down.

"Lefebvre." He looked up and frowned. Came over.

"You, is it? Going to go following me about? Going to go on asking whether I killed her? What the hell does it matter whether I killed her or not?"

"Drive you home?"

"Gone in for the taxi business?"

"Glad to lend a hand."

"But there's an ulterior motive. There always is."

"Apart from hoping you'll lead me to the letterbox of the Russian Secret Service? Where d'you want to go?" He slung his bags on the back seat.

"I have a studio." Nothing to do with artists. Euphemism for a one-room apartment, generally very small. Down past the University and next the ruins of Vauban's beautiful Citadel is a large area upon which the Army sat obstinately for many years, before the message trickled through that German invasions were no longer imminent. The speculating builders fell upon this with glee. Blocks run up cheap were sold dear. Bits fall off. The whole quarter has the look of cheap finery caught in the rain.

"I'd ask you up. Not much welcome to offer." The gloomy, chilly day – he'd have welcomed Dracula's company. The clumps of vulgarly yellow flowering bushes, which the municipal gardeners dot about in odd corners, serve only to make these streets more depressing.

"Horrible forsythia," said Lefebvre. It was worse upstairs, in a smell of dust and neglect, between the carpeting and the wallpaper both in builders' taste. Investment property, rented out on short leases. Temp. accom. for lonely people. The desolation could be masked by living things – plants, birds, wives. He ran a finger along the windowsill and looked at it with disgust while turning a radiator on.

"I can make you coffee, at least." There were a few items of mass-produced furniture. It seemed a wretched place for such a man.

"I needed a pied-à-terre while I was working in Germany," he explained defensively. "This is handy for the autobahn. I know this town well; used to live near here. As you know, of course. Silberstein said you'd make a better impression than some private detective, probably a crooked ex-cop.

"So tell me. How long do they expect me to sit here? Serge is all jovial optimism: how much weight do I give that?"

"If the judge is obstinate you can get a show-cause hearing and a court order. It could be worse, you know. Not long ago they kept a woman in jug for a year on suspicion. Her husband – it's true that appearances were against her. They got a confession finally out of someone; I forget the details. Hard on her. She sued for compensation, of course . . ."

"Quite so," grimly. "A grudging few thousand francs five years late. Less than what was spent on lawyers: most consoling."

"The man in that case was dead, and no question. Your best bet is that your wife will show a sign of life." I had to pick the words with some care. Lefebvre didn't smoke. I could do so for both of us.

"That damn wallpaper," staring at it. "Change it and you only benefit the owner." But he had pictures to hang.

"You might," I said colourlessly, "have some excellent reason for denial or concealment. A man's wife disappeared. They found her seven years later, still in her car, under deep water in a disused gravel-pit. He could show that she'd had psychiatric treatment and had threatened suicide. But tongues were not lacking to accuse him. These suspicions are always difficult to shift."

"You're being sympathetic now, Castang, are you?"

"Professionally, no. My job is to find out facts, where there are any."

"Good cop, are you?"

"So-so."

"You gave me a cock-and-bull story, up there in the North. How did you get involved in this?"

"Arlette Davidson, who knew me slightly from another occasion, asked my advice."

"Bloody woman." He poured out some more coffee. "So I put on the apron, give this dump a scrub. Paint some pictures . . . Apart from my wife sending a postcard saying here I am, this is me, that thing in the picture is a Pyramid, I don't see much that I can do."

"I can still, maybe, spend a little time looking. I wonder whether you'd object to that." I was looking at him.

"Object why?"

"Same basis as before. A fee and expenses."

"Look where?"

"A place in Germany. Just a thread of an idea. It wouldn't take long." But he showed no reaction. Not even any curiosity.

"I don't have a bottomless chequebook. But if you think it worth a gamble . . ."

"And I don't want you to think I'm milking you. It shouldn't take above a day. Who knows, it might get you off a hook." I was waiting for him to ask where I found a thread, but he only said, "I'll have to do some shopping this afternoon . . . Go ahead," dully. "Keep me informed. Or Serge. I suppose it hardly matters which."

I left. I shut the door behind me the usual way, trying to close it gently and having to slam it. Lousy door. Give a breaker about fifteen seconds to knock it over. Not that he'd find much to get, inside. Just that a cop takes notice, professionally. The lift was at that floor, as does happen sometimes. In a minute I was on the street. I didn't look back up at the windows, either the clean ones, with pot plants and washed curtains, or the dingy ones like his. 'I picked it because the light's good,' he had said indifferently. Odd man. I could understand the judge's puzzlement. There were moments one would go bail for his innocence, and a minute later one could feel convinced he was as guilty as hell.

I made a couple of phone calls. Vera said without enthusiasm that she could manage without me for another day or so. "As long as that's all it is . . ." As for the office, they sounded like they'd be perfectly happy if I never got back. I almost caught a train then and there. I was even stupidly tempted to toss a coin.

There was a magazine kiosk next the phonebox. I could choose between *Penthouse* and *True Detective*. I wasn't sure which would afford the best value.

How the hell should I know how my mind works? Some women write poetry while doing the ironing. A Nobel Prize winner got the idea of a lifetime over a glass of beer, at ten thousand feet above Denver, Colorado. People sing, or lie upon sofas. I had been sitting in the castle, in Guy Lefebvre's workroom. Nice chair of mahogany and buttoned leather; it tilted and it swivelled. I was doing both. Nice room, handsome of proportion, well lit. I'd stay here if it were mine. But I'm not married to Sibille.

A business nicely organised. I couldn't recall whether she had secretarial training. Her schoolgirlish handwriting is clear, her files are applepie. Guy is meticulous in his own way, but muddled, inclined to reminders on the backs of envelopes. He had taken some files to Strasbourg. How would he manage without his secretary?

She went to houses with him, a great asset. Notes on shorthand pad; ready with all sorts of information that Guy had mislaid or attributed wrong. 'Thingummy . . . Whatsisname' . . . Wouldn't some of these customer-relations get a bit closer, sometimes? Would there be anything in these files that might provide answers? Going through them would be dog work . . . Mm, a lot of German names. Hence of course Strasbourg. A base close by.

Seeing a historic name I reached out. Idle curiosity is no vice in a cop. Idler the better. Over yonder there's still a bit of the old upper crust; estate-owning, castle-owning. People after Sibille's heart. Maybe this should be looked at.

The file told little; was properly professional. Like any architect – specifications, working drawings, scale drawings and detail: the notes of contract and supply: carefully factored accounts: a bit of correspondence; in English, the lingua franca of business.

'Dear Franz'. Which means nothing. Everyone uses first names now, secretaries included. 'I am sorry to hear the little trees are not doing well. Guy will be across soon and will look into it. This will be better than consulting Hon, whom he finds unreliable.' Quite. Footnote, handwritten.

'Thank you so much for the Parzifal reference, which makes me proud and happy. Of this more soon, I hope, since G. says that no time should be lost. Yours, S.'

Little-trees is quite normal. Parzifal-reference?

I put the file back. They were in order, with revision dates five years from inception. This one was two years old.

Something was scratching at the back of my mind. I found it in the books in Sibille's room, which I had scanned without much interest. Medieval history, I suppose, of that vaguely occult nature which appeals to many: treasure-hunting stuff. Rosicrucians and Templars, Masonic origins. Alchemists. Yes, a half-dozen titles with 'Grail' in them. Mm, I know nothing about Parzifal. The kind of subject in which a baronial German gentleman might be interested. Shared with Sibille . . . nothing says it's more than a bit of common ground but make a note. Religious interest? – medieval mysticism.

You see, a thing of the bear-it-in-mind type is an attraction to gurus. In middle-aged women a need for gurus. Religious sects proliferate, and account yearly for a number of disappearances, a few of which may be sinister.

Tactful enquiry needed, from the gendarmerie.

Yes, I was assured, such had been done. And yes, the examining magistrate had asked for a customer list. He had ordered a number of traces put through, including the usual signal to Interpol.

I wasn't greatly impressed (I did not say so). A surprising number of castles in our dear Fatherland, including some very lush ones, are the property of sects (extremely reticent about the sources of their income). Very touchy indeed, they get, about their privacy. The gendarmerie is nothing if not thorough, but there are plenty of these places in other countries, including – unsurprisingly – Switzerland.

Nor do I get excited by an Interpol trace. The 'customer list' by definition is a collection of magnates, and the local maré-chaussée is chary of treading upon such people's toes. The most done, I could imagine, would be a polite phone-call.

'You've seen nothing by any chance of a certain Madame X, about whom we've received enquiries? No knowledge of her whereabouts? Sorry to have troubled you.' I forget how many Interpol traces there are a year; several hundred. Last seen wearing a red anorak outside Bologna railway station – most helpful. It's the same as the old ladies who live alone in the eighteenth arrondissement of Paris and get attacked for their pension money.

There is just not enough Policía to go round.

Sibille doesn't have to go to Mexico. She could vanish any-where in Europe and as Guy finds with business, Strasbourg is a good starting-point.

And back in Strasbourg I gave Dr Davidson a ring.

"I'm a bit puzzled."

"Are you now?" Sympathetic, but unsurprised.

"I'm in need of an expert. I dare say you can find me one. Medieval literature perhaps, or history."

"The University could cope with that. Would you like to be a wee bit more precise?" I did my best. "Ho. I'll see what the ancient seat can provide and ring you back." . . .

"Breuil is our man. By a great stroke of luck we're on speaking terms. He's a moral philosopher, the way I'm a moral sociologist, meaning we tell theologians they don't know what they're talking about. I've given him a ring. Beard him in his lair and he'll elucidate. Don't expect it to be lucid on that account. The place is full of internationally-acclaimed authorities upon languages they don't know."

Cops go in for sociology too, unmoral as a rule. A whole patch of little winding streets called after Roman Emperors. The pattern then, as it is today. The speculator got his fingers on a parcel of land and developed it into desirable residences, for no doubt a packet. The Emperors had gone in for solid, ugly houses of the 'twenties, jammed close together. The windows were too small; the front gardens tiny. The smallest bush took away what light there was and looked instantly overgrown: no Lefebvre customers here. But an oasis of quiet and redolent of respectability: eminently suitable for academics. They'd be worth a lot of money. Out-in-the-country when built and now practically in the middle of the damn city.

Detective lost his way crawling about in the hydrangea bushes but found Professor Breuil behind an oval brass plate and a front door with little bits of stained glass, leaving a cramped hall, full of umbrellas, in pitch darkness. The traditional bourgeoisie does not allow cops in the livingroom. The diningroom had intricate oily furniture and oily paintings in intricate gilt frames. Dining doesn't mean one gets a drink.

A square shaved French face of intellectual cut; silver shoe-brush hair. Frowning as he listened, but polite.

"Mm, that's a lot of questions within a short space. I can't attempt a synthesis but I understand your puzzlement. A current throughout Europe, entwining Byzantine ideas with Celtic and Teutonic thought. I can find you Grail castles pretty well everywhere. Brittany, Cornwall, right down to Spain. Arthurian romances.

"Tradition of mystical, alchemical, philosophic thought, perfectly respectable. Right down to Dr Jung, psychoanalysts in Zürich. Paracelsus, Meister Eckhardt – are you acquainted with the poets at all? Tristan legend, Gottfried von Strassburg right here. Wolfram von – that's the Parzifal thing which interests you. Meistersingers but forget about Wagner; muddled it all up for his own purposes.

"You'll find secret societies, every imaginable sort; occult nonsense and folk proposing to reinstate the Merovingian dynasty. Grail, Templar treasures – a magnetic quality about these legends; understandably attracts all sorts of riffraff. Hitler himself got fascinated with the Lance from the Hofburg in Vienna. Thought to be the Holy Lance, symbolic of the Holy Roman Empire. One of their titles, recall, was Apostolic. Carried it off to Nuremburg, with the idea of consolidating his grip upon Germanic imagination. There are pockets, as you know, of neo-Nazi belief scattered about, taking hold of these myths to reinforce and inflame their own fanaticism. This woman you're looking for could have got into queer company, and found herself in Queer Street.

"If the man you mention is really from an old family, such a connexion is not perhaps very likely: they mostly take a dim view of such nonsense.

"Quite possible, on the other hand, is something esoteric.

"The Staufenberg is in Swabia; castle ruins on the hill. The family is extinct: the Popes of the time had them assassinated to the last male child. Collateral branch, I suppose – not properly my subject. Certainly one still finds very old families still living on their estates: some extraordinary castles in the Neckar valley. North of here come to that, in the Palatinate, there's at least one with a strong claim to be the original Grail castle.

"But you're not interested in the meaning or purpose of this, as I understand. A policeman, with what is called your feet on the ground." I summoned an idiot grin.

"Just the possible whereabouts of a middle-aged lady with an interest in esoteric belief."

"Stranger things have been known," coming with me to the door. A woman popped her head out of the kitchen. "Quite all right, Madame Breuil, we have matters in hand."

"I do beg your pardon; I thought it was the gas man."

"Ritual," holding the front door, "ceremony, initiations. Powerful grip upon the untrained mind."

The Rhine crossing, ten minutes from Strasbourg, is the traditional entry to Southern Germany: the Europa Bridge is sym-

bolic, if you care to put it that way, of the presentday bond
between the two countries. Whether you are talking politics or
economics, they can't do without each other. Simple as that. I
know the crossing well: have, indeed, uneasy memories of it.
Were it not for the physical reality of the river you'd scarcely
notice the crossing. Both sets of uniforms lounge at both ends:
there isn't even a pretence at checking more passports than are
needed to prevent their falling asleep. Unless of course there
were to be a terrorist scare. We have our Action-Directe and
they have their Red-Fraction and you can't tell them apart. They
don't, after all, wear uniforms.

The Karlsruhe–Basel autoroute is ten minutes beyond. Press
the right foot a little deeper and you're in either Stuttgart or
Frankfurt in two hours. The Swiss border is one hour. This has
really been Hitler's longest-lasting contribution. True, there are
still a few grandpas left to bore us with their war memories.
Waiting I suppose for Rudolf Hess to celebrate his hundredth
birthday, in Spandau Prison.

I found a pleasant, green land; hills and valleys largely
unspoilt, still much farmed. The quiet villages have not changed
much in a hundred years. Central Europe is still lovely; on a
sunny day in spring it clutches the heart. Sage-green and ochre-
yellow houses, little onion-domed churches, baroque plaster-
work and fountains with flowers. As Guy says, 'I love Germany.'
Our NATO Forces with their missiles, the long-'n'-the-short-'n'-
the tall, have learned to keep themselves unobtrusive. You can
always try telling yourself they aren't even there. As for the
Commies, quite a lot of people go to Hungary now and come
home saying it almost looks like Europe. I overran my turn-off,
had forty minutes on twisty country roads. Didn't feel a sense of
strain.

The Freiherr has a nice house. To be honest I like houses like
roast beef, underdone; stone plain and not rusticated; landscapes
not too lush. The Residenz was a jump beyond the ruins of the
bandit hold, with nineteenth-century additions I don't care for,
-ations of castel and crenel: too many belfries, pigeonhouses and

weathercocks. If only they'd left the original Lustschloss alone.
The marvellous garden was all in terraces.

"Expensive, eh?" said Franz, laughing.

I'd had a vague idea of threading the patient way past
majordomos, with a supercilious footman to see I did not make
off with portable objects. The country-gentleman had simplicity
even before charm and opened the door himself. And has Franz
charm! Old-fashioned: he's Conrad Veidt And Basil Rathbone.
Wears a wonderful suit, soft cloudy grey and forest-green with
silver embroidery. Assuming I wanted a high-class seducer of
wives I had come to the right shop. But this charm is made of
poise and manners; comes, when real, of a perfect simplicity.
And when they're that goodlooking one thinks they can't have
brains. Franz has plenty. I tried to explain, in my comic German.
He had understood before I was past my first tonguetied line and
said so in better French than mine.

"The house is for show to tourists and I am one of the museum
pieces, so for the sake of privacy we'll go outside." He took me
to a sunken garden, cypresses and grass and a small slow fountain
and we sat on a marble bench. The trouble with the gardens had
been so lavish a design, needing such numbers of hobbits, that
he had set Lefebvre the task of making it run with one-man-and-
a-boy.

"I don't have much money: it was all in idiotic things like coal
and steel. Daimler-Benz was not thought a suitable investment
for gentlemen." He was using words to study me, looking for the
little sign or the servile smile. We took a walk, up wide shallow
steps flanked with urns.

"I'm generally to be found hereabouts with a wheelbarrow. If
I had Sibille here I'd put her to work. I could do with her. My
wife is not physically very strong. The house is her domain, she
flits about; we'll meet her in a little.

"Your point is perfectly sound. Sibille was happy here, felt at
home. The Parzifal thing, 'durch Mitleid wissend' applies almost
literally: present baronial fantasies and bygone baronial hanker-
ings. And nostalgia: under certain skies the hills and woods take

on a Scottish look. Much of the building could have been designed by Norman Shaw: that flushed, congested Edwardian manner. Hereabout we abolished a lot of pergolas, birch with the bark left on, bowers of Gloire de Dijon. Inside there's a hall with antlers and a vast gothic fireplace.

"Edward looked good in this costume. Spoke of course better German than we did: Wilhelm was his first cousin. One sees them very well; overcoats with fur collars, gamekeepers assembling huge piles of pheasants and blowing horns. Whole wild boar at table, apple in teeth.

"We longed for turbaned Hindu servants, terribly frustrated about the silly little bits of Africa painted yellow on the map: massacring Herreros; order brought to the natives just as intelligent people were realising that empires were things to get rid of. Poor Sibille could still see herself plumed and spurred, galloping a carthorse across limitless frozen lakes in the east.

"It interests me as part of my being and fibre which I have learned to wear lightly. Sibille worries me, taking too much greedily to heart – as too many of us did. Like the Catholic converts one used to see, wallowing in black lace mantillas, ecstatic over some old Fascist Eminenza.

"You've seen the Capucin crypt in Wien, the Habsburg tombs? Ever read Roth's *Radetzky Marsch*? Heard the anecdotes of Sissi on the hunting field with her horsy English lover, Bay Middleton? Whacko!" I liked him, his kindness towards his ridiculous forebears.

I found him still less pious about objects: the picture gallery and the cabinets of china; suits of armour and trophies of weapons.

"Genu-yne bullet holes," pointing an amused finger at the broad stomach in a watered-silk waistcoat of a periwigged Field Marshal. "American soldiery iconoclastic, French plain barbaric but both highly destructive. I could almost have wished they'd set the whole lot alight. An endless purgatory of insurers, restorers – bankers – policemen! Earnest civil servants from culturally-minded Ministries. I can never get rid of any of it.

Nobody wants it but they insist it all stays sacrosanct." The private apartments were pretty, the books magnificent; Franz sniffy about woodworm and dry rot. "And now exhausted by our tour we'll have some plonk." Which was in keeping, and quite marvellous: pungent scents, sunlit and southern, of verbena and lemon thyme and ripe citrus; and here too we met his wife, a ravishing pale ashblonde with extraordinary skin, smelling delicious and rather like the wine. A lot of good words like fragrant have been spoilt for us by advertising agencies so that one is ashamed now to use them.

"If Sibille had run away? And come here? I'd have been pleased; I'm quite fond of her. Tiresome little ways, yes; I've a dotty female cousin rather like that: one must make allowances.

"But I can't see her deserting her husband: she's fiercely conscientious. Unless it would be to join the Poor Clares, but then she isn't Catholic. A pity almost, she has the nature to enjoy it, but very Scawtch, you know. Didn't like sex; one used to think, Oh, poor Guy." I didn't feel able to ask this elegant, very-well-brought-up and highly-virtuous lady to go into details, with Franz there heaving with giggles.

He walked with me to where I'd left the car. On a more sombre note, he said he did not believe in Guy killing anyone.

"And yet maybe I'd qualify that. Too much respect for life, one would say. Guy, you know, says trees are closer to us than animals. There's a ruthless side to him though. I've known him merciless to what he calls a bad tree. Still, a human being . . . I could never accept him as the completely amoral class of individual that is so frequent now, which will kill anything or everybody who stands in the way of their desires." We were both standing with our elbows on the car roof. A smell of hot dusty metal.

"I'd be bound to say though that I've known both soldiers and civilians, and of every imaginable type – peasants, urban workers, bourgeois; honest selfrespecting people – who simply hated militarism, brutalisation, violence of every sort. And who suddenly went mad under provocation. Some wanton destruction, a

169

comrade horribly mutilated. Even a triviality. Going blood-crazed, vicious, mataglap. Unable to control a need to kill."

"That is my experience."

"God help me," said Franz, "I've known it happen to me."

I turned the selfdrive in, back in Strasbourg. Wrote out an expense note. One day, a couple of meals, some petrol. My free railway pass . . . but hours spent on the road count too. Thinking time. But it was at an end, now. No useful work for a commissaire of Police Judiciaire. Less still for the private eye. Nothing left but a few legal formalities, some face-saving bargaining to be gone through by practised professionals. The examining magistrate: Maître Serge Silberstein. Nobody can know. No one ever will know.

Except of course for Guy and Sibille.

But that is their affair. Finish.

And of course it had only just started. But there was no possible means of anticipating that.

Editorial note: A.D.

There indeed it should have finished, with a whimper, distinctly. And since it would have been of interest to absolutely no one – save, as Castang points out sourly, to Guy and Sibille – I would not be writing this. An explanation is necessary. Trying to piece bits together later, dredging about in my disorderly memory, my over-active imagination, my plain dunderdom stupidity and other such factors, I understood that the answer lay with Vera Castang.

I did not know her at all then, and do not know her well now. Some light was provided from my acquaintance with her husband, the Man as she calls him. Some from Arlette's acquaintance with her. The two women have things in common. Dissimilar on the face of things. Arlette is not just tall, noisy, a notable nosyparker, handsome in a weatherbeaten way, French, opinionated, full of French fads and nonsense notions. Intelligent to be sure, and sensitive, and given to showing both in tiresome French ways.

Vera is thin, small-boned, mousy of hair and manner. Dia-

*mond-shaped Slav face which is quite plain, can blossom into
startling beauty but one would never call it pretty. Some sort of
paraplegia has left her with a limp. She has nice legs, and seems
to have no bottom at all. A meagre little woman. Furthermore she
is shy, quiet and not much given to utterance with people she does
not know well.*

*Getting her to talk was not easy. She wrote things down for me,
but these were spare, patchy, not very helpful. She was not
articulate on tape. Either Castang or Arlette – or both – did
something to persuade her to open. I don't know what. Not as
with Arlette by making her drunk. It doesn't matter. Once she did
open she was a floodgate. The tape was full of long pauses,
silences, sudden breaks, reactions and refusals. I've made what
job I can of smoothing all this out. We aren't after any exercise in
literary style, thank heaven. The abrupt transitions and interjections – oh well, it took days to put all this together.*

VERA CASTANG . . .

Man came home, from what he called a wildgoose chase. A
phrase sounding odd to our ears. I can't remember seeing wild
geese since I was a child. I suppose one might see them still in
Scotland? Norway? As a child I saw storks. That country is now
the land where the forests have died. I get very depressed. What
birds will my children see? Every day brings new word; the
merciless greed of man. The farmers have saturated the land
with artificial fertilisers. These have now polluted all the water
tables. This is the country of rain, and what is in the rain? My
children drink water and what is it doing to them?

I am being silly as usual. I have been trying to remember what
I thought while Henri was away. I got upset. I get upset when he
is away. I am supposed to control this. I do not get any better at
selfcontrol. I think I get sillier. He was away upon a silly errand,
I thought. I was reading about a small town in Florida. They
have twice as many cases of AID-syndrome, and why? They are

bitten by mosquitoes from Lake Okeechobee: they are poor and have no airconditioners. Twice as much malaria and tuberculosis and twenty more vile things. Lake Okie-what-is-it sounds a silly place and typically Florida. Far away and don't worry. But it's all around us here too. There are many more plagues waiting for us. It is childish being like this. It only happens to me when Henri is away.

The people are driven, worse than geese, intoxicated by toys, given no chance of any second for rest and thought, harried towards death.

Henri laughs. He is right. For we eat the bread of the government, and without it . . .

I am sorry: it is finished now. It was only a cafard, a depression. The sheer stupidity, hideous and purposeless, of this existence we are tied to.

Henri got back after jogtrot hours in the train: it is a slow train because it comes from Italy and is always full of poor people with cardboard suitcases, lashed with string. I have been through Strasbourg but know nothing of it. Oh, says Henri vaguely, it's part of the Empire. The English lost their empire, got pushed back on to their island and still feel grievances about this. France still lives surrounded by colonies. Less noticeable since the peoples' skins are the same colour.

I remember: the man who killed his wife. Or didn't. It was official business but no part of Henri's. He got himself tangled in it by the Davidson woman. Arlette: I rather like her. And after all this nobody has still the remotest notion whether he killed her or didn't.

I got interested: it is a grave mistake. I take things much too seriously. Henri is a professional; by that I mean that he deals with serious things by treating them unseriously. 'Get rid of the scenario,' he says. It's a standing joke.

Because there exists a ridiculous libretto somewhere. Donizetti or Bellini wanted to take a shot at it. The woman teases her husband by refusing to sleep with him and arranging to be seen with a young man in compromising position. She's supposed to love her husband but be too frustrated to express it. Pardonably exasperated he belts her, which succeeds in arousing her erotic capacities. All is then well. This opera was not written and one does see why. Maria Callas did not mind going mad, jumping off precipices, being knifed, and so forth: did draw the line at being stripped naked and whipped on stage. I cannot blame her.

I like opera; I get highly emotional about it. And when Tosca shoves the knife into that horrible policeman I understand perfectly. Yah, she says, killed by a woman! Are you suffering? Do you feel it? Good! That she should then feel awful, put candles round the body, and pray for forgiveness is dead right. Women do such things. Me too. I don't know anybody who does the other. And Henri adds that in police experience he hasn't met them at all frequently. Am I a prude, a repressed and dirty-minded puritan?

I do not think so. I have to admit that Czech schoolgirls were strictly brought up. I have my moments too of erotic fantasy; it's just that I don't talk about them very much in public. As for the Viennese bourgeoisie which so needed disentangling by Dr F., think of their world. They died of typhoid and diphtheria and scarlet fever. The treatments for polio or tuberculosis, for epilepsy or syphilis! Crude . . . Cholera was still a threat and physical hygiene pushed under the bed. Hardly surprising that their minds were pretty septic too.

But sex is fashionable, and governments encourage it. Keeps the people's mind off serious subjects. I find modesty an under-rated virtue. I see no need to show my tits on the beach or my underclothes in the street. We don't have to go shouting it from the housetops. But that said, sex is still quite a high-power emotion. Even made trivial or frivolous, under pretence of freeing us from inhibition. Read the book, see the play or the movie, and you'd hardly believe it. They're in bed all the time with the world and his wife and nobody cares a damn.

Don't you believe it. There are plenty of oldfashioned women like me. There are women too like Tosca who'd put a knife into Scarpia instead of settling for a quick fuck. We take sex seriously.

Henri says he's thought about it. Has asked. Has looked. Has turned nothing much up. She seemed to have been a fairly bottled-up, tightly-screwed-down sort of woman. Well, so am I, really. He smiles. 'Not quite the same.'

He mentions this Lady-Macbeth notion of Mrs Davidson. I can see that he's quite taken with it. In this scenario the Lefebvre woman – Sibille she's called – was madly, morbidly ambitious. He was unable to cope with this. She, uh, I mean Arlette, thinks that instead of putting the dagger into poor old Duncan, and then stupid honest Banquo in the cover-up, he put it into her instead. I don't quite get this. No, says Henri, nor do I, akshally.

I've no idea. Is this morbid sort of ambition a sort of substitute for sex?

Think of politicians, he says. Impossible ever to imagine them in bed with their wives – or even other people's wives.

True, really. And then?

People interested in power, he says, aren't really very strong on sex. Mean to say, power is an all-absorbing interest.

I've thought about this. True, Queen Elizabeth: sex life something of an enigma. Quite a facile hypothesis to suppose she was obsessed by power and just hadn't any sex life. I don't know much about James I. Mary Queen of Scots is said to have been frigid. Anyhow, Shakespeare writing about power decided to leave sex out of Macbeth. Everyone has asked whether she was a sexy woman and got a pretty dusty answer.

The fact that it never seems to work on the stage seems to indicate that it reads better than it acts.

Oh well, the hell . . . I may as well admit that I like constructing a scenario too, and not the Italian one. Maybe it does involve my going mad in a white nighty, at that.

With Henri away I tend to live on cups of coffee and cans of sardines off the edge of the kitchen table.

With him back I try to make an effort. He likes his fleshpots, the poor old boy.

And that's a rank piece of hypocrisy. I like them too.

So when he phoned to say he'd be back that evening but

174

lateish, I thought of a party. The butcher didn't have any steak I fancied; all looked much too fresh. Steak is boring anyhow. One thing we can get still is real chickens, I mean *real*, free range and fed on nice things. I found a nice one. I cut it up. The backbone, and the winglets and odds-and-ends went for stock, with white wine and potherbs and coriander: there has to be a stock you can really jump up and down on. One poaches the pieces of chicken in this, and one drops in – cooking them just enough to brighten the colour – pieces of spring vegetables cut quite thin. French beans, zucchini, mushrooms: stuff like that. Baby potatoes must simmer a bit longer, but most of them you drop in, and fish out after about three minutes. You have to keep the pot just on boiling point and have the pot where you can crouch round it – like the three witches. Nose of Turk and Tartar's lips. It's a variation on the Belgian 'waterzooi'.

I had a bottle of rather good champagne, to give us an appetite. What Kipling, in 'The Bull that Thought', called one of our better-class tisanes. And a Jurançon, to give us another appetite after. Yes I am sexy. Now and then. A good yellow Arbois does well too, with this dish.

I remember a moment in Spain. A howling desert somewhere in Aragon. Not a tree to be seen. We were quite high, on a saddle between peaks. We'd lost our way, and then got a flat and had to change the wheel. It was pitch dark by then, the wind wailing and that snow that is like sand. Little but nasty, tiny stinging particles. We found shelter at last, quite isolated, the Inn of the Three Witches. But when we got in – Henri grumbling terribly – there was a great black hearth. And immense logs of coal burning bright blue and green. The food was uneatable – I don't remember – chick peas and stewed goat. The sheets were damp and we nearly froze to death in bed. Henri totally stocious on Rioja and Osborne, raping me blind with wolves all round us. Wonderful. It's a sight too cosy sometimes in this goddamn flat.

Still, it's big, it's modern, it's well built. And it's posh, you know; they put in an open hearth. I have regrets, often, for the cottage we left behind. We had applewood to burn there. What we get here is scrub willow as often as not. But I picked some good birch logs. They fell suddenly into a lovely pattern, so that I got my sketch block and started to draw them. Nothing serious, you know, things one draws to keep the hand supple. I like to draw people now. I'll never be really good, I know that. But whatever one paints, abstract or semi or figurative or whatever, only the human figure is really worthwhile. Henri there with his shoes and socks off and rather drunk by that time.

I'm really hopeless at explaining this; it's gone all telescoped together. I drew Arlette later on. Those high-bridged southern faces full of bone in the cheek and forehead, wonderful orbits of the eyes, nose like a ship's prow, the men often go fleshy in middle age. Arlette's gone thin, you see cords in her neck. Good segments to the body, high-waisted and splendid long thighs. Fine carriage of the head, a lovely port of shoulders. The most beautiful thing she has is her walk.

I'm saying absolutely everything, aren't I, bar coming to the point? Well, here it is, at last.

All the men had made up their mind that Sibille had run away somewhere. It doesn't matter whether it be Switzerland or Mexico. She had simply taken off, after Lefebvre left her standing there by the roadside. You can argue her motives any way you like.

But all the women, you see, ended up feeling sure that she was dead. And if she was dead, then he'd killed her. I don't know how nor why. I'm pretty sure it was an accident.

HENRI CASTANG . . .

I walk to the office. Sounds like a routine, and is. I'm getting middle-aged, I suppose.

I used to bicycle. That was in a bigger city, where I had further to go. The position on a bicycle is painful to my arm. Bits of my left elbow are artificial. Taking the car is ridiculous. We live now near the middle of a mediumsized town, and the office is ten minutes' walk. A cop is not supposed to have any private life, and the walk serves to occlude – is that the word? – private personality and warm up the machinery of a middle-grade civil servant. One of the most irritating aspects of this Lefebvre business has been its unofficial, off-duty nature.

This day was official and on-duty, very, because I had to go to the Palace of Justice, and my steps would not totter towards the gallery of judges of instruction, but to the quite handsome oakpanelled dignities of the Assize Court. Elena was due to be tried. Time had passed. It was with a minute shock that I realised how little time, by judicial standards. Alice Jimenez is a quick worker. To be sure, little in this affair was obscure. Little to be contested, haggled over, argued four different ways. Few nice points, fine sharp quillets of the law. It had come on yesterday afternoon, after the President had made a brisk clearance of a thoroughly stupid post-office hold-up, and it was known that the President was anxious to get through this one with as little to-do as might be because there was a tedious and involved rape case to come, the sort where the court is cleared. Having the timing right puts the Court in a good mood. A pleader who goes on too long and causes frowns and pointed glances at the clock can add eighteen months to your sentence.

Since all the formalities of establishing that Elena really was Elena, and not Madame Sans-Gêne the washerwoman, had been got over the evening before, as well as the Prosecutor's opening speech (said by my spies to be quiet in tone and fair in manner), the witnesses would come on early. The weather forecast said scattered showers: the sun shone. The Door-warden, an elderly fussy soul, a sort of Victorian beadle, whisked me into a room with *Private* written on the door. Police witnesses are privileged to remain uncontaminated by the common herd in the anteroom. The beadle was all smiles this morning, false teeth falsely genial. It was not long before I heard him call me.

Twenty minutes. The President is smoothly rehearsed, has in any case the dossier with my depositions and conclusions open in front of him, and I know my own answers off by heart. What am I doing there at all? Simply, the law requires that the debates in court should be public, oral, and contradictory.

The President puts you through your paces, with formal courtesy. The Prosecutor, sitting slightly sideways with his legs crossed, making little of his dread red robe, asks casually, softly, for a few details to be clarified: dates, times, exits and entrances burnished to a Swiss exactitude. Just so did it happen, is all his case, and by no hairsbreadth did it vary from what I am telling the Court.

Beautifully shaved, in fact Gillette-gleaming the President inclines his head a little.

"La Défense."

The defence advocate is a man; neat, middle-aged and greying just a little, sober and unemotional. Quite right. Nobody wants even the prettiest of women advocates right now. Without passion he will tell the court that the life of a woman in this world is harsh, and that fidelity, love, and courage do not make it less so. A man has used this woman ill, and another man must say so, in terms the men of the court and the jury must take to heart. So few words, please, but good ones, and no damned advocacy.

So he is as quiet, and as courteous, as the President has been. And not a word is said about Olga – who will be produced immediately after lunch, meticulously drilled in her part.

"So at that moment, Monsieur le Commissaire, when you brought home to her what she had done and the enormity of it, have you anything to tell the Court of her attitude?" I have not looked towards Elena, whom I know to be sitting there, white and small between two burly dark-uniformed angels.

"She made no attempt at denial or excuse. It was my impression that she accepted her responsibilities with calm and courage."

"She was collected, thus. How would you define that – chilly? Indifferent?"

"By no means. You have to take into account the effects of shock, strain, fatigue."

"She did not quite realise, perhaps, all the implications of what she had done, nor the inevitable consequences?"

"You had better ask a doctor, I should think, about the technicalities of delayed shock. And the physiological condition of his patient."

"He did not see her until later. You were there. A simple opinion, Commissaire, based upon your experience and observation."

"Then yes, acceptance, understanding, but bewilderment."

"Perhaps remorse?"

"I can certainly accept that."

"If I were to say that she showed outward sign of pain inflicted upon her victim as well as upon herself, could you accept that?"

"I could."

"I want to see it clear, and that the Court may see it clear. Her outward expressions could be seen as those of suffering and remorse for what had happened?"

"Yes. I can say that. I cannot qualify it further. I am not an interpreter."

"Thank you, Commissaire, I have no more to ask."

Another sign of middle age is the collecting of accessories. When I stopped carrying a gun Vera gave me a walking stick. I have got attached to it. Others have pipes, umbrellas, briefcases. I appear to be emphasising the bureaucratic nature of this business. The truth is that there is very little difference between the head of a PJ 'satellite' (all the big populous districts have a couple of outlying offices besides the central 'Regional Service') and that of Bridges-and-Roadways. Or the Public Finances, officially (humourlessly) known as The Treasure.

The Office is situated in a gloomy building, of grimy brickwork and windows that are too small, and of no architectural merit whatever. It's a town of some eighty thousand people. One way or another I am responsible for half a million. Sounds a lot. Ultimately, my superior up in Lille has roughly three million under his (highlypolished) aegis. I don't notice him losing any sleep.

The PJ is concerned with crime. There are other kinds of police charged with security, order, counter-espionage and so forth; all troublesome to get on with. There is also the Gendarmerie, a paramilitary body like the fire-brigade and concerned with just-about-anything in small towns and country districts. Rivalries and jealousies are commonplace: one must keep them all soothed. Nearly all the work is of a papery nature. I am not Baron Scarpia with the torture chamber in the next room, though one or two of my colleagues occasionally pretend to be. I bear more resemblance to Captain Queeg finding out who ate the strawberries.

While I had been away upon my odyssey I had phoned in, roughly every time I changed socks, and been told that there was nothing very urgent afoot. I hadn't expected the contrary. Violent crime is relatively rare in our part of the world. We don't get tumbled out at three in the morning with tales of mad bombers and bank break-ins all *that* often. Our police forces, under their numerous separate hats, are badly trained, underequipped, over-armed, and subjected to a great deal of political pressure. They could also be a lot worse.

Thus, while Captain Queeg had been laid up with a slight touch of bronchitis, the office had jogtrotted along quietly enough. Today I would have a lot of traffic that had accumulated upon my desk, most of it encrusted horseshit. I would have reassuring noises to make in the direction of my superiors. Downward there must be some taking in of slack in reins-of-discipline and fusses over petty cash accounts. There would be the usual argument about holidays in the coming months of July and August. There would be judges of instruction, who have this tiresome habit of delivering rogatory commissions, often from far-off places. Very much an ordinary working day.

There was also a worry. Following the travels I had put in a brief report, redrafted to make it briefer, stating the opinion that there were no grounds visible to Magoo for pursuits and persecutions of the Citizen Lefebvre. This was in contradiction to forcibly expressed convictions held by a number of women. I should much prefer to pay no further attention to these.

I was met by Madame Metz. Something of a pest. She drops things. Not only upon the floor, and in preference things that will bounce, scatter, roll considerable distances. She also drops allusions, hints, leers, and lewd insinuations.

"Lot of work for you," brightly. I nodded. I could fend her off with my stick. If I need a weapon it is as good as a gun. Like Long John Silver's crutch. It is also a useful piece of propaganda: people think my leg is bad, which it isn't. It serves other public-relations purposes, like leaning on it with what Vera calls 'the look of negligent woodcraft' which I understand to be a quotation. We are supposed to carry guns. A totem, like a medal blessed by the Pope. Protect you from catching cancer or getting shot. Varennes, my female inspector, a nice girl, carries a big gun behind, sometimes in front of her large well-rounded hip. She has a steady supply of jokes about Castang's stick.

There was indeed a lot of work. A two-way traffic of paper. Up, because the troops are occupied upon mountains of written reports. 'Verbal process', meaning evidential statements from people who saw a car but can't remember the colour. Down, because from Lille and Paris come showers of directives and instructions; prolix, ambiguous and tautological, in that administrative jargon which is the special contribution of the United States to scholarship, and proliferates with equal mastery in German, French or Hungarian.

A noise like a road-drill means that Madame Metz is grinding coffee. She has been known to knock over a kilo tin of coffee-beans as well as paperclips, staplers, telephones.

I exaggerate? Yes. But so do innumerable wives, countless husbands, exposed day after day to the domestic noises, smells, and irritating habits of their consorts. One cannot measure these exasperations. There is no seismograph for the way people clean their teeth or blow their nose or yawn. It's the same in an office. Madame Metz may have disagreeable if commonplace mannerisms; she is a competent, punctual, and conscientious secretary. And she has to put up with me. She does this well. She has been the wife – for thirty years – of a cop. Officially he has retired. I use him, and he is better than useful, as investigator and enforcer too in tricky, generally squalid affairs. Monsieur Metz is blunt, insensitive; not very likeable. He has to be these things.

I dare say that at home he is tedious. He is the sort of man who says 'How goes the enemy?' every night at eleven, turns the television off, emits a borborygme and says 'Time for shuteye'. The point – hereabout – is that he has not killed her. Nor she him.

She brought me coffee. There were no hairpins in it, nor dandruff, though God knows what is stuck in the filter. Now when she brings anything she puts her hands on the table and leans on them. She likes too to run a finger along the surface and then inspect the result, because of a guerilla warfare she conducts with our cleaning-lady.

Now if I were to say that her hands are fat and moist I'd be open to the charge of dramatising my dislike; rightly. The fact is that anyone's hands on the desk create irritation. This is why there is a standing instruction to traffic cops: do not touch the car.

Is there a correlation between tactlessness and a warm heart? If, however politely, I were to ask her to move her paws off my table, her feelings would be hurt. Efficiency would suffer.

Monsieur Metz comes into the office around once a week for instructions or discussion, and generally manages to fart. I have sometimes said 'You overeat'. Makes no difference. The window is open anyhow. I get up and open it further and he doesn't even notice. The man is older than I am and does a lot he isn't paid for. I can't read him off like a girl of Varennes' age. I could tell him, and do, that he is a gross and revolting personage. He gets called much worse every day, and doesn't pay a blind bit of heed.

The paper had really piled up during the days I had been away. Sure ninety per cent is meaningless garbage. I used never to look at it until Richard forced me to. One learns to understand. A Minister not long ago got sucked into a fraud. He claimed his signature had been forged. He was simply countersigning things his assistant put in front of him.

I left the letters till last: I like to open them myself. Many are anonymous and most are illiterate. Some are pathetic. A largish number are in the cumbersome verbiage the French adopt when addressing an official; grovelling circumlocutions that always end by begging one to acknowledge the assurance of the writer's distinguished consideration. The poison pen often thinks that obsequity masks the venom.

And there are also numbers of ingenious devices in the mail. Some just smell; others are trickier.

There are clerical types, used to handling paper, rather handy with the scissors and paste and given to the timehonoured method of snipping out the printed word. Others, inhibited by the strange respect of the semiliterate for print – they call a magazine a 'book' – go to heavy-breathing pains in reproducing print with a ballpoint. The envelope tells a lot and this one a jewel in a sea of baser metal than silver. Lined, stamp on straight, address centred, legible to all, a thing dating from bygone days before zip codes and labels stuck on by a computer that can't spell. One would almost expect the letter inside to be from Victoria by the Grace of God, making known By These Presents. The paper was of good standard quality and folded by a meticulous hand so that the edges matched exactly. No signature could be more eponymous than that of Guy Lefebvre. No handwriting could better be called holograph. The margins and the paragraphing, the fine italic script. Real gold nib. No lousy felt tips here. The graphic artist betrays himself when writing a telephone number on the back of an envelope from the Inland Revenue Service. His letter, quite short, may betray a lot of things, and may conceal more.

I forgot the mass of printed forms and blurry woggly typescript. (IBMs have not exactly trickled down: most of us are making do with the 1924 Underwood which has been dropped on the floor by generations before Madame Metz.)

'I must not trouble you further to speculate upon my wife's possible whereabouts. I set her free, and there is no use or purpose in looking for her.' I am not a psychiatrist thank heaven, and I'm not even particularly well read in criminology, but this phrase 'set free' has been used before in ambiguous circumstances.

'I cannot see that the interests of justice are served' could almost be Silberstein talking. But 'You are the only person who has come near a just estimate' . . . 'We failed to understand love' . . . 'I have not known how to make friends'.

'One learns, I should hope, to come to terms with pain. I do not know whether pain will agree to come to terms with me.' One could say a lot about this; and suppose more. It is not my job to make suppositions.

'If you hear of me again, which is unlikely, I should be glad if the thought which then crossed your mind were friendly.' Self-pity? Stoicism? Both, no doubt: there's a good deal of both around at all times.

Even if this were a suicide note, what did or should I propose to do about it? The sensible answer is, as it frequently must be, nothing. It was, however, an annoyingly official sort of communication. I ask nothing better than to forget Guy Lefebvre and all his conceivable works. Doesn't look though as though I'm going to be allowed to. If I put a match to this it's no longer official, is it? Doesn't exist any more.

Looked at again, definitely a suicide note. One gets rid of this with a phonecall to the local commissariat of the Municipal Police in Strasbourg. Not the PJ. Or the Social Assistance Bureau. Or Arlette Davidson, who specialises in such things. She started this; let her finish it.

These half-assed solutions did not recommend themselves to my judgment. Looked at a third time, this was a cry for help. I'm not sure I can disregard it. What a bloody infernal nuisance this fellow is. Can't even consult Vera. Know already what *she'd* say. She'd sit, and drink coffee, and smoke. Bundle of nerves and sensitivities. But there's a solid, serene centre of decision. Now I sit and drink coffee and smoke, and wonder where what passes for my mind has got to. Now all right: I've plenty of work to do.

I remember getting home. One of those details that strike one and stay in the mind against all reason. A can of Russian sprats from Riga. I complained about these; they were dark brown. Isn't Riga like Stockholm; known for tar? Sprats, I said, ought to be silver, and ought to come in nice little wooden boxes – with silver paper on the inside – from Cuxhaven. 'There weren't any,' said Vera, 'and the other day there was sour herring, and it was sodden with chemical vinegar, and you made a great scene throwing it in the bin and shouting Bomb Cuxhaven.' True, true, and only Jews know how to make Baltic herring. Life is full of these major difficulties. The PJ Commissaire, at the office measured and tactful, comes home and makes a childish scene about herring.

The Commissaire is a prudent man. Sometimes he's too prudent. One has to take a risk from time to time.

Vera has these damned English writers she makes quotations from. I was brought up like a good French child on Dumas. I thought of the moment in the Fronde, when the rioting crowd besieges the Palais-Royal, demanding to see the king. The guards grit their teeth and get set for a massacre. The queen paces about, ready to order an open fire, and d'Artagnan simply says, 'Let them in.'

It's said to be a historical fact: one wonders who in reality had the intelligence to say that. Nobody now takes risks. They call it prudence: it's better when called cowardice, which is its name. Look at insurance people, who are goddamn paid for taking risks. You wonder why their premium is so hideously high. About a third of it covers the real, actuarial risk; another third is what they call costs, and the rest is stuck on happily for pure profit. And they get away with it by appealing to what they call prudence, playing upon fear.

I'm getting middle-aged and it's time I stopped taking risks and stayed at home. And forgot about things which are none of my business.

Vera reads poetry, and reads bits to me. They stick in my head now and again. Running there now is a piece taught me – don't worry, it's nice and short – by another woman: Judith, a Spanish woman, rather odd, wife of my former boss Commissaire Richard. Great gardener. Now if your wife had thought of asking her, when down in that part of the world: she, I think, would be likely to understand Guy Lefebvre.

> *Ocasiones me figuro*
> *que soy de veras un arbol.*
> *Lo miro al viento y me rio,*
> *la raiz crujiendo abajo.*
> *Si me desmiento en la vida,*
> *acuestenme de un hachazo.*

I don't know whether you speak it; I only patter a bit, but in a rough version: There are times when I think I am in truth a tree. I look at the wind and I laugh, my root cracking beneath me. Should I be mistaken in my life, then cut me down with an axeblow.

There should be a cop or two somewhere who's a poet but I have to do my best secondhand.

I heard that evening; Elena had got eighteen months. With time served and remission, less than half that. It will be less than the time it takes to bring a baby to full term. Heavy? Severe? All prison sentences are both.

There are always two victims in a homicide case. 'Cider as well as 'cided. Everyone concerned had done their job.

GUY LEFEBVRE . . .

I've got the habit now. I started writing when I was in jug. What it is for I do not really know. I'm telling myself that it helps, in the end. What they call the final analysis. Odd, but I'm finding existence very odd. I feel completely apathetic. The judge made it a condition that I stay here; I don't know for how long. He has this idea still lodged in his head that I killed Sibille. My counsel, Serge Silberstein, clucks and tuts and makes reassuring noises. I pass on to him the four or five customers in Germany who are getting rather agitato at my doing nothing. Won't be long now, he says. To illustrate, he tells a grim tale; to him a black comedy which he finds wildly funny: I should laugh too.

There is an old woman in Nancy whose husband disappeared. A highly complicated tale ensues of the sort lawyers love, a very French story, all about money, of course. The point is that a great cloud of suspicion exists: a strong presumption, much stronger than could ever exist against myself, says Serge laughing horribly, that the old lady made away with him. The judge of instruction up there is much embarrassed ('a perfect epidemic', amidst more merry mirth) by there not being any body: he can't prove a homicide when he can't find a corpse. Quite, say I moving my jaw-muscles around.

One of the things which puzzled them was finding, in the garage or cellar, I forget, a chain saw, of which the old lady gave no very clear explanation: what could she want with such an object? The latest development, ho-ho-ho, Serge fair splitting himself, is that in some weedy watercourse a long long time later a fisherman has made the macabre discovery of bits of humanity now pretty difficult to identify, but, say the pathologists, dismembered it would appear with a chain saw. 'She must have been watching American horror movies' – the point he is making, between giggles, is that the judge has got this old woman in jug 'and isn't very inclined to let her out'. Further developments are expected . . .

There was a moment when I got pretty depressed, the judge making a great to-do about the exact point where Sibille got out of the car. How was I supposed to pinpoint that? All those roads look the same and I had other things on my mind at the time than marking a tree with a blaze. It frightened me because I could imagine the judge ordering teams of gendarmerie snuffling about with spades for an eternity while I sat in their jail. A nightmare idea, which haunted me until Castang said drily that they wouldn't, because they wouldn't know where to begin.

I would have got into a terrible state. I am still asking myself why I didn't. But ever since that day I have felt a sort of anaesthesia. I don't know; I don't care. I have no idea whether this is a normal reaction, or how long it will last. The psychiatrists who examined me seemed to think that it was. I wasn't very impressed with them.

They said I was perfectly sane. So I am. Suffering to be sure from; so I am. Unbalance of various sorts 'well compensated': mildly dotty, I suppose they mean. I want to give great anguished howls. Sibille, come back.

Yes, I know I have to live with it. I have still this numbness, this stupefied inability to comprehend what has happened. I don't seem to grasp at all. I loved her, is all I can repeat.

I asked the judge how I was supposed to work and carry on my livelihood, stuck here in this town. I don't know, in fact, how it would be if I were on a site. I can't seem to keep anything in my head. I'd stand there and stutter, I suspect. It's just as well to my mind that he hesitates still before making up his mind to 'classify' as Serge calls it. Apart from missing the way Sibille wrote things in her notebook – had it all in her head . . . there's something gone wrong with my imagination, would it be? I mean, my ability to visualise; the sense that tells me 'There, put it *there*'; and I know exactly what, and how I am to do it. Frankly, on a site, with an owner, havering about like this – I'd get the bloody sack.

Luckily I do have some working drawings cut and dried from before all this, for two or three clients whom I am putting off, telling them I'm having treatment for a slight rheumatic condition that has been bothering me. Acupuncture or whatever: taking rather longer than was anticipated. They're being very patient about it all. But what will happen to me when I start fresh work, on something new?

The judge made rather a dusty answer. 'Your client is a painter,' he said to Serge in a nasty-sounding voice. 'He can paint, can't he?'

True. I can paint. Just as Sibille would have liked. Ever since the 'big breakthrough' in New York she has been – had been – going on at me. Planning and making a garden is years of endless work. Seeing – she says, said – the sheer time involved, the effort and labour and dependence upon others and the caprices of clients and their obstinacy and bad taste; yes, one can make a long long list of all the handicaps. Not even well paid when you count it up.

Whereas a painting, as opposed to a set of working drawings, takes no more than a few weeks. Sometimes only days.

Pretty specious argument, all this.

But Sibille perhaps will have her way after all. The joke will be on me.

To see myself on the familiar 'first day' (always a pleasant experience) is now impossible for me: I mean the moment in a new house, looking out, listening to the owner's whims and prejudices; ideas, if any – have I any? The fresh feeling of getting on to the terrain and knowing the lie and exposure, the contouring, the texture of the soil between the fingers. Without Sibille it seems unthinkable. Times one saw the whole thing straight off, the pivot on which it would all turn, so that one could point to the exact spot and say 'There'.

She has never been here. Before setting out I had planned some little apartment of this sort – a 'studio' they call it – for there is six months' work over there and I needed a working base. And after the 'episode on the road' as I am coming to call it, I went straight on with my intention. Why not? A simple need such as any house agent could fill readily. Keep it for six months – and go south for the winter . . . What has changed?

A macho kind of vanity is at work here; a thing of 'I'm tough. It's only a woman!' Shouldn't one be riding off into the sunset, Gary Cooper straight-arrow and tall in the saddle; or that other symbolic figure of our youth, Bogart hardmouthed steering the boat into a quartering sea. This is idiotic rubbish but this, we thought, was the way we were supposed to behave. Castrated or not.

And that is just how I feel. I keep telling myself how ridiculous it is. I have kept my Cooper-figure. I'm one kilo heavier than when I was twentyfive, and my face looks a lot better now than when I was that age. Narcissism, is it? No, damn it, I mean I'd have no trouble finding girls. Except that I don't want any. Heaven's name, I could go straight to any employment agency. 'I want a secretary. Has to be first class, really sharp on the chasing-up level. Must be fluent too in English and German; the transatlantic telephone must possess no terrors. Pretty, of course, intelligent, usual steno and typing skills. Able on occasion to do personal assistance, you know, sew on a button, whip up a meal. I like to have the back of my neck massaged when I'm tired, now and then.'

'Certainly sir. And naturally, she has to be ready to sleep with you whenever you want? Banishment to the outer room when you prefer to be on your own. What I mean – tactful . . .'

'Oh yes – er – definitely!' Must have tact. Can't have them asking awkward questions, like what's the matter with you then, impotent? Can't get it up, huh?

Need to be pretty young and remarkably hopeful. And at that it wouldn't last six weeks. There is also the question of expense. I am no economist. I have indeed only vaguish notions of my own yearly income or what taxes I pay: hell, this is what secretaries are for. It's all in the file, Miss Jones: look it up. She would, I fear, be exceedingly expensive, not to say extravagant. Sneering at my little economies. As for getting into bed – is it a prostitute you want? Normal requirement: I'll look up callgirls in the yellow pages. Fair or dark?

No, er, don't bother. You might put the kettle on for tea, would you?

Sibille faced poverty without turning a hair. It is indeed a naturally-acquired skill of upperclass girls: they've been trained not to think of money as something you turn on the tap for. She was a good and careful needlewoman, who turned the collars on my shirts and darned her own stockings. Never left a room without switching the lights off. Wasted nothing. Her one known extravagance was taking showers. She never even had a cleaning woman until she got her castle. Scotch, silly people would say: rubbish, any Italian girl would be the same. Only the nouveaux riches are wasteful and that is out of vanity. I myself was brought up in a bourgeois household perfectly French. Meanness: my father went about sticking pieces of soap together and was forever complaining about over-lavish use of lavatory paper. It was in pure reaction that in our early married years I bought things which shocked her, like whisky in France – or asparagus in England . . .

I must get out of here. I am seeing her. Physically. She presses upon my eyeballs. A damned painful sensation.

Sibille, you are . . . Now I am shocked. The thought of the sexy-secretary left me like a damp dishcloth. Thinking of Sibille I am a stallion.

Old billygoat, you mean, don't you.

So I am going to work. I am going to find something to paint. Strasbourg is a 'picturesque' city.

Just the trouble, that. The touristy bits are not in the slightest my cup-of-tea. The town has quarters as dreary and ugly as you could hope to find in Novosibirsk.

Stupid comparison, in the first place because I've never been there and know nothing about it. I was being facetious because it has a comic name. Second, since as I understand these Siberian towns have been made from nothing inside a century and to me are irrelevant. I should have said Wolverhampton, or Charleroi;

the iron towns. Dinosaur towns which have no longer any reason for existing, but they're part of history and I like them. What would be the feelings of an intelligent dinosaur, looking around at the new world and knowing very clearly his condemnation?

Strasbourg isn't on the Rhine at all: looking as I do at terrain one can see why. The valley was very waterish, flooding every time the snow melts in Switzerland. They built the medieval town a mile or so back around a little hill; barely a bump but enough for drainage and even protection from invaders: the causeway across the watermeadows was easy to defend. It was always an important road because as far as I can make out there was a river crossing here from very early times. I suppose that sandbanks and islets made fording easier and a bridge must have followed pretty soon: the way to the rich lands of South Germany and the Danube. It is the main line of the immense century-millennia-long-movement of peoples from the east towards the sunset: Europa the Abend-land, the little peninsula that points to the west. And here they picked their way across a trivial barrier, between the reeds and scrag willow, putting planks down so as not to get their feet wet, organising it better as the train of carts got heavier. I, a dinosaur, lifted my neck from marshy shallows to watch. Strasbourg was a place to dry one's boots and cook a steak. The inhabitants must have got rich, charging tolls for the passage and portage-ways.

The pilgrims went on, across the strip of rich corn- and wine-land, climbing the wooded rocky barrier of the Vosges, past the sacred mountain of the Donon, pausing for breath at the windswept Lorraine plateau; plodding (I think of the women and children rather than the fast-galloping outriders) towards the other crossings, the Moselle and the Meuse, the Marne and the Seine; always with their heads lifted up, towards the sunset.

I have been left behind on the causeway, now crossing canals and threading mean suburbs, but still called the Route du Rhin. Struggling against my apathy I have made a kind of habit of walking here, to the bridge and back. It would be about ten kilometres in all. Afternoon stroll. I am used to a life spent outdoors.

I notice that I have spent much breath, trying to explain – to myself more than anyone else – what the attraction, a strong magnet, of this area can possibly be. I cannot understand why it should mean much to me, as plainly it does. It has in itself no interest. I am here, I had better remind myself, to work. The antidote and the only one I know of.

There are chestnut trees along the canal, and bordering much of the Route du Rhin. Old, weary specimens, ill and wretched. Attacked the year round by toxic fumes. In winter the road is heavily salted: the Germans forbid it but in France nothing must ever be allowed to hinder or diminish the sacred wheel-box. We should not forget that the automobile was the most disastrous of our inventions. Until, that is, nuclear power stations. The effects of which are not yet felt; but look around at the damage done by the internal combustion motor and one can make a guess.

One would give those trees no chance of survival. Shrunken and hurt they still stand. Moreover they are lopped in the crudest fashion by municipal command: sabred: the amputations left untreated. Eyeless, fingerless, limbless lepers. And still in spring they find the courage to make leaf and even bloom in defiance of municipal hygiene. Those tall pinkish-white blossoms are nothing wonderful. Now fallen, filling gutters with pale tobacco. I do not know how to word my admiration for the courage of these disgraced and despised trees. Let them be a lesson to me.

I am leading a peculiar life: sober, almost godly. I eat little, drink little. Think little, and still too much? I seem to sleep still, fairly well. That's a thing which frightens me. So I follow the good-old-English precept of schoolchild years: plenty of exercise; all that's needed now is for me to start taking cold showers.

For I go out too at night. What should I do shut up in this box? Look at the infantile television? Six stations and more if I want them, and all dishing out the same babypap – oh yes, one can get porno movies now at three in the morning:

that'll be something, when sleep starts to come hard. More self-condolence there again: work is what I want.

At night I walk into the town. A quarter of an hour's easy stroll, along the pleasant, tree-lined Boulevard de la Victoire, and over the river; nice these summer evenings and for the most part quietish. The river – that's the Ill, flows into the Rhine a few miles further downstream – offers nice promenades along the banks, rather as though I were someone's quite friendly labrador dog.

I like it best when it rains. I have a meal – monotonous, heavy, the choice between frites and noodles – and some local wine in a corner of a café: the pink is good; the white I find too acid. Sometimes I pick noisy cafés with vulgar guffawing and accordion music: heavy-jointed local folklore in a patois I cannot follow.

The whores do not bother me, and I have no desire to bother them. I never was, it is true, more than a lukewarm amateur even when a boy. I am susceptible enough. Fastidious? A shrinking violet? I've never had much confidence in my powers of seduction. But Sibille did not cheat: nor did she allow cheating. Strength of character. Yes, and a mighty penetrating look. Before the word narcissus crops up again I may as well say I've no great opinion of myself and am not unduly fascinated by the contemplation of what I call a pretty dull chap.

It can't last, this existence, can it? Pottering out at night, leaf blown by the wind. Patterns develop. There are two or three places now where I stop for a glass of wine and where they greet me; a nod, a near-smile. I recognise certain faces; of nocturnal joggers, men who walk dogs, men who prowl, men who stay in the café and soak. In a town of this size how many are there wandering, driven by compulsions? I go sometimes to the cinema; sit alone in the dark and watch people do meaningless things, mouthing and jerking on the screen.

HENRI CASTANG . . .

It has taken me a fortnight. I have found a piece of official business which I can cook into a pretext for a couple of days' absence. I do not plan anything in particular. A 'planque'? The word is ridiculous in the circumstances. I haven't done one for years. It's a job for a junior – the technical term for surveillance of a place where one has reason to believe a crime is planned. And the people frequenting the neighbourhood. Vile job. Can take a long time. Squinting out of some cramped and uncomfortable hiding place. Pissing in a milk bottle. One needs a whole team: they relay one another.

There exists also a technique, usable on occasion, called an open planque. You show yourself deliberately in unexpected places at irregular intervals. You don't have to follow the chap about. The idea is to shake his nerve and get him rattled. It doesn't work, quite often, the way you expect. Or want.

GUY LEFEBVRE . . .

The 'click' at last to set me working. Came about in an amusing fashion. I was down by the river, in the usual way; I could never tell what I was doing there. The Rhine itself is virtually canalised at this point, an unimpressive ditch not much bigger than the Thames, say, at Westminster. Only the massive, weighty roll of the current warns one. The embankment is revetted. Both here and in the little town of Kehl on the German shore the banks, upstream of the bridge, have been parked, in flat and quite uninteresting style: gravelled walks, a few trees, benches for strollers. It does improve the shabby, slipshod look of the approaches. The grass is mowed and the bushes trim. Children pedal tricycles, women push prams, men walk with half an abstracted eye to guard against the dog getting into bad company. Nothing animates the scene. A slow thickness of blood; dark and stagnant.

I was slouching along the verge when I saw a little old man, a 'petit vieux' approaching me in a brisk hobble: the liveliness caught my eye. Beautifully dressed up, cap à pie. A check overcoat looking new and loud – it was a lowering chilly day. Twinkling polished shoes, shirt with a modish sporty cut and a rich silk tie; sharp-pressed legs. On top a curlybrimmed hat with a fresh ribbon. He looked highly rakish, helping himself along with a cane that was newly varnished, had chased silver bands and a bone crook. As he came nearer he was still older than I had thought; eighty, the prehistoric saurian look of an old Mexican peasant – no; birdy and brilliant, the rapid eye of a cultivated Jewish gentleman.

My curiosity amused him. He planted the stick, leaned on it with both hands.

"Well, my young friend. Why so sad?" It pleased me to be young, and it pleased me to be a friend. Strasbourg to be sure is a civilised city, with a large and prosperous Jewish population; the Contades quarter swarms with darting shrieking children, their bright-embroidered little skullcaps pinned on with kirbi-grips. But there is also, never quite absent in France, the dull-eyed, heavy suspicious look of the man who says of course he isn't antiSemitic, but . . . Perhaps I had smiled without realising; he was an invigorating sight.

"I'm sorry. I find it depressing. Doesn't smell too good either." There was the sharp, unpleasantly chemical smell of cement dust from somewhere, the sickly reek of cellulose.

He chuckled, glimmering. Lifted up a finger, going to 'make a quotation'.

He launched into the classical German that every educated Strasbourgeois can speak. "'Freundlich grüssend und verheis-send / Lockt hinab des Stromes Pracht.'" For the ignorant French he started to add the translation.

"'Doch ich kenn ihn' – I know him," wagging the finger,

finding me funny, "'oben gleissend', a surface glitter, but – 'Birgt sein Innres Tod und Nacht' – underneath is Death and Night."

"Yes indeed: who is that?"

"Heine, young gentleman." I am well into my fifties but I was a boy to him. "Stranger?"

"Not altogether. But you would call me so."

"Remember it. No one better than le petit père Heine. The friendly greeting, the splendour of the river. Not what you'd call evident. Hereabout Disguised," enjoying this notion greatly.

"Make no mistake – lockt hinab – pulls me down under to his depths. Take a ride on that," pointing suddenly with his stick. One of the big smart pleasure cruisers of the K–D line had come stealing noiselessly downriver. Swinging now thwart stream, for the entry to the Strasbourg harbour. People sat on deckchairs, muffled against the cold: whitejacketed stewards bustled with trays of drinks. The old gentleman sniggered.

"Great fun. Soon be out of this, comfy on the promenade deck, rug over your knees against the draught, snap your fingers for the Black Label on-the-rocks, great big ol' Nikon resting on your lap – bit topheavy with the telephoto lens. Down in lovely Rudesheim in no time. Vineyard bower, big pretty girl trotting up with the bottle and glasses, smells a bit sweaty, but no matter, sunlit skin."

"Loreleis and whatever."

"Always a few lonely American females." In English; his sharp ear had caught my accent. His own fairish newyorker. "Retired schoolmarms, stout matrons from Minneapolis, nice girls from Duluth, Grand Rapids. In pairs but you fix the dogfaced one up with the steward." He went off again.

"'Berg und Burgen schaun herunter / In den spiegelhellen Rhein' – isn't that lovely, mirror-clear," shaking with laughter, "but don't fall in, he'll pull you down. Set to music by Schumann, grand meaty stuff." He hummed, in a tune even I could recognise. "Tja, young friend, don't let me keep you."

A big motor barge was forcing its way up, loaded to the gunwales, kicking up a bow-wave like a ploughshare to the hard stamp of the diesel. A hand in a cowboy shirt, whistling, his hands in his pockets, strolled along the catwalk, and pleasure flooded me. What magic had the old boy wrought? The French side is starboard coming up: it passed close in. The wash clacked rhythmically, a series of hard slaps upon the oily stones of the revetment. Two more were coming down on the other side; light, the rust-streaked, redlead-coloured hulls towering high, engines idling in an easy-riding thud that just reached me. They gave the brave plodding camel a friendly toot passing, the way the big TIR trucks will flip their lights to a mate.

My hands itched for board and pencil. I was still alive! The westering sun found a sudden gap in the low sky, and lit a lovely cloudscape with gold that snapped on the thick roily water: a greasy Grüss is the kiss of the Rhinemaiden. But I could paint again.

CHARLES-GABRIEL ERLANGER
Procureur de la République . . .

I have consented to this interview, Professor Davidson, upon the conditions stated, and speak with you now on this clear understanding – agreed? There are questions which will not be put? Very well.

Since the affair is judged, I can comment to some extent, in private. The two matters are linked as you rightly point out. Of the political aspect – which will not be spoken of – I confine myself to the bald statement: it caused evident embarrassment; was of some delicacy.

Nor do I propose to deal with matters of international law. A riot – commotion – upheaval – upon a bridge between two countries . . . does this bridge join, or separate? At what exact point is sovereignty said to be exercised? I do not deny your right to show an interest: I say merely that I shall disappoint it.

The fact, further, that a senior officer of Police Judiciaire . . .

Fortunately, he was able to extricate himself. Fortunately for himself . . . well well, I can agree with you that the criminological aspect is of interest. There we find common ground. As soon as it was realised that the link, here, between a commonplace affair under the criminal code and this . . . the link existed. It was formed by, rested upon the personality of this woman. Lady Macbeth – you are of course joking – no? Well, I'll go a certain way with you on that but you'll agree it's needlessly melodramatic. As a lawyer, the point that I wished to make is this; it was evident that I should ask Boislevant – you know him, I believe? – to get to the bottom of the affair, since he had conducted the original enquiry. Which is classified, naturally, in every sense of that unhappy word.

As you know, under French law, it was possible for the advocate to plead – he's a clever fellow, Silberstein – that no terrorist act had been committed or even planned. Student high jinks, I wasn't going to have that. He was attempting to lay a foundation for undermining the self-defence plea of the functionaries who rightly, quite rightly, used force: that is what they are given weapons for; I don't propose to discuss it. I took the affair seriously, I chose to prosecute in person before the Court. I have nothing to add to what I had to say before the tribunal, and there's an end to it.

JEAN-CLAUDE COURBET
Physics student, Strasbourg University:
statement . . .

Ed. Note. *This while cut and condensed is in substance the same as his initial statement to the police, and that made before the tribunal. No special tribunal, be it noted: the decision was made for purely political reasons to play the affair down and conduct the hearings on a low key. Since, as we have already heard, the Procureur, a senior legal official, chose to appear in person as Advocate General prosecuting for the government, a great deal was argued in court that is quite irrelevant here. I was fortunate in managing to get access to the records of the examining magistrate.*

LADY MACBETH

*Jean-Claude's arguments, what might be called propaganda, with
which I find myself in sympathy, are no more than adumbrated:
as the magistrate kept saying, 'We are only concerned with the
facts.' Jean-Claude maintained robustly that this was nonsense,
and so it is. However, the 'non-factual' bits have been covered
pretty well in the recollections kindly made for me by Commissaire
Castang, and in that remarkable document which he subsequently
recovered, Guy Lefebvre's 'diary'.*

*I note, finally, that I did not see the police 'verbal-process'
transcript. But I was present in court throughout the hearings, and
have no reason to believe that Jean-Claude concealed or withheld
anything important. This is I think the clearest and most succinct
of his different statements, the most trustworthy. For brevity, the
magistrate's interjections, questions and comments have been
eliminated. – A.D.*

Dead bloody simple, Mister. I don't know your title. Since you
call me Mister, that's all right with me. Call me by my first name
if you could wish and I'll call you Théodule or Hippolyte – to
quote General de Gaulle.

That's correct; French citizen, French parents both sides,
French as you could wish. Alsace is France, isn't it? Or so they
claim. Born right here in Strasbourg, Steckelburger, blood and
bone. You can take note I'm not any special sort of political
fanatic about the liberation of Alsace. Liberation of bloody well
everybody is what interests me. I haven't prejudices or worries
about Jews or Arabs or any other group: just us chickens, the
Europeans.

The Tchernobyl thing just about put the lid on for us. That's
right, the Russian reactor. That particular piece of childishness –
look, you keep asking for what's relevant. I'm telling you! As
long as you can't grasp what we were doing on the bridge in the
first instance.

When we heard about the fallout in Germany we went and
measured it. For Godsake, I'm a physics student. We have
instruments rather more precise than supermarket geiger-

counters. Those were showing up the radiation all right; just hold it over a lettuceleaf and listen to it clatter. Yes, this was in Germany. Man, I can see you don't know much about Germany. What d'you think? Germans to you are a lot of tourists, come over here in big cars with lots of money, specially for the pleasure of having it stolen in restaurants where everything is smeared with raspberry jam and it costs a week's working wage? Of course I have friends. Yes indeed, a lot are students. Heidelberg, Freiburg, anywhere you like, Tübingen, Esslingen and a lot more, just ordinary people. I even know a German judge of instruction!

All right, I'm sorry. I realise I'm being aggressive. I have no wish to be. I don't try to justify myself; I don't need to. I don't need to defend anything; on the contrary, I welcome the opportunity.

You have a lot of legal charges there and you expect me to take that shit seriously? Riotous assembly . . . Yes yes, rebellion and outrage towards ze defenders of Ze Public Order. Damage to public property. And you could find a whole lot more. Let's see, you have illegal possession of explosives, haven't you? Why not conspiracy to overthrow the government or the State, or the Nation or a few more of these benighted imbecile concepts? That's all cock, as you very well know; there wasn't explosive enough to blow up a phonebox: a firework display is all it was. Scrape it all together and you've enough for six months' jug. I should be frightened or something? As a student I'm deferred for military service but try calling me up and I'll serve another six for refusal to go near your stupid useless army.

What? Pacifist, anarchist, what does that mean? Like people talking about methodology. Exactly the same as worrying whether Alsace is French or German, according to whether you live on the left bank or the right of the Rhine: it's the same people, waving flags won't alter that. Yes, I should think we can change the subject!

All right, chronology, I'll give it to you. A couple of us were up in the hills. Sorry yes, the Vosges. The Schwarzwald is something else, even though trees die in both. I'm being precise. To be still more so, myself and Bernd, or Bernd first. My car. It's an old Renault. It's one degree less busted than Bernd's. We were just driving around. Interested in a whole lot of things none of which would interest you. Ethnology, prehistory, geology, botany; what d'you want, a list? Mister, do you really think a physics student is interested only in physics? The crap they teach us at the university is good for nothing but to pass exams with. It's all physics. It's all metaphysics too but I don't expect you – no, I thought so.

No, I don't think I could point to it on the map with exactitude. I can try if you like but I can't give you any guarantee. Sure I know this countryside. There's a lot of it, you know. Some of those roads are not much better than paths.

Well in point of fact, that's not far out. It can be a short cut and if you mistake the way it's just the opposite. All right, never mind. You don't meet many people round there; the odd car, the odd tourist. Hikers, yes, maybe hunters in the season. I've understood already. It's the woman who interests you. I don't know why and I don't want to know why.

She was walking along by the side of the road. Correct, she was carrying an overnight bag. No, she didn't make any sign. She was plainly tired. When we slowed down she put her hand up over her eye, like this. Plainly too she was hurt. So we asked if she wanted a lift and she said she'd be grateful. Why not? That she'd think we'd rape her or something? Mister, I can only say you're out of your mind. That's the trouble with all you bourgeois. You're afraid of everything and everybody. Trust no one, and who will ever trust you? All right, be it as it may. Said she'd like a lift to the town. I didn't look what time. Late in the afternoon. We were going back to the barn anyhow.

Mister, we didn't ask. Do you crossexamine everyone you meet, or only professionally? What business was it of ours? People have their private lives. She had a black eye. Her cheek was bruised and swollen so we found a clean rag and soaked it in cold water to make a compress. We stopped on the way down. I don't know, fifty kilometres on. To get some icecubes, and we had some coffee. I couldn't care less whether they noticed or not; d'you think I'm inventing all this? Rested she felt better. As one does. Talked a bit. As one does. Said she didn't want to go home. Couldn't say I blamed her if it were the husband who sloshed her. But refrained from comment. No, I wasn't curious. There is also such a thing as tact. What we did ask was what she proposed to do. Thought of going to a hotel. Had a credit card and didn't want to use it.

God, it's like talking to the man from Mars. Why the hell not? I wasn't going to ask her home. I've a shitty student trap under the eaves. Bernd's got a big place. So we drove there, didn't stop in Strasbourg, it's only ten kilometres out the far side.

Ask Bernd – no you can't, haw haw, he's German, you'll have to have him extradited. Yes I dare say you can find means, go right ahead, he hasn't anything to hide any more than me. Christ, you've a filthy mind, the moment a man and a woman are together in a house you see them in bed. Sometimes Bernd has girls there and sometimes he doesn't; d'you think I write it in my diary? No-he-isn't-homosexual. And neither am I. Sibille's a woman of fifty odd. Is she my mother on that account, no-she-isn't, she's just a friend, like anyone else.

You mean you've been looking for her for eight *months?* Well, excuse me if I laugh. The great police apparatus. Stop and ask us for identity cards all the time, frightened we might be Red Fraction. She has a perfectly good passport. Sure she went out. Didn't want to cross the border to here; don't blame her. One can have a trauma that stays longer than a black eye. And I'm sorry, I find you perfectly ridiculous, on this subject as on the other. We drive to and fro all the time. Sometimes they look at our cards and sometimes they don't. There are, what? – ten thousand people in this town who go to and fro every day. Jesus, there's even a bus line. That frontier doesn't exist, except that everything's a lot cheaper the far side.

So right, to get back to the point at long last, we thought we'd make it exist. That nuclear cloud, according to the gendarmerie it stopped dead in the middle of the Rhine because being Russian it didn't dare cross over into France without permission of the Authorities. Oh you're not finished yet? Sorry, ask whatever you like. Bernd's house? It's an old mill.

What?

Say that again.

Are you telling me that Sibille's dead?

GUY LEFEBVRE . . .

Heartened. Better, I felt forgiven. Furthermore the Rhine can be one long smudge from Basel to Rotterdam – the Lorelei would do well to stop combing that goddamn golden hair and reach for the shampoo – I can paint it. A new bridge with a curve to match that of the power cables on the big cantilevered pylons – French nuclear electricity for poor hungry Germany. I am out of date. The coal and iron which built empires for enlightened capitalists, people with progressive views and names like Schlumburger, the forgemasters who put up these Victorian 'social dwellings' for their workers, have made way for the silicon industries. Which I do not understand – what are semi-conductors; what are these chips they talk of? They seem at least to be clean and small. I can't say I subscribe to the schoolgirl gush whereby we'll all be good and happy if we just let them take over, and listen to their sage advice.

A drawing board, a few sheets of cartridge paper. For different Rhines, different bridges. One sits here on the park's terrace, with a good view of this large, undistinguished concrete structure, and one starts by letting the mind sink back into the past. Impressionist sketches; pencil, some watercolour. I can see something coming of this.

The first would have been of wood, on piles sunk into the sandbars. Carried away a few times, no doubt, by floodwater. I could do some research. Had the Romans already bridged the stream, to link Gaul with their lifeline of German provinces? –

Augsburg! and the Danubian outposts all the way to Dacia. Better to let the fantasy run free. A Gothic bridge – crocketed and pinnacled, in the lovely flamboyant of the Strasbourg cathedral. A classical bridge, say of the mid-eighteenth century. Like that one, excellent and still doing duty, over the Herault at Gignac. Would make a good ruin in the style of Piranesi. Just upstream from there is a charming tiny suspension bridge. Ironwork! A tremendous monument to the Assyrian empire of the iron men. Should it be cantilevered, like the Forth, or suspension like the Brooklyn? Which was the Tay? It broke in a great storm – 1876? '67? Look that one up.

Why not do all of them, one after the other, and all in ruins? That is the point of the operation.

Scattered about here are a number of memorials from the last war, including a tank left here on the terrace, absurdly small and pathetic. I presume the Germans blew the last bridge up in their retreat. This big lump in front of me would take a lot of blowing up. Some ambitious terrorists might manage it. Would make quite a spectacular operation. It would need surely a deal of explosive even strategically placed. Their usual line is to pack an old car with plastic. Which would knock a fine hole in the roadway and break the parapets, but probably wouldn't affect the bridge in the structural, engineering sense. Their objective, which is propaganda, would of course be attained . . . but that idea does not interest me.

My mind fantasised, but I was at work. A simple perspective of the bridge and the banks. Both are flexible. Back in the studio one will bend the bridge, bend the landscape, articulate.

My eye took in two figures in the foreground. Two young men on a bench. They were sitting doing nothing, looking at me with the tolerant indifference of anybody, all over the world, who watches one sketching. Always found funny, in a goodhumoured way. I absorbed them, half-consciously, there on the periphery. Students no doubt: there are plenty around, though this is further out of the town than one usually sees them. Medical, law, theology: there's every school you can think of in Strasbourg.

Architecture, perhaps. I had a swimmy moment of sentimentality, seeing myself as a student. Before Sibille. They were looking at the bridge, back towards me, as though judgmatical about my perspective.

I slid the sketch under, repinning a fresh sheet. I was irritated now at the big thing, ready to do it violence, drop the whole centre span in the river. I began a caricature: bump – silly bridge. Germany cut off – Continent Isolated! Polizei, gendarmerie, customs men running about like blue-arsed flies.

I looked up aware of something bigger behind me than the usual inquisitive child. One of the students, studying my sketch and grinning.

"I'll do a better one when the dust has settled." I am not good at humour. I just sound facetious. But he laughed.

"Cartoonist?"

"No, architect, Sunday painter." Simplest explanation. "I didn't like the bridge so I made other plans for it." The other had come to look too: they sniggered.

"You're an anarchist," he said, amused.

"Something like that," I agreed. They strolled off, heads together, talking seriously. Lecture time?

I started another drawing, the gothic this time. A very early gothic, almost still romanesque, the lower arches round and heavy and the upper pointed, beginning to reach upward; the gothic as I love it best at its beginnings. Like Durham, Laon, lovely Laon with the oxen in the tower, the beautiful oxen who have hauled the great stone blocks.

I do not wish to sentimentalise. A satiric effect perhaps. But beware the San-Luis-Rey stuff, the bridge broken between Sibille and myself. The swaying fragile catwalk crossed by the trudging peasant and his burdened donkey.

This bridge is only a bureaucratic statement, a table of stressed concrete carrying four lines of wheels while ensuring room for the river convoys beneath. It is now inadequate. They are planning another bridge; a little higher up.

The two boys were still there. Studying their lecture-notes now; still glancing up at me from time to time.

When I next looked up myself I had a slight shock. There was a figure on the bridge. It was too far for me to distinguish detail, but the port, the carriage of the head, recalled Castang, that police officer who said – kindly enough – that he had no good reason to believe in my criminal . . . what will we call it? But who, underneath, believes that I killed my wife.

I must have imagined this. I imagine more. Bridges, huh? Nice drawings, such as a gallery has liked, more galleries go on liking. Sibille's delight. Castang, a professional, with work to do, has certainly more useful occupations than nosing around after me. I did not kill Sibille. I managed to kill something of myself. Do not fall back into this attitudinising. That is all it is; selfpity. You are a good garden architect. Graphically a clean draughtsman. A pen-and-ink line. A delicate colour sense. This does not make you a painter. Sibille with her insane ambitions; her 'metaphysical' talk; her distorted mind.

I have, simply, like every architect of any use, a romantic imagination. One is, virtually always, frustrated of one's Xanadus. The best American architects – take Pei, that tricky diamond cut thing (Detroit is it, or Dallas?) – at their best they have magic casements opening on perilous seas. And I, I have the right to put a bloody weeping willow aslant across the brook. Fair enough; that is my speed. I play games, I grow lianas and giant treeferns up Roebling's gothic towers, I let palm trees and sequoias explode in the Grand Central train shed: does that make me Bernini?

HENRI CASTANG . . .

I thought it would be a simple enough matter. Saying it like this in cold blood sounds bad: break someone's nerve. Brutal gestapo stuff. I suppose it is, in a way, but it's an ordinary piece of police procedure. I wanted the answer.

Truth is something else, mostly less simple than we try to make it in criminal affairs. Some of the truth, say; a truth. Lefebvre had gone on repeating No-I-didn't-kill-her through a pretty heavy barrage. He had been some weeks in jug: observed in numerous sessions of questioning by a shrewd and experienced judge of instruction. He had gone through detailed physical and psychological examination. For what it's worth I had myself done work on his background. Serge Silberstein had seen and spoken with him throughout the whole time: that's likewise a skilled and experienced criminal pleader, whose opinion I wouldn't take lightly.

Naturally, he follows the rules, the deontology of his profession. He doesn't want a client he *knows* to be guilty. He doesn't want to plead extenuating circumstances but an acquittal plain and simple: better still the prosecution case dropped for notorious insufficiency. Serge allowed himself a comment to me; as he could, knowing that I was nowise officially involved. 'Guy's an enigma; I'm damned if I can make him out. I feel quite sure he didn't kill her. But he behaves like a guilty man. What is he guilty of?'

That worries me. Worries the judge and plainly still does since instead of closing the file he was dragging his feet. Something wrong there.

This flaw in Lefebvre – or in his tale, it's the same thing – could be found, I felt pretty sure, by pushing him a bit. It's not technically illegal. No rule of procedure or ethics forbids putting pressure upon a suspect through surveillance. Defending advocates are piously shocked and use words like 'waylaying', but a trial judge will tell a jury not to feel shocked. The examining magistrate hadn't enough evidence to have Lefebvre networked by the local PJ. I don't know what he was waiting for – heavenly enlightenment perhaps?

I had followed Guy a bit, for a couple of days. It was not difficult with such a creature of habit. You do not need to imagine me hanging about in doorways in the pouring rain. Taking samples was enough; the compulsive walking both by day and in the evenings. His unawareness made it easy. People often get a feeling of their footsteps being dogged but Guy was by that time so wrapped up in himself he never noticed. Driven back upon his own resources he was carrying on an intense inner dialogue. I hardly saw him talking to people – a woman in a bookshop, an official in the bank. He wrote a lot of letters. I was not at all surprised to find the 'diary': I'd been expecting something of the sort. Had to get all the talk off his chest somehow. The chief screw at the jail told me he was the – common – type who writes it all down at immense length and carries bundles of documents about with him. They go on explaining it to themselves until they have the story arranged to their satisfaction. Altering a detail here or there, justifying themselves through thick and thin. Lefebvre was honest with himself but yielded to this commonplace obsession.

There on the bridge I let him see me. It didn't register much so I did it again at the end of his drawing session. That clicked all right: he was startled enough to drop his board, and the sheets were only held with diagonal elastics. Took him a moment to get all that together, and by then of course I was strolling away – towards the German side of the bridge, as though I had business there and no interest in Guy at all. I wanted that doubt in his mind. It's quite an habitual technique, as you probably know.

That evening after some bird-dogging from far back he had lost his wariness and I thought right, I'll move in on you. When he got near where he usually ate I nipped around the corner and got in ahead.

It's a biggish place, but at that time fairly crowded. I was lucky to get a table across from him, and it took a moment before he noticed me. He looked thoroughly alarmed and as though about to bolt. That's a risk one takes. But usually the compulsion to talk gets the better of them. In general it is vanity, the conviction of being cleverer than stupid cops and the fatal attraction of making complications; a display, a good performance. I had forgotten that Lefebvre was English. He came across and said "Share your table?" as though I were doing him the favour.

I can't try and reproduce his conversation. The food was unimportant; it is one of those beerpalaces with waiters in red jackets and a pile of noodles with everything. One drinks a lot. Guy I found as enthusiastic about the pinot noir, which is as near as Alsace gets to red wine, as myself; and if anything the looser tongue was my own. He was perfectly ready to talk about Sibille.

"I'm wondering myself" – scraps of his dialogue can be reproduced because they have stayed in my mind: I am trained to remember, and a little later to put the same question again, and notice variations in the answer – "how I can possibly survive without her."

"Survive?"

"Yes. As you see, I am accident-prone. One of those people, they're quite common, to whom lamentable things happen. Generally comic. We tread in the dogshit. Waiters spill things on us. Airlines lose our luggage. We are arrested by the police for a resemblance to a wanted fugitive. I would never try to smuggle anything past a customs officer. I have, you see, that furtive air of slinking guilt."

"Sibille was a safety net?"

"A good definition. To whom else could it happen that deserted by his wife – in itself a ridiculous and undignified happening – he finds himself accused of killing her."

"I've heard a lot about her, and much of it conflicting opinion."

"I should have thought you were used to that. She was a bundle of conflicts. I valued above all her competence."

"It struck me how often a comparison got made with Lady Macbeth."

Guy was mildly amused.

"Mm, Macbeth was a good soldier, from what I've been told. Liked by his troops, looked after their boots and their rations. Respected by other commanders – he and Banquo got on well. Pretty useful general. Up to that irresolute streak, and the fatal

210

gift of imagination. I find myself empathising. I don't know much about generals. We never know much about their wives, do we? Whoever heard of Mrs Wellington?"

"Women provide strength of character. Common sense. Judgment. As well as ambition." He played with his glass, twiddling it.

"Indeed, Sibille was all those things. Not much intelligence, I suppose, but it was always assumed I had enough for both."

"Well-matched pair."

"Certainly. I learned to rely upon her in all my dealings. She saw a need to protect. And to push." It was an attractive feature in him, this detachment. Or would one call it self-indulgent? "She had the force and tenacity I lack."

"And would you agree that she became over-dominant and that you came to resent this?"

"You're beginning to sound like my examining magistrate," said Guy.

"He hasn't taken me into his confidence."

"How does it go then? – that Macbeth finding that his wife has put him properly in the shit slips her ratpoison in the cocoa?"

"That wouldn't, perhaps, be thought entirely illogical?"

Lefebvre came out of a reverie.

"You don't know anything about art, do you?"

"No, for that you'd have to ask my wife."

"Forget this Macbeth nonsense. So far as the cliché goes, so good. Yes, Sibille saw herself as the key to advancement, the motor of ambition, the spur to success. She started to think she knew something about art. Very annoying. One doesn't kill people on this account."

That pink plonk is easy to drink. I could say now that it got to Guy. Except that it got to me in equal proportion. I held no advantage over him. I get rhetorical too after a bottle of this stuff – and we were well into our second.

"What's art?" asked Lefebvre quite crossly.

"I can say I like this or I don't like that, but nobody's going to listen."

"Sensible of you. It's taste or feeling? Not just proportion. Why are Jews better at it, d'you think? Why were Greeks good and Romans bad? What's special about quattrocento Italy or seventeenth-century Holland?"

"I've no idea," in some alarm. Guy gave me an amiable smile.

"I'm not about to get aggressive. You want to understand Sibille, here's a path for you to follow. We can't define art in engineering terms; it's a metaphysical thing, okay?

"Like many stolid-seeming women in middle age, menopause or whatever, Sibille got bitten by metaphysics."

I have only Guy's word to go by. He was being, I think, honest with himself.

She began to think she understood his business better than he did. A bossy soul, and used to his being disorganised – uncoordinated? – and ambitious for him. Ambitious too for material success. Nothing crude, like furs and diamonds, but she wanted her castle. Wealth. And fun – she'd had little in her life. Power.

Guy was evasive about this. We were both a bit incoherent at this stage. But Arlette – your wife – saw things clearly, I believe, on that occasion in New York. That, we're told, is the pinnacle, in the commercial sense. Get it made there; you're made.

I'm no judge of pictures. Those paintings seem to me witty, original, accomplished; that's as far as I can go.

A good judge would maybe think them nothing wonderful. And that's the view Guy takes. He used the word 'défoulement' which doesn't translate easily: a break-out, a violent sense of relief, and in compensation for some constraint. Better still the expression 'fuite en avant' – Flucht nach vorn, what's it in English? An advance can also be a flight: progress is still an evasion, dodging the real issue. I have put it clumsily: a cop doesn't pretend to judge such things. But this I think is why Vera, best placed even without having met him to understand someone like Guy, urged me to look for the answer. Sibille's wish to commercialise a private, inward expression was to him unforgivable. Making a whore of him. She stabbed something

212

sacred. Didn't Macbeth feel that knifing the king was peculiarly dreadful? It was not ordinary blood.

Violence is not always brutal. Guy was both gentle and violent. Catch a pacifist upon a raw edge. The word 'écorché' comes to mind; means skinned or flayed and is used in French to describe the vulnerable sensitivities of people like this: raw edges all over. Whereas a cop – he has grown an extra skin, corned and calloused by professionalism.

I had to learn that Vera could be hit hard and would laugh. Hit a sacred place and she'll throw an axe at your head. But everybody as I believe has a secret, vulnerable joint. Don't touch them there.

After Guy left me, I could not see much doubt left. A thing which worried the judge was giving me too some pretty close thought. I mean disposing of a body. Have you ever dug a grave? Even if you choose your garden, under the currant bushes where the soil is easiest, you'll find it very hard work. Specialised, in fact. You cannot get round this by saying that Lefebvre was an experienced gardener and had a spade in the car. In fact he would know – of all people – that you have to go deep into subsoil. Compacted stuff, and stones. The topsoil is thin, in the Vosges, and rock near the surface. The gendarmerie knew this, if the judge didn't. The fact caused a 'suspension of belief'.

You might recall, though, a fact blurred by the passage of time. That back in nineteen-fourteen, during what we used to call the Great War, the front line ran through these hills. If you know where to look, and I dare say that Lefebvre did, under seventy years' woodland growth can be found the traces.

I don't know about trenches. But there are fortified emplacements, casemates and gun platforms, pillboxes and bunkers; storage too for matériel and ammunition. Compared with the soft chalk of the Somme – a countryside I know better – this rocky ground presented enormous difficulties. But as far as I know the lines here were static for many years, and in that time the soldiery was kept well occupied.

The woodcutters know all about this, and while the theory was afloat that Sibille had encountered some drunken oaf in a neck of the woods the gendarmerie had certainly done some rummaging. There are also disused mines in this part of the world. I wonder how well all of this is mapped – and how thorough, if at all, were the researches. And since I have no official standing or authority; since moreover the district is enormous; nobody will thank me for enquiring. Over a hundred miles of line. Both French and German, front and support. Not like in the North. After the first few weeks all notion of attack was given up. The terrain is just too difficult.

I feel strongly that this is the answer but what am I to do? Go look for myself? – no, get Lefebvre to show me . . .

When he left me that night, he was a very shaken man.

GUY LEFEBVRE . . .

Understanding women! I'm not much good at that. I seem, to myself at least, to be an instinctive sort of man. Unravelling the motives for people's behaviour, making psychological observations, this has all passed me by. Novels in France are full of this elaborate analysis. I am not intelligent enough, or I don't have this sort of mind. I read, of course. One can't be forever poring over technical blurp and seedsmen's catalogues. I find that English novels bore me too. They seem invariably to be about class differences. Well, leaving the country was largely to get away from all that. I like crime stories. But it's not remarkable, I should think, that I've rather gone off crime tales lately.

I've been kept hanging about since they let me out of jail. I haven't been able to get on with work, and time hung heavy. Now that I can paint again, things will be better. But I have read a lot. In the quarter here is the usual 'university bookshop' heavy with the amazing variety of stuff students are nowadays supposed to eat – and digest, good heaven. But it has a foreign language section run by an enchanting woman – enchanting, I mean, in her gentleness, inner quiet, serenity. So unlike my stormy world.

She has a roomful of paperbacks and I have unearthed a splendid thing which I have heard spoken of but never read. This is a picture of life unrolling from a childhood in the First War until almost the present day – there are several volumes. It is called 'The Music of Time'. I have been reading this mesmerised. Some is familiar to me. To have had oneself a childhood in England in the years before the war adds much to the flavour. But most was to me a discovery. I admit I found some of the wartime memoirs lengthy, but if I may quote: 'The sense – essential to mature enjoyment of any classic – of being entirely free from responsibility to pause for a second over anything that threatened the least sign of tedium' – this I suppose is 'mandarin' but I like this stately language.

And why this lengthy digression which 'threatens tedium'? There are a great many characters in this series. They talk about a great many things. Including, very often, women. It has had much to teach me. I noted three of these remarks which struck me with a particular force.

'All women – some men – command a power of projecting around them a vast resentment.'

'How dexterously women can take in the ideas of a man, then out-manoeuvre him with his own arguments.'

'I've come to the conclusion the characteristic women most detest in a man is unselfishness.'

A good writer brings you up with a jolt, like this. I wouldn't have thought of these, alone.

I had a ghastly night. The state between waking and dreaming in which one treads the borderline of both. What is true, what is false? Memories too clear and yet not clear enough, hideously vivid and impossible in their exaggerations. Nightmarish – yes. Some of my drawings are like this too. I must have slept, and probably for many hours. I felt this morning as though I had not slept at all. The only remedy for this is work.

Remedies! As well suggest counting sheep, or Chew each mouthful thirty times. Or Write it all down and you'll feel better. So many jokes get made about Dear Diary, appurtenance of

schoolgirls and elderly politicians, both gushing about that
heavenly butcher's boy glimpsed this afternoon.

Why not tell the truth? That writer, so civilised that it is
impossible to imagine him strike a servant, tear a girl's shoulder
strap, even raise his voice, is frightening. The timed and measured periods, delivered in a dry quiet voice, tell of fearful things.
Such detachment is the more effective.

I got out of bed at last and went to make some coffee. I
bought myself a loaf of German wholemeal bread, fine textured
and delicious-smelling: I was looking forward greatly to this. The
coffeemaker gurgled quietly in its corner. I put on a little
saucepan to boil an egg. A gleam of morning sunlight slipped in
from the balcony. The loaf, aromatic, waited on its board.
Butter. Marmalade. A Chardin breakfast-piece. At the moment
I laid hands upon the loaf to cut the first slice, I clenched my fist
upon the knife holding it underhanded like a dagger and drove
it through two three four times into the wood beneath. I stood
there for a moment appalled. I laid hold of the wounded loaf
with both hands, I could not bear the sight, I tore it into
fragments and flung it into the garbage bin.

My father, Victorian, materialist and I suppose rather dull
provincial business man, and a great believer in conventional
manners, had a mystic respect for bread. He could not bear to
see it wasted, and as a child I had to eat the stalest heels. It
might not be thrown away. It might not be mishandled. I have
been punished for dropping a piece upon the floor. To break
bread was an act accompanied by a silent word, of gratitude and
of blessing. The old man's bloody atavistic, I can remember
thinking. And I was astonished by my own atavism. I was also
terribly shaken. I drank some coffee, before writing this. But I
have eaten nothing.

Despair? Yes. And black hatred? I am afraid so. The thought
– make no mistake, the fact – of the treachery comes up into my
face, off this paper; a choking greasy black smoke forming
between the lines, between the characters shaped by my ink
and my hand. I write with an ordinary Sheaffer fountain-pen.

True, an expensive model. Silver. Given me, as it happens, many years ago, upon my birthday; by Sibille.

Treachery? Is that not an absurd word to use? Ludicrous, even? Treason: connotations of school historybooks: people clapped in the Tower, put up against the wall. Way of getting rid of inconvenient political rivals: coup d'état stuff. Is there any real treachery? – save between man and wife. Even that, for who swears allegiance these days? It's a piece of paper, to be torn up the moment it no longer suits one of the parties. If I talk of treason the judge of instruction will look at me with a kind of humorous indulgence. Well really; isn't that just a thought psychotic? Some policeman, like Castang, an honest man but dulled and imperceptive – how could a professional be anything else – would laugh. Treason! Haven't heard that one before advanced as a motive for homicide. Only the State is allowed that specious argument.

Yes, treason. Exactly like Macbeth. The more because it was Sibille herself who set so high a value upon fidelity, purity, faith. One of her sisters is called Faith. Prudence would have been more to the point.

I will not speak of it, ever, to the judge, to Castang, to anyone concerned with the odious farce they term Justice.

I should have killed her. I wanted to. I wish I had. Like the bread.

And now I have. The symbol is more real to me than any reality. The reality was a trivial affair.

But let them go on imagining I killed her. They cannot prove it. I cannot disprove it. It is the truth, now. Then I had no knife.

The reality was so filthily petty. All it amounted to was that I had been driving all day. Sibille beside me distilling poison into my ear. I had argued at first. For an hour and more I had taken refuge in silence. Nothing, ever, could stop her when once she had made her mind up to something.

Of course I was very tired, physically as well as nervously. Stupidly, upon those back roads I think I know, and have the vanity to say so, I succeeded in losing my way and taking a completely false path, that far from being a short cut added indeed a loop on. So unbearably trivial. I stopped the car and was rubbing my eyes. And Sibille chose that moment to begin a commonplace, nagging, fishwife's whine.

I turned, from behind the wheel, and drove my fist straight into her face. I need no policeman, no judge, to convince me of the gravity of this.

And yet to Justice that would be merely a domestic tiff, wouldn't it? The harder grain in our daily bread. Common assault. Grounds for divorce, no doubt. And how many men would you not still find to applaud. Good God, man, so you gave her a slap; you'd ha' done better to take the whip to her but under the circumstances, absolutely right, old chap, not a doubt of it.

It was not a really hard blow. Not enough, I believe, to give her more than a respectable shiner, a real oeil-au-beurre-noir. One need only think of the position in the driving seat of a car; adapted for driving, but for no other movement: one is indeed so hampered as to be almost helpless. But of course it had force enough to kill her, and it did.

She was stunned: her head went back and banged the door-post. I twisted on the seat. Into an attitude of defence, for I thought she'd go at me tooth and nail. She was a strong woman, and a wild cat when provoked. But she looked at me, and said nothing. We stared at one another like that, for a longish instant. She put her hand out then, calm and quiet, clicked the safety belt loose, opened the door and got out, still saying nothing. She took her jacket, her handbag. She opened the back and took her overnight bag. Without a further glance she slammed the door – not hard, more contemptuously. And walked away, unhurried, back up the road. She didn't need to say anything. I knew well enough I had killed her. She was a woman of dignity and pride. Like a cat, which if paralysed by a bullet will try to raise its head and stare into your eye, quite unafraid, waiting for the death blow. I have seen their eyes. No hatred left there. Scarcely even a reproach. What else had one ever expected, from anything as contemptible as man?

I was stunned myself. I did nothing. I went on sitting. When Sibille was, I suppose, a hundred metres away, walking evenly, unhurried, her head up, I started the motor and drove away.

To police and to magistrates I have told nothing but the truth. They understand nothing, but what can one expect from such people? Sibille is dead and so am I.

How should they? From my own wife I had thought I had some right to understanding. And at times coaxingly, at times angrily, at one moment all sweet reason and the next the wildest most total illogic. She cajoled and threatened, returning again and again. It had been going on for months.

I have been trying to remember joy, to set against all this evil. I have come back to September past, to a moment just before nightfall when that wonderful dark green light makes the commonest orange marigold flame like a blastfurnace. My host, a rich, jovial Bavarian business man (the sort of house with a bathroom to each person and all equipped with jacuzzis), had been entertaining us to dinner. A very good dinner indeed. I may call these pleasures vulgar and costly. The description is accurate but not necessarily pejorative: the big table of burnished hardwood, the Meissen china and Baccarat glass and the fine lustre jug full of roses – the food and the wine. It was his everyday style: they believe in doing themselves well. Perhaps towards the end I felt overwhelmed. I wanted silence and I didn't want cognac. I excused myself. He chuckled at me, indulgent, by then used to my small eccentricities. I took my Cuban cigar outside: they taste best at this hour when the dew falls and the flowers glow. Yes, there is a lot to be said for wealth.

His house was upon a hillside, a piece of land that had been a smart deal he was fond of telling; a battle won and the municipal authority (of some thirty thousand souls, outside city limits while still on the S-Bahn) thoroughly, splendidly foxed – he had a magnificent view. Behind the house the ground sloped steeply up: with considerable pains I had fought off his concrete and bulldozers. I had built a drystone terrace upon two levels, for under the surface I had found lovely irregular slabs, and with pickaxe and crowbar – one great beauty defied us – I refused to let the workmen use dynamite (they love dynamite) and made it the startingpoint of a fountain. My hands were in a woeful state but that evening I had turned the water on and after days of nagging, occasionally roaring, he was happy. So was I. The sunset was over but there was a lovely apricot afterglow. I paced up and down. The topsoil was raked but had still to be turfed. In another day I would be done. The bill – thanks to Sibille – would be exact; not an ounce of fat on it. Every cubic centimetre costed and quantified. He could audit it and he would. But once he was satisfied, that fat man's cheque would be on my table. That was business. He wouldn't delay payment for six months in order to have the interest on the sum, which is what others would call business. I had a fingerstall on a badly bruised thumb; my nails were cut and scratched.

Memories like this you don't have from a picture. The french windows were open in the house below. I could hear Sibille's voice laughing and talking. They would be out in a moment. He has sixteen bathrooms but enjoys pissing in a flowerpot.

I have no children but I had made a living thing. That I call happiness.

Well, I am better now. I will take my sketching things down to the river and work on my bridges. I've had nothing to eat: yoh – as they say in Alsace – there's a perfectly good pub down there.

Will I read all this stuff over some day, and shake my head over it, laughing a little?

HENRI CASTANG . . .

I have to laugh a little. At myself. How idiotic was my pretty little theory. It is often so in police work. Mean to say, there's old Castang being the smyler-with-the-knyf, thinking he has Lefebvre properly bent, waggle him a bit today and he'll fall apart. And the next cliché that comes to mind is the one about mice-and-men: Steinbeck's story of Lennie, who was going to get a little farm . . .

I had already pulled the gag of showing myself on the bridge, so had to introduce what Richard used to call 'elegant variation', after some clown had put a phrase in a report like 'a certain number of' instead of 'some'.

And then I became aware of those two boys, the ones looking like students: were students. They had been taking what seemed an undue interest in friend-Guy the day before, and once is happenstance and twice is coincidence. James Bond thought only the third was enemy action, but a trained cop is no great believer in coincidence. They were much too bloody animated. People on their lawful occasions don't scratch and fidget that way. Guy was a lesson in concentration. He never noticed me at all. Right; do a job, do it whole heart, and the hell with the audience. When, for example, Madeleine Renaud does 'Oh Les Beaux Jours!' which I suppose she has done three thousand times I do not believe that secretly she's thinking of the cake for tea. Say what you like about him Guy is a good pro. When, indeed, he began to bite his nails and stare, I had the notion that it was the two boys getting to him, subconscious. They were concentrating upon him so hard that he was unhappy and didn't know why. It was a nasty day, overcast with puffs and gusts of warm sour-smelling wind: in fact it was sinister and this too troubled Lefebvre. He packed up well ahead of time, and at that moment the less jumpy of the two boys went after him. And I thought it well to go after both. All done by stages; tactical withdrawals.

You see, it had added to my curiosity that they had noticed *me*, and had moreover a shrewdish notion who and what I was. The plainclothes cop in army boots and a dirty trenchcoat with his hat down over his eyes belongs with Hercule Poirot, but he does give off a smell. Any footstep-dogging was thus from way way back, but I was helped by knowing Lefebvre's patterns. Not only is he blind as a bat to whatever does not interest him, and right now he is only interested in himself – but he is a creature of rigid habit. Take away that underground garage and he literally would not know where to park his car. He's even vexed when he doesn't get the same slot!

The boy who had my particular interest looked to be a man of action. He was black, to my way of thinking Antillais. The ones from these islands, with the appalling tradition of servitude and negritude in which they are kept pinned by a benevolent French administration, when good are very good: they have to be. Outstanding athletes with sharp alert minds, often formidably goodlooking. They are mostly no longer intact; there's the trouble. The natural warmth and generosity has been corroded too far by the bitterness: there is a feral streak and a fanaticism. They can be evil, and they don't like cops. This one was a smiler, and might carry a knife. A bright-looking merry boy of twenty-two or thereabout, neither big nor small but put together with that loose and supple articulation that is one of their gifts. He was not built strongly: he might have made a good hop-step-and-jumper. Or a three-thousand metre steeplechase. It is about that far, from the Pont du Rhin back to the Esplanade quarter.

Guy, encumbered by sketching material, had brought the car today. He had no notion of being followed. As well for him. The little Fiat, itself inconspicuous and fairly dirty, was nearly in his pocket, raising prudent cop eyebrows. By going through a red light I contrived to reach the catacombs on time. These underground parkings are happy-valley for the evilly-disposed. Dim and smelly, since parsimony ensures that the lighting should be as feeble as the ventilation, they are unsafe. Yes, there are surveillance cameras, manned by some fatso in a cabin at ten minutes' walk. You can do what you choose, some choices pretty subhuman. There is nobody much about, in mid-afternoon. Teatime in England. A moment for toasting crumpets, gleefully cosy on the sofa, Dr Watson's boots steaming on the fender.

Guy put parcels on the car roof, dropped his keys on the dank concrete, went all round the car wondering whether the doors were locked. I was grateful for his absentmindedness. Blackshadow used it to make sure nobody was about. Armpits stuffed with art, Guy was now trying to get his hat straight.

I have many reasons for disliking guns and one is they're so little use except for shooting people. Point the stupid thing and say hands up, and your average criminal runs away, knowing perfectly that it's forbidden to shoot him. Worse, he might shoot you, creating a bad temptation to get it in first. You can hit him with it, always assuming that you're close enough, and that he's obliging enough to stand still. But an ordinary walking-stick doubles your reach for a start. You can prod with it, fencer-wise; nastier than it sounds. Reversed, it can trip the dodging foot. On a shinbone it will paralyse. But being behind an active and athletic young gentleman is a help. You can hook his ankle or give it a smart tap. I like safety margins so I tapped him first and hooked him after. If he had already started his bombs-away I might have tried for the small of his back. Above the knee is right for a lathi, but that is a lot heavier. I hope I don't sound as though I enjoyed any of this. It takes training and experience. The young man showed signs of fight. I banged his head on the floor, which was dirty as well as dangerous. But, to paraphrase President Coolidge, there existed a necessity for becoming excited. During all this time Guy stood there being astonished.

There were things more urgent than explanation. I had no cop paraphernalia like handcuffs. Nor any handy substitutes like wire coathangers, the inner tubes of bicycles. Stupid Guy didn't even have any string. What he did have was the plastic straps with which gardeners stake young trees. Tongue through loop and they are toothed down one side. Ratchet effect. Bad for the circulation but so are handcuffs. I had to choke the boy a bit with the stick on his throat. But it wasn't just a mugger. I went over him and he had a gun. The idea floating in my head of People's Army began to take shape.

"Well," said Guy, by now quite jaunty, "it never occurred to me that I'd be saved from a bandit by the cop who thinks I killed my wife. I am doubly fortunate. I'm grateful. I'm also shaking a bit; that was a nasty experience. You were very professional about it. What does one do with muggers?"

"Lefebvre, listen to me carefully. Pay close attention. Go home and lock your door. Bolt it. Do not answer it. I'll phone you." He started being startled again. "And don't go out for a walk." I got rid of him. I had to concentrate upon Sam. I did not know what he or his friends were up to but this was serious. "Walk quietly," I told him. "I have your gun."

The local police were not much interested in a garage-cockroach, even in possession-of-a-prohibited-weapon, though they admired the improvised handcuffs. They were a little flustered to learn that I was a senior PJ officer; more so to be told to get DST and look sharp about it.

This is the counterespionage service. They have offices in major towns. We do not have much to do with them, and as a rule there's not a lot of love lost. They much dislike infringements upon their precious territory and especially by other kinds of cops.

The duty officer was an inspector of forty-odd, with the local meaty build and pungent accent. Vexed, and rude.

After all, my story sounded silly. A man sits sketching the bridge. People take an interest. Local layabout decides to mug him: easy target. So what? And Sam wasn't saying anything, except that his real name was Gilbert, which we knew from his papers. What did we have on him? Nothing much; even shopping him for the gun was small fry. He had only to sit tight, watch us waste time, and laugh. His jumping Guy – convincing me that their purpose was serious – might have only been to bundle an inconvenient witness out of the way. It might have been to acquire a hostage. But the People's Army is totally unpredicta-

ble. The idea could have been to suppress Lefebvre altogether.
'Proof' in the criminal code is only obtained when one has a
beginning of execution. We have to wait for the bank hold-up to
begin: short of that the only charge we've got is association of
wrongdoers and conspiracy. But alone, unarmed, unprepared, I
couldn't take any risks with Guy Lefebvre. It could have been
his life. Sibille had nothing to do with it.

The irony, and let's call it comedy, of all this escaped me, I
am bound to admit, at the time.

The clown from DST was irritating me, had noticed as much,
and was piling it on. He started to interrogate Gilbert, using the
arrogant colonial 'thee', speaking pidgin-arab French, calling
him Boy. He knew well enough that I had no authority over his
service, and that short of pulling my commissaire rank (creating
thereby an enormous, disproportionate umbrage) there was little
I could do.

This wasted more time. And where was my identifying witness? I could not keep Lefebvre under wraps. And what was the
odd thing about him? That he had been making drawings of the
bridge, as and when demolished by large quantities of explosive.
Very peculiar story, Monsieur Castang (by this time we had a
senior officer on the scene, decidedly sarcastic at my expense).

Well, from there on you know roughly what happened. Next
thing we were all down at the bridge and it wasn't just a French
uproar but a German one too. Was there a terrorist action
planned by any goddamn People's Army we've ever heard of
(and a great many we haven't: there are new ones all the time)?
And great goddamn, who, what, where?

You have probably been across that infernal bridge fifty or a
hundred times without paying any heed to it. At the German
end you run straight past the police post and slap into the town
of Kehl, with an awkward crossroad first thing. It was rush-hour,
with impatient workers pouring across back to the French side
and creating the usual traffic jam. On the French bank the road
doubles round an island of buildings – there is an absurd tourist
bureau, a couple of little shops and even a church, and the

frontier and customs posts are to the side of these: there are a number of escape paths, including those into the park. These approaches – and getaways – complicate affairs: it was decided that here was the likeliest point of attack. Police and Polizei started showing zeal all over the shop. I may say that on three or four occasions demonstrations have taken place on this bridge – and created a considerable nuisance. Complete blockage even by daylight and with plenty of warning. Farmers for example, at any moment liable to pounce, and dreaded by every force of Policía in Europe; scourge of the battlefield, those échelons of trundling tractors, cows let loose in the Préfecture, mountains of produce dumped on the roadway with a hideous facility for becoming unhygienic over about five minutes. And as for turning on the tap to one of our monstrous lakes – floods of milk and wine cascading in the gutters . . . surrealist sight. It comes to mind because the black comedy serves to point up, the more, the black waste of it all.

I was in the middle of all this, dragging Guy around. I could identify the other boy, the French one. But what others were there? If they found him a witness worth suppressing, it was on the cards that he might recognise a silhouette, a profile. He'd been sketching the scene, a landscape with figures he did not need or want and hadn't focussed upon. But his eye was a good one. They'd undoubtedly been observing, planning, quietly measuring. Anything at all which hadn't registered at the time, but were now suddenly to look familiar – hey, that blue raincoat.

The standing orders are always the same. Clear the public from the suspected area. Terrorists like crowded public places for being difficult to evacuate, and precisely because a lot of folk are carrying shopping bags, parcels of every shape and sort, while you're trying to identify the one looking negligently abandoned and the people with the over-casual air. A bridge sounds easy on the face of it: exit at both ends. And a big disposal area. Cast the eye upon the suspicious object, you've only to chuck it over the parapet, it'll go pop in the river.

Quite wrong, because you aren't supposed to touch it. On the

contrary because the detonating mechanisms are delicately trig-
gered. Matter as you know, or perhaps you don't know, of
making an electric contact; two poles that have to touch, and
once they've pulled the string even turning or poking it can be
fatal. So one avoids heroic acts – call the specialist chap in the
Michelin-Man outfit.

A bridge carrying motor traffic is in fact far from easy, because
you can't turn traffic round. Hideously inflexible. All these
people too, short-tempered after a rough day, longing for home
and supper, told to get into reverse and crawl back to Germany
while more every second pile up behind. 'And those behind cried
Forward, while those in front cried Back' – the balls-up is
inevitable, classic. Even on an ordinary day Kehl can get like the
Place de la Concorde. German cops working to turn them aside,
but there's no room. One side of that crossroad is the railway
station and the other a narrow shopping street.

The logical thing would have been exactly the opposite: freeze
the crossroad but let everything on the bridge forward into
France. The emergency plan does in fact provide – but I can't
blame them; buildings there with big glass windows, if there's a
blast there's nothing worse than shards of glass. They are quite
appallingly lethal. The man had a horrible recollection of other
bad bangs – Bologna railway-station.

You might remember a scene in a movie where the ranch
catches fire and the black overseer wakes up the boss lady with
the phrase 'God is coming.' It was at this moment that God
started. Guy had felt the thunder brewing, hours back. It had
added to his feeling of unease; the still afternoon and the puffs
of warm wind. In May and June thereabouts, it's to be expected.
The odd one can be very nasty. Hail can strip all the vines,
flatten the growing corn, smash the greenhouses. Nobody had
noticed the sky steadily darkening.

I can't remember hail. You might think it impossible to forget
a detail like that, but I can't. I don't remember the street lights.
You'd suppose they'd be photo-sensitive. What I do remember
is all those loonies turning on their car lights. It is a reflex, I
suppose. One is taught to switch on in a rainstorm. The twilight

was growing too. Parking lights would be all right, but people here have the bad habit of turning on headlights in the mid-afternoon. You can't teach them that one sees less that way instead of more. Supposedly dipped, and three in five are ill-adjusted or even deliberately crooked. When the rain really came down we were all plain blinded.

Thunder is a funny thing at the best of times. Some people feel crushed and numbed, and others are excited and stimulated. But out in the open everyone feels vulnerable. In the town there is shelter. Everyone dives into the pub, laughing and flapping their wet trousers – guffaws and drinks all round. But if it takes you out in the open field . . . Perhaps you've never had this experience. Even more on a bridge, over water. That river is sinister at the best of times and has always obsessed the imagi-nation of the people living on its banks. I can understand. It is easy to feel that the solid ground is giving way beneath you. You'll have noticed no doubt that our famous technological society is peculiarly vulnerable to being reminded of God. When a hurricane blows on the north coast – from Finisterre right up to Hamburg you bejesus get it rubbed in. Was it Xerxes who ordered the sea flogged for disobeying the Emperor's orders?

It sent everybody barmy. You can understand that the bomb scare had already run like electricity way past both ends of the bridge. Nobody can stop people getting out of cars to peer about and yack any rumour down the line – bomb-bomb-bomb. The electricity overhead compounded the madness. One would think the rain would at least keep them shut safe inside the box. Not a bit – milling about in the roadway and on the pavements. Crowd control, as you probably know with unhappy memories of horrors in football stadiums, is one of the nastier cop jobs, because crowds are unpredictable. The power of the god Pan. I don't think anyone actually jumped in the water. But at the approaches people were trying to get over into the park. And that was naturally the one thing the cops of both nationalities were determined to prevent. Such a jolly laugh we do have about it all. There wasn't a shadow of a bomb, we've all said. One of the biggest D-notices ever known got dropped on the press and every other medium known, but all the governments in creation can't arrest the Arab Telephone.

So that the official story has been very loud and earnest. A pacifist group of vaguely green colouration had planned an anti-nuclear demonstration. This has the merit of being perfectly true. Naughty green people, irresponsible isolated elements, trying to be nasty to our kind paternalist guys who hand out electric power like Father Christmas and have lots over to sell to the Germans. Our dear Mother France terribly upset at this hideous ingratitude.

Nasty too to good godfearing Nato-loyal Germans. Beastly pacifists. We hope the judicial authorities in both countries warm their bottoms good and proper.

So the unhappy coincidence, ya, of the rush-hour and the stupid thunderstorm, all very banal but contributing to the hysteria for which we shall rightly be chided in the editorial columns of Serious Weeklies. The Police are not to be blamed for a certain quantity of Nervousness.

Nobody, but nobody, has been let in upon the truth. There was a bomb there. A bright idea of Lady Macbeth's.

Editorial note: A.D.
The gapped structure of this dossier, designed to spare the reader much that was pedantic, was always evident. The difficulties of editing into manageable shape were nowhere more apparent than in its conclusion.

Of this there exist at least three versions, two in the shape of official reports, constructed by evidence given before boards of enquiry, and designed to satisfy the French and the West German governments that what happened on the bridge which joins, or if you prefer which separates, the two Republics, was no more than an unfortunate occurrence. No reader will be surprised to hear that these are largely whitewash. If there had been confusion, incompetence or brutality, it must be the other party's fault. It wouldn't do to say so, for fear of creating a diplomatic incident.

Best, thus, to insist that the police on both sides behaved fault-
lessly. No official censure took place, because none was
recommended.

The third version is Castang's own, most of it 'as told to' myself.
But he did not want it on tape, understandably. Jokes made about
Official Secrets Acts had likewise to be censored. Castang, more-
over, adopts a frivolous manner to mask serious intent. He
appears most cynical when holding deep convictions.

So that I had to piece together his indiscretions, attempting to
make subjective impression into an objective narrative. This has
meant that the reported thoughts and sayings of the essential
witness to this part of the narrative, the man 'Bernd', have been
paraphrased, filtered if you prefer, through Castang's eyes and
ears to my own.

ON THE BRIDGE: conversations with Bernd

Naturally, everyone on the bridge not wearing a police uniform
was rounded up for control of identity. At the French end of the
bridge Castang would have shown his card and passed. At the
German end the mood of obstinate thoroughness meant they
didn't even look. 'Everybody to the control please: pass along.'
Not wanting any explanations. He didn't make any. Effaced
obedience was the line to take. His professional standing was
ambiguous. Off duty? Not the moment to show interest in Guy
and Sibille – chief interest there right now being medico-legal, of
a bleak nature.

At the control post there was a Great Stone Face, taking cards
one by one and slipping them into his little gadget. Bright light.
Other kinds of light, ultraviolet which shows up falsifications and
deletions. Takes a photo, and stores numbers in a computer
memory. Stoneface studied the tricolor card with care, and
Castang's face with more. Terrorists have often dressed up as
cops, and they have been known to masquerade as plainclothes

officers. After a moment of hesitation his fingers tapped out a number on the keyboard in front of him.

Castang's heart sank a little – this is no business of mine but he told me later that he hadn't thought of this earlier, mind on other things, but he wasn't very anxious to have his identity verified by the Bundeskriminalamt computer, having been involved upon a time in doings upon German soil that shaded even technical legality unpleasantly close, needing subsequent diplomatic lubrication.*

He couldn't see the screen, which naturally was turned away from him but though the stone face did not change, the read-out was too long and too complicated. One can never get off a computer. The best one can manage is additions and annotations. A reference, for example, to a senior official in the Polizeipräsidium of the city of Munich. All rather ominous.

"I am afraid, Herr Castang, I must ask you to wait."

"Yes. Uh, Herr Wachtmeister, I think it would be as well if I were to have a word with the chief."

"He is occupied. I do not know when he will find the time. Step in here," unbolting the door beside his wicket. "No disturbance, please." No point either in arguing. Back room. All the appearance of a waiting room but the door bolts and there is steel mesh on the window.

He had two or three neighbours, and acquired a couple more, but only one was interesting. A thickset, strongly built man of thirty-odd. A heavy, smouldering face; troubled, and lined with worry, upon which he had imposed calm. Dark hair and thick eyebrows and jaw carelessly shaved. Celtic face. Blunt massive hands of a manual worker, the nails short; dirty but not with deep-sunk grime. Check shirt, leather belt, jeans, canvas shoes; all shabby and fairly grubby, but thought and character in the face.

"Cigarette?"

* This episode is described in a previously published work, *Wolf-night*, by the same author.

"Thanks. French?" The accent heard even in one word.

"Yes."

"I don't know who you are. But I've seen you. On the bridge, right? Yesterday."

"That's right."

This was Bernd Schuster. It isn't his real name. He deserves some protection. He chose this pseudonym and it illustrates a certain humour. 'Or Paul Breitner if you prefer that.' I like Bernd better. Both were footballers of much talent; the providers, who roam about in midfield, collect a ball and run with it, creating a threat, pulling defenders out of position with sudden changes of pace and direction, giving a long pass to a lurking attacker. Both were exactly what the national football team most needed. Neither made any real international career. 'Bad characters' both, forever at odds with the manager, trainer, and most of the other players. Given in consequence to self-imposed exiles, sardonically watching the team run hard, show aggressivity and physical strength, courage and tenacity – and somehow never scoring enough goals.

Philosophers are much pleased by these football metaphors and Bernd, while jeering, was – is – a political philosopher.

He was touchy to begin with. He had failed in his objective and was embittered, and with strangers showed that German readiness to be rubbed the wrong way.

'I'm the prognathous Westphalian business man. Behind me is a little whitefaced Jew in a bathchair.'

'Who on earth said that?' asked Castang, startled.

'Old fascist called John Buchan half a century ago and Brits go on believing it. Bullying fatnecked Junker Prussian officer. Wear perfume. Pederast tendencies unheard-of in Brit Guard regiments. I'm a Hun. Cut nuns' tits off, throw babies in air, catch them on point of bayonet.' He had the not uncommon trick of unconsciously mimicking the stranger's defective German: Castang's is fluent but ungrammatical: my own just the opposite, so stilted that I sound like Bernd imitating Neville Chamberlain.

'What utter balls,' said Castang.

Bernd had been arrested (he had been nothing but open about his rôle) for organising and carrying through the original idea of the demonstration. Well-known local troublemaker, on the computer for twenty such adventures, at the Frankfurt airport (you might recall the conflict over driving a new runway through good woodland), at a dozen nuclear power stations, at the places where the US Army planted cruise missiles upon German soil. Tactically an old hand in the combats against military or economic pollution and destruction these last ten years – 'Well, it's all the same war.' Strategically unhappy with the basic pacifist dilemma: all experience shows that only non-violence is valid, but how, in combating violence, does one avoid infection? 'It's catching like the cholera.' Common ground here with Castang: 'a cop is a professional of violence. We are simply the fist of the pen-pushing army.'

Finding themselves thus thrown together, Castang and Bernd fell into conversation: the beginnings were probably 'Got a light?'

"Did you have anything to do with the demonstration?"

"No." If not a contemptuous intonation, close to it.

"What are they holding you for?"

"They live in hope of catching me on a criminal charge which would stick. Conspiracy would do them nicely."

"You know the people involved then?"

"Acquainted," said Bernd shrugging. "I wasn't encouraging them. Demonstrations need meticulous planning, whether it's a bomb or just sitting on the railway line. I could use the word scruple, in the moral sense. Some are without it; I'm burdened with it. The authorities don't distinguish. Everything outside their book is terrorism. They do distinguish between the professional and the amateur. So they'll realise quite quickly that this was not my work. Right now they're angry because they've been made to look amateur as well as foolish."

"Much my conclusion, and we're embarked in the same boat."

"Then allow me to introduce myself. Schuster, professional terrorist."

"Castang, professional policeman." They shook hands formally and with enjoyment. "My interest was in the woman. Sibille Lefebvre – you may know her under another name."

"Know her well under this one. She lived in my house for six weeks – on and off for six months."

"She's given me some trouble."

"She's about to give everyone a lot more. She was an amateur terrorist; bane of my existence." And all this time, thought Castang, I've been trying to find my way on the map, until this moment when I at last realised that I was holding it upside down.

Near his home, there is a ship canal, crossed at one point by the main road on a swing bridge. He watches still, absorbed as in childhood, while the ponderous mass slides home. As a child, he had wondered how men got them to fit with such minute exactitude.

"Now I see why she often reminded people of Lady Macbeth."

Bernd cocked his head, amused.

"Very like. There was a real amateur. With a ha'porth of sense she'd have found professional assassins. Must have been plenty of disgruntled soldiery about. Give them a good bribe, brief them carefully, the job done congratulate them lavishly, fill them up with drinks, show them to the little wicket gate and hop – down the oubliette."

"Just so."

"But converts to a cause are more catholic than the Pope. Especially the women. You'll have noticed how the Red Fraction keeps going – on women, and of just that sort." Castang has remembered the sister, Faith, telling him how they had been brought up as children 'to give one more'.

"I'd like to know more about all this – about her. It isn't, now, going to be the subject of any official action; I mean of mine. It was thought, you see, that her husband must have killed her." Bernd thought, and nodded.

"It can do no harm, now that she's dead."

"Now that they're both dead . . ."

A uniformed policeman came in and said, "Herr Kommissar," in a sepulchral voice of deep disapproval.

"Come and see me any time," said Bernd, grinning. "Once we're both free of the bureaucratic entanglements."

Bernd lived in an old mill. Nothing very romantic or picturesque: a quadrangle of massive stonework converted into four or five apartments. It stood among willowtrees on a laneway, two minutes' drive outside a neighbouring village. Brown water flowed lazily under old masonry: fish plopped in the former race. The little river pottered off into a gentle, traditional landscape. Sturminster Newton, in the middle of Baden-Württemberg. Ducks and moorhens sheltered in the overgrown waterside coverts: while Castang watched, a hare lolloped across a field. Maize, wheat, lucerne. Birds sang, and appletrees grew along the lane's verges. Saving electricity pylons there was nothing to tell one that this century, dragging towards an unquiet end, was the twentieth. But in the paved yard were two cars; one the colour of canned tomato soup, the other of a chemical orange lollipop. Still, there were windowboxes also. Geraniums, and petunias.

Bernd let him in, to a simply-furnished livingroom with whitewashed walls, many shelves of books, a homespun look to furniture and covers, a table untidy with papers and typewriter.

"You're open, here."

"Perfectly," agreed Bernd. "I've been clandestine in my time, but there's no point in it. They come down on me now and again. They've been known to appear with a search warrant and rummage about. If I have anything secret, I know how to keep it so . . . I'm a declared enemy of the state, and I run my business openly."

"And you sheltered Sibille openly," amused. All the pompous nomenklatura of Interpol and maréchaussée, gendarmes and carabinieri and the terrifying Bundesgrenzschütz, but to whom it had not occurred that a Missing Person had found shelter with an enemy-of-the-state prominently booked on all their computers.

"She was – I ought to say seemed – no more than superficially hurt. I have a spare room here. It has happened before that people have asked to rest or recover from a hard time. I leave them be. Chuck them out if they become troublesome or create a pigsty.

"She was quiet, controlled, orderly. She pulled her weight – cleaned the place, did the housekeeping. She cooked! – it's nice to have a woman about who can cook; it becomes a rarity. By oneself . . . cans of ravioli, a chop thrown in the pan. Indeed she helped me a lot; tidied files, cleared a great stack of old paper: did a lot of my typing . . ."

Bernd stopped to collect his thoughts; to answer the unspoken question.

"I've known more of these women, who turn terrorist. Some are dead . . . Others – say that I've lost sight of them; leave it at that. Noticeably how many of the killers are girls, some quite young. People can't understand, repeat that English cliché about the female of the species being deadlier. Or they think an impressionable young woman has been perverted by association with some sadistic psychopath. It isn't like that at all . . . Pathetic they are, and psycho as is obvious. You'll find them cooking meals, sweeping and tidying the safe house, caring tenderly for the geraniums in the windowbox.

"The psychiatrist? – I suppose he'd say schizo, a great gaping crack right across the personality, but I see it as a wound, which gapes, yes, and refuses to heal. You'll find it in them all, a great hurt inflicted and they can't recover. They've tried. Loving a dog, a flower. Whatever is vulnerable and easily destroyed.

"Sibille spoke little; I know little. With hindsight – now – I can recognise the terrible pride, the loneliness. The horrible human being, there is the enemy, who somewhere along the line – they can't forgive themselves, you know. I knew one who wanted a baby. The obvious reason she couldn't was being on the run? No – she could not force herself to bring a baby into such a horrible world.

"I know this much; you might know more. She was wrapped up in her man, not just the centre of her world but the meaning of her existence, and she pushed him hard – too hard. He gave her a black eye, that's nothing, but she saw it as a rejection, a refusal, of all her love and loyalty and her lifelong effort. That's only my guess. It shot her down, broke her wing. They get the death wish then, you know. They want to go to the guillotine in bare feet, and what happens? We shut them up in Stammheim Prison." He stopped again, as though trying to recall a half-forgotten phrase.

"Call it stupid, insensitive of me; I wasn't to know she was a hurt hawk." To Castang's look of query Bernd replied with the quotation.

"'We had fed him six weeks, I gave him freedom. / He wandered over the foreland hill and returned in the evening, / Asking for death.'"

Ah! He would ask for the reference. Vera would like that.

"She went off. I thought no more about her. Then she came back."

"You didn't sleep with her?"

"No. I was between girls as it happened. But no, it never came up. So that it created no obstacle. I don't harry them. If it comes about naturally . . . but she respected my privacy, as well as her own. And that, as you understand, made her easy to live with. We were quite comfortable together," and only on that last phrase did he allow a 'wry' intonation.

"She didn't speak of what had happened?"

"No. I am observant, yes, I am experienced, yes. Nothing beyond that. She didn't lack intelligence. That's a thing another man notices quicker than a husband, perhaps. Frequent source of discord, I'd say. Man who underestimates his woman, gives her an unfair advantage over him. Which if honest she doesn't want, which in any case she resents." Castang nodded.

"Suppose now I did a little drawing of the husband, who's a bright chap, artist, gifted. Kindhearted and generous. Do you see him at all? Generous and selfish; easygoing and obstinate."

"Not a clever mix."

"Nor with the woman you're describing."

"She had that ferocious sense of virtue," said Bernd slowly. "Good in the sense of fidelity, loyalty . . ."

"Yes, I heard a lot about her honour."

"But when it turns into that awful moral righteousness. The women in the Red Fraction are like that. Mistake to think of them as anarchic or amoral: it's quite the contrary. Nothing you can do or say will ever persuade them they might be wrong. They burn with fanatic zeal but it goes all the way down to moral bedrock. So that I have myself to blame, a good bit. It was through me she got into the protest groups."

"While she was away, where did she go?"

"Up along the border, Saarbrücken way. Name of Cattenom mean anything to you?" with a flicker of smile.

Too much, to be sure, thought Castang; our lovely big new nuclear power station, such an object of pride that one does a little wonder why it needed tucking away into one of the remotest corners of France. An afternoon stroll from Belgium, Luxembourg, Germany. Cooled by the water of the Moselle river at just the moment this ceases to be French: convenient of it. The thing had not exactly promoted international harmony and goodwill.

"She wanted to be where the action was," with the ghost of a smile.

"And then she came back: tragically. Hideous great tragedy? No, small domestic incident."

"But a diplomatic incident."

"Po po po," said Castang. "The police shoot so many people. Everyone satisfied. Terrorists ought to be shot. Great mistake when they aren't. The other great mistake is getting married."

The ghost had become a broad grin. Like Vera, Bernd had a quotation for that one.

"'My experience teaches me, Lady Dedlock, that most of the people I know would do far better to leave marriage alone. It is at the bottom of three-fourths of their troubles.'"

"You're as bad as my wife."

"And you aren't exactly a typical police officer: would you say?" Bernd's tone was kind. "Like a drink?" he added, for consolation. Irish whiskey, helpfully called Paddy for those in some doubt.

Castang's usual reply is that his wife's Czech: this is a bit thin.

"No, but what's typical? Are you a typical German?" Bernd, pouring paddy into two mustard glasses, was untroubled.

"I wish I were. But there are more of us here than in most places. Natural, since we're in the front line. Prosit. You want ice or something?"

"Good God, no."

"Isn't it time we stopped worrying about our collective unconscious and began constructing? I find it funny. They have to go on blaming us. Now we're the woolly idealists, the sentimental pacifists, the weak-kneed noncombatants. Good old Hitler! In those days we had a really solid barrier against the Bolsheviks. We must make sure, now, that we lose this war too."

"Is it certain?" asked Castang.

"There are those who hold that the powerstations are our secret weapon. Since a calamity there is inevitable, the sooner and the bigger the better. Right here in Western Europe. That the shock wave created would be big enough to stop atom-splitting once and for all."

"You believe that?"

"No. The number of lives lost in a war has never even postponed the next war."

"So that after us it's the deluge. Hasn't that been said by every generation?"

"The skin-of-our-teeth theory. Since we came through the ice, and the floods, and the wars, we can survive anything. Those are the ones who go to New Zealand and make electricity by wind power. Nice wind! By courtesy of a breakfast food. Cream of

Mush brings you fibrosis of the lung. Quite quick, and not unduly painful."

To defy the wind Castang lit a deathdealing cigarette and Bernd's laugh filled the room.

"There are also those who believe in skipping while there's still time. Build a big rocket. Not these stupid little things with barely enough power to get up there among the garbage bins. Strike out for a comet. Water there. So, it's thought, means to support life. Lucky old comet."

"You hadn't planned on going along?" asked Castang politely.

"It wouldn't work, would it? As long as any people were planning to go along."

Castang had been seeking a quotation of his very own, for some time, and now found the deathbed line from Humphrey Bogart.

"'I never should have switched from Scotch to Martinis.'"

"And I'd always thought of a French police officer as the lowest form of human life – barring, that is, our own!"

"No, they wouldn't bring me along."

"You've got the message, mate. Apart from presidents, Nobel-prizewinners, and a few generals, who's on the list?"

"You've made your point," said Castang, suddenly fierce. "Despair. You're pulling the roof in on us, is that it?"

"Not quite," said Bernd, imperturbable. "That's what the terrorists do. That's their argument. Since the world is horrible, impossible, knock it down. I survive since I'm the toughest guy with the biggest gun. They have a vague idea of purifying later. Love among the ruins. Come on, you and I know better."

"So you have another answer?"

"A sentimental one only," now perfectly serious. "But sentiment, you see, is worth more than intellect. Intellect says that there's nothing there, out the far side. Only the big sleep. Emotion says there's just a chance that the world might be well worth leaving. Hasn't it struck you – that this was Sibille's conclusion?"

"A suicide, deliberately sought? It has struck me. I have not the right to make it my conclusion. And what about poor old Guy? He hadn't thought about it. He saw only his woman, who meant his whole life to him. And made for her."

"He was a gardener, wasn't he?"

"Yes, and a good one."

"Oh, I think Sibille would want to take him with her. He wouldn't have wanted a world with no gardens."

"And you?"

"I don't believe in suicide. We Germans have done enough of that."

"So you'll die standing up. With your boots on?" Shouting.

"That is a sentimental brutality," said Bernd in a gentle voice. "Put it that I believe in defending indefensible positions."

"Yes indeed, I saw him again," said Castang. "In Cologne." He likes the old Rhineland city, so civilised a place that neither bomb nor bayonet could ever change its character. He feels well there; that's not just the admirable beer. Or all that art. It's a considerable place too for traffic in drugs; the official reason, at least, for his being there. He likes the town, and he likes the people; an independent lot, with no great opinion of the German government. Any German government, he says with relish, or any other either. That is probably the heart of his contentment. It is a bloody-minded place, a people inclined to do the opposite of what they're told; in brief a Fronde city, and Castang is a frondeur.

Nor is it far away: two hours by the autoroute, the same as Paris and in no sense to him a foreign town.

Autumn it had been, nigh on six months after the calamity. Castang would like to say he has forgotten all about Guy and Sibille Lefebvre. He hasn't. The whole area, like the tender pink flesh over a healing burn, is unpleasantly sensitive to any careless touch. He makes a show of shrugging this off. It all happened, he says, at a vile time of year, neither late spring nor early summer, when one tends to complain that there has been no proper spring and that summer is never coming.

And it had dragged on, administrative bumbledom irritatingly compounding the ever-present paperwork, chronically neglected, endemic. The pathological metaphor for this would be a bronchitis. Picked up in a moment of imprudence, out without a scarf some fickle March evening, and nagging on drearily into June.

But in autumn he is happy. Green dales full of early morning mist, hills gold and brown and yellow swimming in hot sunlight, and even close to cities there are harvesty vintagey smells challenging the murky reek of chemicals. Castang goes swinging round a corner in the inner city – ludicrous double sidestep, twinned mumble of smiling excuse – slap up against Bernd. The pleasure is genuine, stimulating.

"Eh there!" they both say. Not in that much hurry, are you? Where is there a nice pub with one of the sixtynine local sorts? He is looking at the tall girl with Bernd, standing back with the controlled boredom of a woman while two men are slapping each other's backs.

"She's a special friend. She's Chilean. Let me present you. This is real dirt, Rafaela – this is Polizei!" Bernd is in form and infected with malicious amusement because the bare word has turned Castang into dogshit on the sidewalk. So that he must make a special effort. She is worth it.

Rafaela is in her early thirties, hard-boned; long fine shins under a wide skirt, narrow supple waist under a big leather belt. Long fine hands and feet, dark hair in a plait on her shoulder. Plenty of Indian blood; the long eyes are those called sloe by people who wouldn't recognise a sloe seeing one in the hedge. They are suspicious and watchful: her experiences with Policía have not been reassuring. In the pub, a careful choice of table, a thorough look through the occupants. In Bernd's company? – doubtless another terrorist. But not Red Fraction.

So that an extra effort is called for. He undoes his jacket, delighted to be wearing no gun, tries his awkward-accent

German on the waitress and on her his low catalan Spanish,
which thank you makes her laugh: hers is no villain-porteno but
the beautiful Spanish of the upper west coast. She'd rather a
Gaffel – elegant cylindrical glass that suits her unringed hand –
to the gaudy bottle of wine he has suggested. Prosit. Her German
is much better than his. The seductions are intense. This too
makes Bernd laugh.

Bernd looks a great deal happier, and less haggard, than when
Castang last saw him. That the two are 'together' is obvious; that
they are matched a probability.

Rafaela is no Sibille. Her he had never seen. Not even dead.
The German Kommissar had been very polite, once Castang had
explained who he was and how he came to be there. And also
very firm. Castang's status, shaky but just coverable in one
republic, is in the other no better than an onlooker's. Of all his
witnesses, he has managed only to put together the wooden
identikit portrait. It was his great handicap throughout; an
immoveable obstacle to reaching the truth: that never did he see
Sibille alive. Left always with abstract, conventional notions of
the northern woman as something stiff and narrow, rigid and
puritanical and – in the long run fatally – fanatical. It has never
satisfied him. Vera, who is Slav, who is both so simple and so
complicated, and who has Been To School and read Ibsen there,
and who has lectured him confusingly about *Hedda Gabler* and
The Doll's House – it has shed no clear light. He knows other
northern women, like nice, nasty, uncomplicated VV, but they
haven't helped him understand Sibille. Probably the kind, civilised, intelligent homosexuals came closest. But what can an old
queen, however charming, know of a woman's passion?

Rafaela is herself a conventional picture of the southern
woman. Hot-blooded you know; passionate – yah, it's the cliché
of the flamenco dancer in a frilly frock. Yes, she is supple and
resilient, she will never be a hurt hawk (even physically, with a
bullet in her, her will to live will astonish and delight her
surgeon). She is intensely female, smelling delicious; lovely-to-
look-at, entrancing to know. Not Sibille.

But she's all you've got. Look at her more closely, across this pub table strewn with beer mats, ashtrays, a small vase with two springs of freesia and one of asparagus fern (not plastic, at least). You will not see Sibille.

Or will you, after all, see what might and should have been?

It's the little things that kill one. Guy kidnapped and never again seen, one would have found Sibille in a white headscarf, walking in slow dignity round the plaza in Buenos Aires. It kicks one again in the gut, this stupid senseless loss of a fine woman. But thank God, Rafaela is alive, here, drinking beer with me on a sunlit terrace in a northern city.

"The world is going to go on then, a little longer?" Castang asks with false innocence.

"I'd like to last through another vintage," says Bernd placidly. Yes; there's a ripeness, a readiness about them.

This has conquered the nihilist discouragement of their last meeting. And effaces fear. Even were he a commonplace 'Green' organiser, preaching no more than ecology and disarmament, Bernd would be vulnerable. There are plenty of violent folk made extremely angry by this. Since he preaches civil disobedience, in a part of the world where there is plenty of reactionary behaviour, he's an obvious candidate for assassination. In the course of a peaceful conversation – the beer, excellent, helps – he floats the notion out.

"She's a work of art," said Bernd, serene. "The fundamental purpose of a work of art is to impose order upon chaos. Within us, or outside. Three more, my dear." The waitress draws little lines upon his beermat. "You remember the story that was the occasion for our meeting?"

Evidently.

"The need people have, of one another."

Goes without saying.

"We have our exits and our entrances. Profoundly unimportant they are. Except to ourselves."

"Genau." Which means roughly 'you've hit it'.

"And to one other. If we're very very lucky. You remember

that little bitch Pandora, frigging about with her box. All the horrors got out, and Hope got stuck inside. Ever occur, to wonder what it looked like? The Nut-cracker Fairy?" Bernd drank his beer. "Don't think I'm going romantic, my time of life. Learned this though: you don't do it alone. Pretty banal thought.

"Just that these last twenty years, while you and I have been adults, solitude has been romanticised. Heroic fantasy of the lonely hero. Ever been to Baden-Baden?"

"Once. I didn't stay." And I don't care to think about it.

"I'm not surprised. The old ladies sit under the plane trees. The gardens are kept beautifully weeded. Appleblossom everywhere! Even on the azalea bushes. Perhaps it's the only place left in the world where the four-piece orchestra plays on the terrace – palm court in wet weather." Bernd showed an unexpected talent for mimicry, becoming an elderly virgin in a black semi-evening, playing the cello and blowing her nose during the violin solo. A smile, inevitably, spread upon Castang's face.

"Don't laugh," said Bernd seriously. "They play 'Tea for two and two for tea', and 'Whenever spring breaks through again' and the old ladies sit still as mice; and instead of grinning like that, think about Sibille and wonder whether we are wrong and they are right." He put his left hand out palm upward among the beer mats, and Rafaela put her right hand into it. "The Fairy in the box looks like her."

Castang is accustomed to being vulnerable, to the malice of certain colleagues, the dislike of certain superiors. It is familiar in every hierarchy, where the jockeying for tenure, prestige, and of course money sees the dull and the crass show a talent for self-advertisement. He defends himself. Over the years he has learned the basic elements of politicking. As a result of the nonsense on the bridge, there was an administrative enquiry. He was detained by this, in Strasbourg, for some days. On the defensive.

I had done nothing (he said) actively blameable. My investigations into the Lefebvre family were formal. Officially countenanced. My interpretation of the mandate that can be read into a 'vacation' was stretched, it's true, to the absolute limit of the elastic. I held that once requested to undertake investigation, on a private basis, 'in the interests of a family', upon payment of a recognised retainer and expenses, I was then free to pursue the enquiry as I thought fit. Nothing in the Code of Criminal Procedure to forbid it . . .

An instructing magistrate is sovereign in his conduct of a criminal enquiry. He authorised these doings. Laid down the condition that my findings should be the subject of detailed written report. All faithfully executed!

Display of shining virtue, in short. It went down fair-ly well. There was some flak from Divisional Commissaire Sabatier. That's my chef, up in Lille. What-the-fuck is Castang doing, down there in Strasbourg, of all places, when he is supposed to be improving public morality in the Pas de Calais? Nothing much was going on, fortunately. I mean at the rank of Commissaire, one rests upon the laurels a good deal. Work is for junior inspectors. Anywhere else it's a sergeant, but in France there's this legal thing about officers of judicial police.

More flak – as was to be expected – from the Regional Service of the PJ in Strasbourg. They took umbrage at my sporting around in their territory; failing to inform them of my presence and purpose. That's the regulation. They made the most of it, mumbling about grave breaches of collegiality and suspected dereliction of duty.

I replied blandly that there was nothing to inform them about. My observance of Monsieur Lefebvre was for the exclusive purpose of shedding light, however hypothetical, upon the whereabouts of Madame Lefebvre, officially a missing person. I begged leave to state that no evidence whatever existed of any criminal act.

Nobody, of course, gives more weight than myself to the interests of collegiality.

But since the Judge of Instruction saw fit to entrust the original enquiry to the gendarmerie, who was I to query a magistrate's motives?

Certainly I admit. Prevarication, impudence, and administrative assholing.

The Enquiry was very much a shades-of-meaning thing. Definitions! Nobody's going to speak of a balls-up on the bridge, are they? These are happenings. We were at great pains to conclude that there had been no administrative malfeasance.

Well, there might be shades of meaning. For example, if we draw a line saying Frontier – and that in itself is a legal fiction – in the exact centre of the Rhine (the East Germans have always been cross that we refused to do this with the Elbe)! Is it crossing the Rio Grande that turns a Mexican into a wetback? So if there is an um, scuffle, on the bridge, is that the territory of the Republik, or of the Republique?

Once international law had settled this, we were much complicated by uncertainties, whether to admit to terrorists, or stoutly to deny that there ever had been any terrorists. The concept of Stout Denial, as defined by P.G. Wodehouse, is rather a feature of enquiries.

Suppose there are any, who do they belong to? The bridge, you see, is a splendid example of amity and cooperation. I mean to say there are French cops at the German end, and German cops up the Republic's ass. Diplomacy was exercised by these and numerous further – had anybody, for instance, given any order to fire? Standing instructions, mumble-mumble, discretion of the agents of Public Order: all that business of Due Procedure. Who goes there? Keys. Whose keys? Queen Elizabeth's Keys. Advance, Bet, or is it Key, and give the password. Any imbecile can see that the Halt-or-I-Fire thing is the best possible argument for not letting them have guns. Guns or hypocrisy, you've got to choose which.

Now let us hypothesize the eventuality of certain emergencies. If a German police officer gives an order, does it imply total and instant compliance by French cops? You know, some clown raised the parallel of civil defence. Suppose, he said, there were

– heaven forbid, we were no end pious – a discharge of radioactive vapour from the nuclear power station in Fessenheim? That's on the Rhine, just a few kilometres upstream. On the French bank, and prevailing winds are westerly. What is the position of French troops in Germany? They become automatically enabled, yes yes, but are they under the command of the German civil authority? The uh, Prefect? Oh! Germány doesn't have Prefects? Well, they must have somebody who wears a uniform and takes command. Who is he? Not a military man? You see, if the Russians come, a German general can command French troops. Heaven help him, but that's another part of the forest.

I am aware. Tittering, aren't I? Being facetious. A parody of the mandarin language known in France as woodentongue is far too easy, and betrays my embarrassment. French is, alas, a language that lends itself to rhetoric. Before one reaches a judgment given by the court, read aloud, generally in a monotone mumble, by the presiding magistrate, there are numerous paragraphs of cautious qualifications known as the Considereds.

Considered that the personage Guy Lefebvre, accorded a measure of provisional liberty – they mean out on bail. Suspicion of killing his wife, since shown to be unfounded. Because behold, here's the wife, described as his conjunct but we know who they mean.

Among the other considereds was one about Castang, rapped on the knuckles for exceeding allowable limits of prudence, but earning a good mark for vigilance. Was he not the first to detect and frustrate and Abort an Odious attempt to destabilise the government of the Republic. Two Republics, dammit.

Foiled by the devotion of the forces-of-order, at imminent risk to their own skin. As for Monsieur Castang, who had lost no time in alerting the responsible authorities, it cannot be held that he failed in the performance of his duties.

There was a sigh of relief, I don't mind saying. These were senior magistrates, judges of the Appeal Court, holding an enquiry in camera. I'm not getting sent to the Bastille this time. But I had another obstacle to pass.

Understand me, mm? France is not like Holland or Scandinavia, you're aware. We've a lot of violence and brutality in our society. It's ingrained in our fibre, and that includes the police. When I say that I greatly dislike this, and try to combat it by precept – I maybe manage example, the odd time – I'm trying not to sound a prig. It's some years ago now, but I've worked Paris streets. I know what it can be like. So that I do have a certain sympathy – no, that's a crappy phrase; I've a fellow-feeling. For the chap. Not for what he's done. I know how much provocation he may have had.

We do try to civilise ourselves. A cop who exceeds his rights and powers, most particularly when there's a loss of life involved, is stood down automatically. Suspended is the technical word. Placed on open arrest as likely as not, and if it looks bad, a judge might order his detention. In any case, there'll be an internal enquiry, apart from anything judicial – that's right; Inspectorate-General. I was no exception. Not that I was charged with anything, or likely to be. Certainly I was not suspended. I was a witness. They were being par-ti-cu-larly punctilious, you understand, on account of the Germans. This was not the ordinary police 'bavure' (the word means a blot; one of our better euphemisms).

They sent an old boy called Boninsegna. Sophisticated old gentleman. I was in luck too – he'd known Richard, my former mentor. But an old cop is an old bastard. He'd been one for forty years and showed no sign of weakening. A listener though; I don't think I've known one so patient. He looked like Teilhard de Chardin, equally prepared for a long long time before mankind gets anywhere near Point Omega.

He asked questions in monosyllables, slowly. He made notes, slowly, upon a roll of paper – where does he get them from? – similar to those in antique cash registers. His handwriting was gothic: small and spiky. The thing stayed in front of him, unrolling towards his right. I learned to watch out for the moments it rolled back to his left. 'That is not what you said earlier.' His teeth were long, and dark brown. His own; I can witness.

Towards the end of the day 'he spoke'.

"There are things which are good not to know. Beware of archives. It is said – you have heard? – that there are ten tons of Gestapo archives, captured by us in Berlin, transferred to Paris.

"Historians express a periodic grievance that these have never been made available for serious research. Thus deprived of a major source, the historian is reduced to speculation concerning the intimate relations between the police of the occupying power and ourselves. The other major source, I mean our own archives, having naturally been burned."

"I should think there were ten tons of paper," I said, "smelly in every way. Rotting, largely illegible – doubtless just as well."

"That is quite correct. People still alive are named. Some may be signatories of a number of these papers. Official reports, no doubt. So many electric light bulbs. So many pairs of boots. A parallel could be found with papers of a similar nature signed by the President of the Austrian Republic. It was thought bizarre that papers known to exist but which had remained unseen for many years should come to light at such a moment. It is a sobering thought, that a momentary concern for the indent, a requisition for paperclips, should come to be scrutinised in the light of history.

"You are wondering about my paper. It is a condensation. It is read by no one but myself. It is in a form readily destructible. Once in Paris I will dictate to my secretary, in a form further condensed. I have learned to be careful what I write, and sign."

He did utter again, somewhat later. He had asked me to go back to the source – and he actually used the phrase 'fons et origo' – of my interest in the Lefebvre family. I had mentioned Elena, the Spanish waitress at the Russian Tea Room. I won't say he let me run because those long brown teeth bit me. Snapping at my ass and I don't exaggerate.

"Easy, eh? Normal straightforward routine, no trouble at all.

Simple, open working woman. And then we get this bourgeoisie, complicating everything, with its tortuous involved values, its weird, far-fetched self-torments, its artificial, unspontaneous attitudes – the hairsplitting that went on. The desiccated analyses of every little spat of vanity . . ." At this tirade he actually smiled. Took off his glasses. No, he didn't clean them 'on the fat end of his tie', but on the front of his pullover. A musty, old-man smell came from him. Clean, but like an office in the Ministry of the Interior. Cleaned every day but smells just the same.

"There are women, and men also; I cannot say whether it be a feminine phenomenon though it is certainly more frequent there. They sit upon a disaster the way a hen sits on an egg, waiting for it to hatch. It could be said that they provoke it, bringing it to the boil. Knowingly? Upon occasion. What strikes one is that they are unable to prevent or avert the calamity, even when it has been clearly seen to be approaching." I wouldn't call this the most penetrating of the comments I have heard upon Sibille. Concerning Elena, it was not the stupidest.

The saying-what-happened is one of the most difficult enterprises imaginable, and that, I suppose, is why I put it off so long. I had to break it down, which was like breaking small sticks of kindling wood by hand, for Boninsegna. Whose official title is Monsieur le Controleur (that's pretty high in the PJ hierarchy: the English would say an Assistant Commissioner).

Very like a performance of *Macbeth*. For a thousand people in the theatre you'll have a thousand opinions of the whys and wherefores. And when you have a real-life drama with a thousand eyewitnesses you'll have a thousand different versions of plain 'what'. Saying that Sibille 'was like' Lady M. is no different to saying the Pope is like Hamlet.

I haven't seen the German enquiry. Unsatisfactory, no doubt. No different from ours in that both exemplify the bureaucratic art of sanitising an occurrence itself unsatisfactory.

If the Germans, as I bet they did (native thoroughness) sent down a Boninsegna – now if you could have got hold of that before it was sanitised, and collated it with the Dead Sea Scroll, you might then have found what the criminal brigade terms a back bearing.

As it is, you'll have to make do with my conditional, suppositional reading. Paraphrased, here it is.

The local protest groups planned simultaneous demonstrations. The symbolic nature of the bridge has not escaped these people: in fact it's a favourite terrain. It is possible to coordinate these things: small farmers in both France and Germany share the same fears and have sometimes blocked the bridge for hours on end. Professionalism, as Bernd has explained, consists also in a feigned legalism: you keep within the letter by serving due notice of your purposes to the police and keeping your spontaneities disciplined . . . Taking the police by surprise bespeaks the amateur.

We can find traces of these schemes. Piles of old auto tyres soaked in petrol. Set alight they make a royal stink, combining an anti-pollution thing with a pretty little glancing reference to South Africa and Daimler-Benz, who do a roaring trade there. A bomb scare would create hysteria in the rush-hour traffic (large numbers of thunderflashes). The police meantime would be pestered by diversions, at the Prefecture, where a tank of liquid manure with its valves jammed open would create a splendid stink of its own; and at the seat of the European Parliament, where craven fears would soak up a whole company of auxiliary riot-police. The entire force of authority would thus be harassed, frustrated and held up to ridicule.

Bernd, professional as he is, turned all this down out of hand. Too difficult to coordinate, too much childish undergraduate humour, and a lot of it too dangerous. Apart from illegality, 'gratuitous' provocation of the police has a bad backfire. They are over-armed and under-trained, a bad combination.

Move when you have the troops, says Bernd. Make your demonstration on a large scale, quietly and with dignity. If the police exercise violence you have the public's sympathy and help. The terrorists say that the public's leaden apathy can only be shaken by fear: Bernd rejoins that violence puts you on the level of the Red Fraction. The student demonstrations in Paris at the close of 1986 form a historic, classic example of how right he is. Bernd dreads nothing more than to see his movement infiltrated by mad ayatollahs. Throwing grenades at American soldiers is not his idea of valid protest.

There was indeed a hard element here. As we all very well know, right-wing opinion will always claim that any demonstration hostile to itself is manipulated by Commie agitators. So that your professional manipulator covers his tracks thereby. It's a very old trick, and the locus classicus is the burning of the Reichstag by the Nazis. A good trick – it is repeated every year.

Bernd got wind of this and tried to have the whole thing called off. 'Prophets are assassinated, be it Christ or Jean Jaurès. I'm not a prophet, I'm a foreman, and the foreman can get himself detested by the workers and the management, for truckling to both. I worry more about being discredited, though it wouldn't surprise me to get shot into the bargain.' Scylla and Charybdis; the agents of provocation and one's own hooligan element; the bicycle-chain brigade. It is the greatest cowards who are the most violent. Crowd-control is the least favourite of the cop's jobs, too.

Bernd did not know that Sibille had been captured by violence. Knowing something of her character, we can understand this better. Not to speak of her background. More Catholic than the Pope? – an easy manipulation. Nobody so far has identified, let alone caught the young woman who told Sibille that thunder-flashes were for schoolchildren. The way with pigs is to chuck in a grenade.

The fact has been glossed, but a grenade was thrown. Please do not underestimate the police. It was a cop who had the courage and the presence of mind to throw it over the parapet. It exploded in the water. There are no fish in the river: Swiss pharmaceutical companies have seen to that. There seem to have been no Rhinemaidens around.

Sibille was holding another grenade, and she was still holding it when it went off.

I do not know whether this was or was not suicide. The Appeal Court judges sitting on the board of enquiry did not pronounce upon the point.

Guy? Poor, blundering Guy, with his talent for doing the wrong thing?

It is possible to argue that he set the whole train going, the day he married her. Or there's a turning on the racecourse at Epsom, where, they say, the Derby is lost or won. The moment of giving her a (richly deserved) black eye; you might call that Tattenham Corner.

Guy was standing there on the bridge, under my wing. I needed him to help smoke out the little group of 'students' (a couple of them real students, manipulated as Sibille was). We got one, as you know. It did us no good. We had nothing much on him bar an attempted mugging. He stuck to his tale, there was little we could link him with, he kept his mouth shut and we had to let him go. Still, we can be grateful to Guy. Their sniggers at his 'bomb drawings' was a mistake and gave them away. They plainly knew too much about the nastier attempt disguised as a 'happening', and realised too late that Guy would make an inconvenient witness to this.

Guy saw no face that I wanted picked out. Instead he saw his wife. Without saying a word he bolted straight for her.

The evidence disintegrates at this point. Yes, including my own. Human behaviour obeys no logic the bureaucrat can follow. Isn't that so, Elena?

Oh, I have the same excuses for meaningless verbiage as the editors of this report. The car headlights, in that sinister twilight; the thunderstorm on the top. No Rhinemaidens about, and I can't answer for Wotan. Alberich was there all right: he always is. Donner arrived.

I can see one thought in Guy's mind, which obliterated all else. There was Eurydice.

You are mine; I am yours: we belong together; in this world or out of it. Can I risk saying it? – I think that this is to be admired.

The witnesses are divided but it seems clear that they joined. By that I mean that I saw them join. Or so I say.

But it must have been Sibille's movement, which I say was to join him. It was taken as a threat, an imminent danger. Several cops have said they saw the grenade. I don't deny that. I find the police reaction entirely reasonable, in the context of no reason at all.

Police instinct was to level the gun, blow them both to kingdom come. That's quite all right. They had both lost all interest in the world. Sibille's grenade would have done the job for them.

No, the autopsies afford no light. The pathologists could do no better than the phrase Vera found for me, from Joseph Conrad. 'Earnestly examining the by-products of a butcher's shop with a view to choosing an inexpensive Sunday dinner.' Ironist, the Pole. Nobody was prepared to say whether it was police bullets or the grenade which killed them. Off the hook, gentlemen. As the report says –

a) there is no evidence that the police killed anybody.

b) if they did there is a clear case for self-defence.

Close the circuit. Lady Macbeth killed Duncan, and her bemused idiot of a man made away with his old comrade-in-arms Banquo; and who is that Third Murderer anyhow? Do we care? They are thin characters and it's difficult to take much interest in either the king or the general.

What is true, and clear, is that Macbeth and his wife destroyed one another. There is the tragedy. Strength and weakness hand in hand. What matter whether the kingdom be the size of Scotland, or that over-tidy four-room apartment of Elena's? What matter gun, knife, or bomb? It's a carnivorous world. We devour one another. Hate is love.

Just in passing, I found a picture in Strasbourg. Don't think I can afford Modern Art: I don't get offered enough bribes, and my wife makes things to hang on our walls. It's just a litho, one of a series a man there did, the Mythology of the Rhine.

Guy, after all, had had the same notion.

It is extremely simple, a sea and a sky, in two shades of blue. The skyline is marked by the cranes and docks of a harbour, in the distance. Swimming in the sky, since the water is just too polluted for them, are the Rhinemaidens. They've won, they've got their gold back, though men, and the gods, have set themselves on fire. Quite tempting to put in a bit of symbolism there; Brunnhilde on her horse, jumping him into the centre of the flames.

No no, here are just the girls, swimming in a free circular pattern. It's a resolution at the end of the road, down there in the estuary. A final harmony. The man who drew it called it 'Eternity in Rotterdam'.

Fair enough, I thought. Little glimmer from that box of stupid Pandora's. Brief, and feeble, as a candle.

But must keep lighting candles, no?